P9-DKF-820

New Hanover County
Public Library

If found, please return to:
201 Chestnut St.
Wilmington, NC 28401
(910) 798-6300
http://www.nhclibrary.org

STEALING SNOW

STEALING

SNOW

DANIELLE
PAIGE

BLOOMSBURY
NEW YORK LONDON OXFORD NEW DELHI SYDNEY

First published in the United States of America in September 2016
by Bloomsbury Children's Books
www.bloomsbury.com

Bloomsbury is a registered trademark of Bloomsbury Publishing Plc

For information about permission to reproduce selections from this book, write to
Permissions, Bloomsbury Children's Books, 1385 Broadway, New York, New York 10018
Bloomsbury books may be purchased for business or promotional use. For information on
bulk purchases please contact Macmillan Corporate and Premium Sales Department at
specialmarkets@macmillan.com

Library of Congress Cataloging-in-Publication Data
Names: Paige, D. M., author.
Title: Stealing Snow / Danielle Paige.
Description: New York : Bloomsbury Children's Books, 2016.
Summary: Seventeen-year-old Snow escapes a mental hospital by racing into the woods
where she finds herself in icy Algid—her true home—with witches, thieves,
an alluring boy named Kai, and she discovers her royal lineage.
Identifiers: LCCN 2016011504
ISBN 978-1-68119-076-1 (hardcover) • ISBN 978-1-68119-077-8 (e-book)
Subjects: | CYAC: Fantasy. | Magic—Fiction. | Secrets—Fiction. |
Love—Fiction. | Kings, queens, rulers, etc.—Fiction. | BISAC: JUVENILE FICTION /
Fantasy & Magic. | JUVENILE FICTION / Love & Romance. | JUVENILE FICTION /
Action & Adventure / General.
Classification: LCC PZ7.P154 St 2016 | DDC [Fic]—dc23
LC record available at https://lccn.loc.gov/2016011504

Book design by John Candell
Typeset by RefineCatch Limited, Bungay, Suffolk
Printed and bound in the U.S.A. by Berryville Graphics Inc., Berryville, Virginia
2 4 6 8 10 9 7 5 3 1

All papers used by Bloomsbury Publishing, Inc., are natural, recyclable products
made from wood grown in well-managed forests. The manufacturing processes
conform to the environmental regulations of the country of origin.

To my family, Mommy, Daddy, Andrea, Josh, Sienna, and Fi, and every girl who wanted to be a princess but became a queen…

FIRST KISSES SOMETIMES WAKE slumbering princesses, undo spells, and spark happily ever afters. Mine broke Bale.

Bale burned down a house when he was six. He was a patient at the Whittaker Psychiatric Institute like me, and he was also my only friend. But there was—he was—something . . . more. I told him to meet me where we could be alone, at the one place where we couldn't see the iron gates that hemmed us in. Our kissing would have a time limit, though. The time it took for the White Coats to notice that we were gone.

Bale met me in the darkest crook of the hall, just as I knew he would. Bale would meet me anywhere.

We were clumsy at first. My eyes were open. He had not leaned down quite far enough. And then we weren't clumsy at all. His lips were warm, and the heat washed over me. I could hear my own heartbeat in my ears. I leaned into him and felt his body against mine. When we finally broke apart, I rocked back on my heels and looked up at him. I felt myself smiling. And I rarely smiled.

"I'm sorry, Snow," he said, looking down at me.

I blinked up at him, confused. He was kidding.

"It was perfect," I asserted. I was not the type to be mushy. But he was not allowed to joke about this. Not ever this.

I pushed his shoulder lightly.

"I see what you are now," he said, grabbing my hand and holding on a little too tight.

"Bale . . ." I felt something snap in my palm, and a sharp pain ran up my wrist and arm. I cried out, but Bale just looked at me with steady eyes, his grip and gaze suddenly cold and unyielding.

Not like a prince at all.

It took three orderlies to get him to let go of my wrist, which I later learned was broken in two places.

As they pulled him away, I noticed through the double-paned windows down the hall that it was snowing. It was too late for snow. It was May. But it was upstate New York, and weirder things had happened. The snow stuck to the glass and melted. I touched the cold pane. If things had played out differently, the snow would have been a perfect punctuation to a perfect moment. Instead it made it that much worse.

Bale went on the cocktail after that. I went on it, too, after they refused to let me see him. That was the usual procedure for Whittaker kids who never outgrew their imaginary friends, the dream catchers and time travelers, the cutters and kids who couldn't eat or couldn't sleep. And for me, who tried to walk through a mirror when I was five. I still have the scars on my face, neck, and arms from the shards of glass, though they've faded now to faint white lines. I assume Becky, the girl next door who I had dragged through the mirror with me, still has them, too.

Dr. Harris said they'd found pills under Bale's bed. He hadn't been taking his meds. He couldn't help what he did to me.

I wasn't sure that was the whole truth, and I didn't care. The broken bones were temporary. What stuck with me was that perfect first kiss. And the shock of what he had said.

That was a year ago. Bale hadn't spoken since.

1

IN THE DISTANCE I *could see a tree that seemed to scrape the sky in* *every direction, with gnarly branches and the strangest, almost lumines-* *cent white wood. The bark was covered from top to bottom in intricate* *carvings. I had seen this tree before. I felt a pull to walk right over to it* *and run my fingers along the carvings. But instead I turned away from* *the tree toward a loud, constant crashing sound: water. It was running* *fast and deep. I looked down and saw that I was hovering on the edge of* *a steep, rugged cliff, when something or someone came at me from behind,* *shoving me hard.*

I fell and fell and fell until my body hit the water. It was freezing *cold. Cold like none I'd ever felt. The water cut at me like little needles* *piercing my skin. And then when I could not stand it a second longer, I* *opened my eyes and saw something in the murky deep: tentacles and gills* *and gnashing teeth coming at me in the icy blue.*

My arms flailed. I needed air. Which was worse? That thing in the water or drowning? I opened my mouth to scream as the thing reached me, wrapping its icy tentacles around my ankle.

♛

When I woke that morning, Vern, one of Whittaker's orderlies, was standing over me.

"Hush, child," she said quietly. She had a syringe in her hand, and she was prepared to use it.

I caught my breath and threw back the covers to check my leg for the mark made by that thing in the water. The sheets were drenched. But it was my sweat. There was no mark and no water creature to blame.

"Snow?"

The orderlies—or White Coats as we liked to call them—weren't really our friends even though they were the only people we saw every single day. Some of them spoke to us. Some mocked us. Some laughed and moved us from locked room to locked room like furniture. But Vernaliz O'Hara was different. She treated me like a person even when I was a completely drugged-out vegetable and even when I had the shakes. She didn't know which person I was at the moment, hence the syringe.

"I'd rather not knock you out today. Your mother is coming," Vern said in her maple-syrupy Southern accent. Her low, long brown ponytail swung behind her as she stepped away from my bed and slipped the syringe back into the pocket of her scrubs. Looking up at her, I marveled at how close her head came to the ceiling. At six feet nine, she was an abnormally tall woman. I half expected to feel a breeze from the whiplash of Vern's hair.

Depending on which patient you asked, Vern was a giantess. Or an Amazon. Or a Jörd, the giant Norse goddess who gave birth to Thor, the god who sometimes shows up in comic book movies. I'd looked up Vern's condition in Dr. Harris's collection of old encyclopedias in the library. Vern suffered from acromegaly, a hormonal condition that occurs when too much growth hormone is produced by the pituitary gland, which resulted in a larger-than-everyone-else Vern. But "suffered" was the wrong word. Vern owned her size, and it made her the perfect muscle for Whittaker. No patient could find his or her way around the wall of woman she was. Not even me.

I held out my hand. "Fine," I mumbled.

"She speaks," Vern assessed, her oversize green eyes lighting up with surprise.

Vern wasn't being sarcastic for a change. Because of the meds, I didn't speak often these days except for swear words. And also because I didn't have anyone I wanted to talk to. Except my mother when she was visiting . . . and of course, Bale.

Vern was the only one of the White Coats I could even stand to be around.

I had bitten Vern once—right after Dr. Harris had told me I couldn't see Bale last year. I had expected Vern to treat me differently after that, but she didn't. She was the same kind Vern. I always wanted to ask her why. But I never did.

"Did you have the dream again?" Vern asked with the same level of anticipation she had for the next episode of *The End of*

Almost, one of her "stories" that we watched during supervised recreation hours.

I shook my head, a lie my body told automatically. They encouraged talking about the subconscious at Whittaker. But I didn't like to. I was determined to keep my dreams mine and no one else's. Even though they were often twisty and dark, they were the only place I got to be close to Bale. I had slipped and told Vern once. A fact she would not let me forget.

Last night's dream had been Bale-free. And a little stranger than usual. The tree was in it again, huge and looming, taking up the whole sky. Then there was that *thing* . . . The memory of it flooded in, distracting me, pulling me back into the cold, dark water. Patiently, Vern waited for me to sit up, pulled out a fresh pair of Whittaker gray sweats for me to wear, and sighed a heavy, breezy exhale that denoted her disappointment.

I slipped out of my paper-thin cotton pajamas in front of her and caught a glimpse of my reflection in the plastic mirror on the door of my closet. Since the kiss, I was still searching for whatever it was about me that had spooked Bale.

My face looked the same to me. Brown eyes. Pale skin because of the lack of sun. The trail of white scars tracked down one side of my body, most densely on my left arm. Despite multiple surgeries, my arm and torso would forever bear the weblike tattoo of the day that had brought me here.

The white streaks that wove through my ash-blond hair had grown only more pronounced this year. Vern blamed it on the new drug cocktail, but I didn't see any other patients going gray, and plenty of us in Ward D were taking the same prescription.

"Maybe we should put some new art up. You're really getting good," said Vern.

I shrugged, but I felt a surge of pride well up underneath the gesture. I had begun drawing as therapy. But I kept doing it for me.

Sometimes I drew the other patients. A lot of my drawings were of Bale. There were dozens of them, in fact. I drew the inmates as they were and as they wanted to be. Wing thought that she was an angel or something, so I gave her wings. Chord believed in time travel, so I'd draw him anywhere or anytime he wanted to be. He once told Bale that he "blinked" from place to place. That was what he called it: blinking. He could come and go from the signing of the Declaration of Independence in a single blink. Time was infinite and different for him. I envied him that. I would give anything to blink back in time to before the kiss with Bale.

Sometimes I sketched Whittaker. The asylum had a lot of rooms. But there was a dividing line between what the parents saw and what the patients saw. My room was pretty spare: white sheets and walls, a white cabinet, a full-length plastic mirror on my closet door, plus a small white desk. The only decorations at all were the drawings hung everywhere with duct tape. I had Vern to thank for that. The rest of Whittaker looked like an English manor —with high ceilings, fancy furniture, and wrought-iron sconces along the walls. The irony was Whittaker wasn't that old. It was built sometime last century. And rural New York was a far cry from England.

Sometimes I sketched my dreams, which ranged from stark, blinding-white landscapes to creepy execution scenes that I couldn't really explain. The worst was the one with me standing on a mountaintop, and below me there were bodies, blue as ice and covered in a blanket of snow. I was smiling in it, like I had a secret.

Or there was the one with the armored executioner who was wielding an ax, about to swing it into something—or *someone*—off the page. I was proud of how I captured the blowback of blood on his armor.

Dr. Harris thought drawing was a good way to channel my anger and imagination by putting pen to paper and seeing the "ridiculous" things in my head. By getting them out of my mind, he thought it would help draw a dividing line between what was real and what was just a fantasy.

It worked for a while, but ultimately Dr. Harris wanted the drawing to be a gateway to my talking about my feelings. That rarely happened—or at least not in the way that he liked.

"Almost time for visiting hours," Vern pressed. She had turned to her cart and was grabbing the familiar tiny white paper cup that contained today's pill.

"What'll it be today, Vern. Sleepy or Dopey?"

I had affectionately named my myriad pills after some of the seven dwarfs. Each one corresponded to the effect it had on my mood. Sleepy made me sleepy; Grumpy, etc. One by one, they all came to represent—even Sneezy.

Today there was a green pill in the little cup.

"Happy." I grimaced. That one didn't really work anymore.

"You are chatty today," Vern half questioned, cocking her head.

I pulled the nondescript hospital uniform shirt over my head, and I pulled on the pants. Vern handed me the paper cup and waited for me to gulp down the pill, which was so big that it scraped down the back of my throat even with a sip of water. Vern took back the cup and waited for me to open my mouth to check that I had actually swallowed the pill.

In that half-a-heartbeat pause, a second of resentment flooded in. It was that moment in our everyday routine that kept us from being friends—that, more than the lock on the door or the syringe in Vern's pocket. It was her job to check, not to trust. And it reminded me every day that even though she was the only person who really talked to me, she was paid to be here.

2

AT VERN'S SKYSCRAPER-ISH SIDE, I walked down the hall of Ward D, peeking inside the small, square double-paned windows to the other rooms along the way that made up the most secure wing of Whittaker. Through the one to my left I could see Wing perched on the edge of her chair, ready to take flight. She couldn't really hurt herself from that high up, but her White Coat, Sarah, a birdlike woman with surprising strength, was attempting to coax her down from the chair anyway. Wing didn't look it, but she was probably the patient the White Coats were most afraid of. One open door, one loose restraint, and Wing would find the highest surface she could and throw herself off it. Wing thought she could fly.

I walked away the second she "took off." There was literally nothing sadder than seeing Wing's face when she landed and realized that her flight was over.

In the next room, Pi was scratching things in his notebook.

He thought he was writing an equation that would save the world, or break it. According to Vern, who liked to fill me in on the other patients, he was done with his alien abduction phase and he had moved on to some new kind of government-conspiracy-cloning thing that involved code breaking.

Magpie's room was empty. But I knew that underneath her mattress there were dozens of tiny things that she'd stolen from all over Whittaker. Magpie was our resident thief and my sometimes nemesis. I had been so distracted with Bale over the years, I hadn't noticed that for the better part of our lives she had a head start on hating me. But I was playing catch-up now. It was something to fill the time, at least.

Then there was Chord, who was just sitting, staring out the window. Statue still, blinking. Finally, I hesitated by the last cell, Bale's. Bale was staring with intent at the wall. By the white-knuckled grip he had on the arms of his chair, I knew he was thinking about fire again. He was probably trying to set fire to the drywall with his mind right now.

Bale came to Whittaker like we all did: against his will. But he also came without a name. He was only six, like me. I had spent a whole year at Whittaker without him. An angry year. A sad year. A lonely year that I would never get back. And then there was Bale.

They said he had been left alone, starving and scrounging for food in an old house. His parents had left him there—parents he said he didn't remember. He was emaciated and dirty when he arrived—and not just from the soot from the flames. They said that he had stood and watched his house burn down after setting it on fire. He didn't try to run away. He just wanted, maybe needed, to watch it burn down to ashes. He claimed that he didn't remember anything about his parents even though he was old enough to remember. Dr. Harris said he was choosing subconsciously or unconsciously to forget. And he didn't know how to read or write, which some of the Whittaker kids made fun of. Just because we all lived in glass houses of insanity didn't mean that we could not be cruel.

That first day he walked through the Whittaker gates, I thought Bale had been sprung directly from my imagination, his red hair spiked up on his head like a little skeleton devil. He looked like he'd literally walked out of the fire instead of just setting one. One of the other kids ran and hid, but I walked right up to him and touched his face to make sure he was real. I can't say that I loved him at first sight, but I've been walking toward Bale from the second I met him.

Bale was a complete mystery to all of us. He didn't even know his own story. I had had so much therapy with art and dolls and stories already that I confused it for play.

"Why don't we make your story up?" I had suggested.

"Why would I want to do that?" he'd asked.

"For fun," I had countered with six-year-old logic. "I do it all the time about other people."

I pulled out my sketch pad and began to write: *Once upon a time* . . .

Bale looked at me like I was crazy, but he didn't retreat. I looked at his profile and drew a quick sketch of him.

"That's me," he'd said, pointing at his own chest. How he

found himself in my collection of rudimentary lines made me want to draw him out, make him tell his story even more.

"Now you tell me who you are," I'd urged, doing my best Dr. Harris impression. "Once upon time, there was a boy named . . . ," I singsonged, and waited.

"Bale," he had replied quickly. "Once upon a time, there was a boy named Bale who lived in a house made of wood. The monster made him cry like no mother or father should. Then his family went away. But made Bale stay. And Bale burned it all down one day."

To this day, I don't know if I remember it right or made it up, but the name Bale stuck and so did his story.

We had different monsters. Mine was my icy anger. Who wouldn't be angry after being locked up all their lives? Bale's was his love of fire. If fire didn't exist, I thought Bale would have been a normal boy. But a world without fire didn't exist any more than a world without air. Would Bale love me, understand me, if fire didn't consume him like it did?

I knew Bale loved me from the first time he saw me have an episode. He was no stranger to anger. And when I was feeling it, the sensation was so strong, it took over my whole body, making me hot and cold all at once. I was never sure if it was better to hold it in or let it out. Fighting against it felt like holding my breath. There was no way the anger wasn't coming out eventually, and my head always hurt from the pressure. Most people usually ran in the other direction when I exploded. But not Bale. He stood right next to me. He didn't touch me. He just stood patiently until I was done. When I stopped seeing red, and the intense, all-consuming wave of anger subsided, and everything in the room finally quieted down, he held my hand. That was when I fell in love with him, too.

I wanted my hand in his from that day to forever. Even if he did break it in two places eventually. Because no one really understood what it was like to live with this kind of rage and pain, like fire and ice, inside you. No one but us. And no matter what ward we were in, we always found our way to each other. Again and again. He made this place a home. Without him, Whittaker was the same thing for me as I'd always thought it was for everyone else: a prison.

I stood in the hallway of Ward D, staring intently at the back of Bale's head, willing him, begging him, to turn around. To look at me now.

He didn't.

Vern gently cupped my arm to get me to keep moving.

"Please . . . just a few more seconds," I pleaded.

She shook her head. "Child, if we could actually cure things by staring long enough, Whittaker wouldn't need to exist."

Begrudgingly, I continued down the hall toward the visitors' lounge.

"You know you're going to have to forgive your mother eventually," Vern said.

I shrugged. Mom had said she loved me. And despite all my problems and her committing me to an insane asylum my whole life, I believed she did, in her way. But after Bale broke my wrist, Dr. Harris had recommended that he and I be separated, and Mom had agreed. She took away the one thing that made Whittaker more than just survivable. He was my only friend. I could not forgive that. I hadn't even tried to.

Vern was still looking at me for a real answer about my mother, but I just shrugged again. Around me the hallway was growing cloudy, but the colors were more vivid than before. My footsteps felt lighter. My Happy dose was working.

"Well, you'll have to. Maybe not today. But soon," Vern said.

"Why?" I bit back—unapologetic.

"Because you only have about three people in the universe to talk to, Snow. And technically Dr. Harris and I are paid to."

I looked sharply at her. She laughed.

"You know you're my favorite, Hannibal Yardley."

That was my nickname because of the biting. She named me after a character who had a penchant for killing and cannibalism in a violent movie we weren't allowed to see. Coming from anyone else, the nickname would have elicited a toothier response and a bit of blood. But from Vern, I took it and kept on walking.

3

AS WE TURNED THE corner to the visitors' lounge, I could see the tapestries and high-backed, overstuffed armchairs where the asylum patients met with their parents once a month. It looked like a drawing room from one of those public television period dramas that Vern liked to watch. Only at Whittaker, the lamps were nailed down to the floor and tea was served lukewarm in paper cups for safety.

Mom was looking at her phone when the guard buzzed us through the double doors. She put it away quickly as if it were contraband. She didn't like to remind me of the things I didn't and couldn't have. We did not have cell phones at Whittaker. We had an ancient cordless phone in the common room that was monitored by the orderlies. Mom stood up and hugged me when I approached, wrapping me in her arms. She smelled of cinnamon and lemon, probably from her morning tea.

I didn't hug her back.

Behind me, the door clicked shut. Vern was giving us privacy, although the big mirror on the wall betrayed the fact that we were always being watched.

"You look happy today, Snow," Mom said, running her fingers through my hair as we sat down across from each other.

Ora Yardley was perfect and beautiful in every way. So much so that every time I saw her, I wondered how we could be from the same DNA. She had the same blond hair as me, which she inexplicably decided to dye auburn, and she had a perky nose that would make a cartoon princess jealous. Today she wore a sleeveless pale-pink sweater dress that skimmed over her curves and showed off her pale porcelain skin. Still, her eyes were my eyes: brown and deep. Her lips were my lips: full, with a tendency toward pouting. But hers were constantly, politely, upturned at the corners while mine went the other way.

Mom continued to stroke my hair. Like Vern, she said it had gone white from the medication I was given at Whittaker. But the way I remember it, my first streaks showed up the day after I walked through the mirror—before the doctors had figured out what drugs to give me. I remember looking in the mirror when I woke up in my new room and there they were.

"Honey, I wish you'd just let me do something about it," Mom tried again.

I pushed her hand away. "I like them."

"Honey," she began again, but she stopped when I pulled away completely.

"I brought you something." She smiled, giggling a little as she reached beneath her chair and pulled out a box. It was plain white and unwrapped, and had likely been searched before I got there. The ribbon was the tiniest bit askew, which was odd, because my mother was all about perfection. But I tore into the bow all the same. Not because the box was pretty, but because it was from my mom. Because it was new. Nothing was new at Whittaker.

Inside the box was a pair of pale-blue mittens. They looked homemade.

"Winter is coming soon," Mom said. "I wanted you to have something new for your walks with Vern."

Mom's smile deepened with the apparent hope that she had picked the right gift. Something to make everything better. Something to bridge the gap between us. Some part of me leaned into her at times like this. I was so close to melting. So close to forgiveness. But I thought back to the day when she and Dr. Harris had made the decision that changed my life.

"I've talked it over with Dr. Harris, and we're in agreement on this," she had said, sitting across from me in the same chair she was in today. "We think that it's best for you and Bale to be kept separate." She had made the decision so easily, like she was insisting on making me wear a helmet for riding my bike, not taking away the love of my life.

I had gotten angry too many times to count, and I felt it again now, the anger bubbling to the surface, but Happy did its job for once and tamped it down. I focused on the mittens in my lap.

"Thanks," I said.

"You're so welcome!" Mom clapped her hands. To her, my not throwing the mittens across the room meant that the gift was a success. When she smiled wide enough, I could see the faint white mark on her cheek pinch. It was the only imperfect thing about her, and it was because of me on the day everything changed. She'd been reading *Alice's Adventures in Wonderland*, and I had taken it literally and tried to walk through the looking glass with my best friend. But I didn't remember that day at all.

I learned from my dad that Becky, the girl I pulled through the mirror, and her family sued us, and we had settled. I never saw her again. But I still wondered about her. My scars had faded over the years, but they were still there, reminding me of how and why this all began. I wondered if Becky was out in the world with her scars, too.

When I first got to the institute, I thought that it was a punishment, a time-out for bad behavior. I sometimes wondered if my parents had just accepted Dr. Harris's diagnosis that day or if they knew when they dropped me off at Whittaker that it was forever.

Mom chatted on about Dad and the house, a place I had not seen in eleven years and couldn't care less about. And a dad who came every other month and on holidays. She must have noticed I was being distant, though, because she suddenly said, "Honey, I know you think that you and Bale are Romeo and Juliet, but this will pass."

I felt my anger notch up a bit, but my fingers started tapping against the leg of my pants and I swallowed down the rage. Mom gently removed the box that the mittens were nestled in and put it on the nailed-down coffee table. She studied me as she leaned back into her seat and re-crossed her legs.

"You think it's love, but it's not. I know what it's like to feel passion and think that you can change someone."

I perked up despite myself. Mom wasn't talking about me anymore. She was talking about herself.

"You tried to change Dad?" I asked. My mom was my mom, but my father was a different story. He was a stranger. Dad could barely handle seeing his crazy daughter on a bimonthly basis. Most of the time I had trouble understanding why they were even together, let alone imagining what Mom had tried to change about him.

"Not Dad," she countered, her voice a little faraway as if she were lost in a memory.

I never thought of Mom being with anyone else.

"The point is you can't change Bale. He's sick, honey. He broke your wrist and that will never be okay."

I closed my eyes, and my fingers tapped against my legs, almost of their own volition. I was getting angrier and itched to sketch something. I needed to calm down, or I would get thrown in solitary.

"When they called me to tell me that he had broken your wrist, I was so scared. Bale's not well." Mom's eyes filled with tears. She reached out and put her hands over mine, stopping my finger taps entirely.

"Does that apply to me, too?" I asked pointedly.

"What do you mean?"

"I mean, if Bale can't get better, that means I can't, either. Right?"

"That's not what I meant," Mom faltered. Her lips formed a thin, tight worry line.

"But it's what you think."

"It's not. I know it's hard for you to believe, but everything I do is out of love, including protecting you."

"Then love me a little less," I said without missing a beat. I didn't know why I said it.

"Impossible," she said automatically.

I crossed my arms and glared at her until she started to deflate.

She gazed at me for a long beat, shoulders hunched, before looking at the mirror on the wall to signal Vern. Our twenty minutes were up. Vern was in the room within seconds.

"Vern, I'd love to see Dr. Harris before I go." My mother bit her lip, and she had a faraway look that I had seen on *The End of Almost* when characters were thinking of things that they shouldn't, but ultimately would, do.

Mom cried a little as she hugged me good-bye. I don't even know if she realized I never hugged her back.

I had a secret, though. I still loved her even though I never ever showed it. But Mom never stopped visiting, never stopped talking, never stopped trying, and I suppose if she had I would have hated her for real then.

I couldn't let her in. I couldn't survive in here if I did. I would have gone soft with longing for what I once had: a pretty little room perfect for a five-year-old me and a mother who stroked my hair at night. We couldn't play mother and daughter in here, until she was ready to take me home and do it for real out there.

"I'll walk you, Ora," Vern said. She told the orderly at the desk to look after me. Then she grabbed a sketch pad and some charcoal and placed them on the coffee table in front of me, next to my new mittens.

"Now, don't get into any trouble." Vern wagged her finger at me.

But for me, it was impossible not to.

4

I HAD STARTED TO sketch last night's dream—the tree and the thing in the water—when Magpie appeared in the doorway, fresh from a walk around the grounds. Her orderly, a short Jamaican woman named Cecilia, let her into the visitors' lounge without noticing me there. She had no doubt gone for a smoke break and Magpie wasn't a runner or violent so she probably thought nothing of leaving her alone. But Magpie did antagonize others. Especially me.

Magpie was wearing coral-pink lipstick today. It didn't quite match her olive-brown complexion, but thieves couldn't be choosers. The coral was the same shade that Elizabeth, the nurse at reception, wore. How Magpie managed to lift it off her was a bit of a mystery, considering that I'd never seen Elizabeth cross the line between the private and the public quarters.

Magpie's actual name was Ophelia. But her nickname came from her penchant for taking things. Magpie didn't just steal physical things. She stole secrets, too. Sometimes I thought that maybe she had all that junk where her soul was supposed to be.

"Not so tough without your firebug?" she taunted.

While she was talking, she twisted her shiny black hair into a knot. I knew I shouldn't let her get to me, but I couldn't stop myself sometimes. Okay, most times. And Magpie usually deserved it.

I'd seen the look on her face when she had stolen something and watched the person look for it, all the while knowing that the missing item was rattling around in her pocket or hidden under her bed. Gleeful. Evil. Magpie had the same look now as she spoke about Bale. Even though she had nothing to do with our separation, she still enjoyed toying with my loss.

"Shut it, Magpie," I snapped. My fingers curled into my palms. *Come on, Happy. Work your magic.* But it was as if the effects of the pill were burning away as my anger rose.

Magpie's expression turned suddenly coy. Like she knew something I didn't. "Well, let me know if you need anything. I can get anything that anyone wants. Anything."

I didn't know where she was going with this. Magpie spoke in riddles sometimes. And depending on my mood, I decided whether or not to play.

She pulled out a packet of matches and tossed them from one hand to the other. Her wicked smile was back, and it was clear she was waiting for me to connect the dots.

I'd always wondered how Bale managed to set fire after fire at the asylum. I always blamed careless orderlies. But Magpie was saying that she could and possibly had given as well as taken.

The anger I'd been holding in since I'd seen my mother boiled over. I felt it inside me like icy-hot flames licking their way up my chest and fighting to get out. I lunged at her with a scream, fury taking over. I grabbed her hair and yanked as hard as I could, but then something weird happened. I expected her to yell or push back. Instead she stopped in her tracks. Her mouth opened, but no sound came out. She fell to the floor and lay completely still.

"Very funny. I am not falling for this," I said, looking down at her seemingly lifeless form.

She did not move.

I knelt down and touched her arm. Her skin was cold. Her lips were blue. Her eyelashes looked suddenly frosty white.

"Hey, not funny," I said again. I was considering doing mouth-to-mouth or chest compressions—not that I knew how to do either, but I'd seen it on TV.

Magpie's eyes blinked open. She looked at me both pleadingly and accusingly at once. Her gaze shifted from me to the door.

The White Coat at the desk who was supposed to be watching me was engrossed in a *People* magazine. I got up and yelled for him.

"It's Magpie! I . . ." My voice trailed off.

"What did you do?" he demanded as he ran over.

I looked down at Magpie, prostrate and unmoving in the center of the floor. Her eyes fluttered once more before they closed entirely.

5

"AREN'T YOU SUPPOSED TO take me back to my room?" I
raised my eyebrows as Vern led me into the common room.

"Just because you went all Hannibal on Magpie doesn't mean
I have to miss what happened to Kayla Blue," Vern explained,
plopping us down on the plastic chairs in front of the common
room TV. She was referring to Rebecca Gershon's daughter on
our favorite show, *The End of Almost*.

On-screen, Kayla Blue was crying her eyes out. She had just
told River that she wasn't the woman he thought she was. His
angular face registered confusion as she explained her complicated
past to him. But within minutes he was back on one knee, pro-
posing to her. The speed of his understanding and his forgiveness
was kind of beautiful. The certainty of his love was something to
be envied even if it was just a story. I found myself leaning in.

All of us at Whittaker learned things from television, because
that was the closest thing we had to school and boys and prom

and friends. But we didn't know what happened between the commercial breaks or after things faded to black. I knew there was a difference between reel life and real life, but the television taught me everything I knew about kisses and dates and broken hearts and family dramas—sometimes all wrapped up in a bow within half-hour or hourly segments.

Kayla Blue had just said "yes" when Vern got a text on her phone. I couldn't read her expression. *Was it about Magpie?*

"Is she . . . ?" I asked, not quite sure how I felt about hearing the answer. I had wanted to hurt her but not badly, and I certainly didn't want her dead.

"Now you care, Yardley?"

I didn't have a defense, exactly, so I shrugged. I was a master at shrugging.

"Looks like Magpie is going to make a full recovery. She was paralyzed temporarily. But she seems to have regained the full use of her extremities. Toes wiggling. Eyes rolling. She's back to herself."

I can't say that I felt relief. But a wave of something came over me just the same.

"Child, I know Magpie has a way of starting things, and I'm not telling you to just ignore her. But sometimes you got to fight quieter. Sometimes you got to pretend a little."

"You're not going to tell me not to fight?"

"Don't quote me on this, or I'll deny it. But I'd be worried if you stopped fighting. That isn't to say you should go around pulling Magpie by the hair. Even if she said something that deserved it."

Vern took me back to my room after that. Tomorrow would be filled with recriminations. Probably a new drug protocol and another visit from my mother. If my parents thought this was serious enough, maybe even my father, too. But since Magpie still breathed in and out and had regained the use of her limbs, there would be no real consequences. Vern knew it and I knew it. But for the hour that we watched *The End of Almost*, Vern thought that my anger had taken another victim. And that I had changed everything.

6

I WAS IN MY room at Whittaker. It was dark, and I was staring into a hand mirror encircled with metal and decorated in symbols and strange writing along the sides. A giant, silver-looking tree covered in carvings took up the entire reflection. And in front of the tree, there was me.

"Bale?" I whispered. He was usually in my dreams, but lately he'd been missing. It was a cruel insult to injury that I didn't get to see him even in my subconscious.

"I'm here, Snow!" he called, his voice hoarse like he'd been crying. Or screaming. "Behind the tree."

My reflection in the glass smirked at me even though my face hadn't moved a muscle. The "me" in the mirror raised her arms even though my own remained at my sides. The arms reached for me, then suddenly one of them pulled back to punch.

"No! Snow, don't!" Bale cried out, but I couldn't see him, and I couldn't stop what happened next as my reflection's fist collided with the mirror.

I covered my face as glass fell into the room, landing on the tile floor all around me. I examined myself for scratches, but somehow none of the shards had touched me. Then, almost against my will, I picked up the pieces and began assembling them into something, despite the fact that my hands stung and every movement drew blood. I placed my handiwork on top of my head, ignoring the pain. I had made a crown that shimmered like ice. A line of blood dripped down its surface.

♛

I woke to the sound of a knock on my door. No one ever knocked at Whittaker.

Then the door opened. It was Dr. Harris.

This had to be bad. The good doctor didn't make room visits. *Did Vern get in trouble for letting me watch TV after I hurt Magpie?* I wondered. I mentally patted myself on the back for thinking of someone else first. There was no seven-dwarf pill for empathy; my concern for Vern was genuine. Dr. Harris had said empathy was good. Little did he know I was already putting what I did to Magpie in my rearview. She had come after me in the visitors' lounge. She had given Bale matches. She had added to Bale's fire. That girl was a bitch, and everyone knew it. She deserved what she got.

"I heard Magpie's fine," I said preemptively.

Dr. Harris wore glasses and a perpetual crease between his stark green eyes that seemed to always stare a little bit too long. Not in a lascivious way, but in an "I want to find out how you tick" kind of way.

I wasn't used to his being in my space or standing upright. He was supposed to be in his office behind a desk, not moving much more than an eyebrow.

"I am here to check on you," Dr. Harris said curtly. "Tell me about what happened."

"Magpie came at me. And I gave it right back. I barely touched her. There's no way I pushed her hard enough for her to be paralyzed, even temporarily. She must have been faking it."

"The doctor says she's fine. Ophelia does tend toward the dramatic. But I am more concerned about you. You were angry. We've talked about this. You have to gain control and learn to express your anger without making it a physical thing."

He waited for me to say something. But I had nothing to add. This was exactly the conversation I was expecting. I just didn't expect to be having it in my room.

"I'm going to try something new with your therapy. You know that we could not keep you in this ward if you had actually . . ." He trailed off, which was unlike him.

Killed Magpie, I thought. That's what he was going to say.

"There isn't anything beyond Ward D," I reminded him. *What more could they do to me?*

"If something had actually happened tonight, the state would have taken you away from me . . . away from Whittaker. Criminal charges would have been pressed. Do you understand?"

I nodded.

"Don't worry, Snow. We will keep you here, where you belong." He almost looked sincere. "I'm going to start you on a new protocol tomorrow."

I gritted my teeth. Another cocktail.

He walked farther into the room, holding out a white cup to me. I hadn't even seen it in his hand. "In the meantime, you need rest. Good rest."

I noticed two White Coats just outside the door, watching, waiting. Just in case things got out of hand. I guess Dr. Harris was more worried about what I did to Magpie than I thought.

"Go on," he said, rattling the pill inside the cup.

I snatched it from his hand and looked inside. The little blue-and-yellow powdered pill I called Sleepy stared up at me. Just looking at it drained all the anger right out of me. And I kind of wanted that pill. I really *was* tired.

"Thatta girl," said Dr. Harris as I swallowed it down and lay back on my pillow. I was already starting to fade out by the time he closed my door. But before I fell asleep, I couldn't help but hear Dr. Harris's voice resonating through my brain. *We will keep you here, where you belong.*

He was wrong. Whittaker wasn't my home. No one deserved to be locked up forever. What was the point of life, then? Didn't he want me to get better?

I didn't know where I belonged, but it wasn't there.

Later, the door to my room opened in the middle of the night, pulling me out of a deep sleep. At first I thought it was Vern doing spot checks. It wasn't. Even through the cloudy, drug-induced haze I could see the boy standing by my bed. He had light-brown hair that fell partly over his eyes and dusted his shoulders, curling slightly at the edges. His features were soft, light eyebrows, small nose, full lips. But I could see a sharp jawline as his face jutted out into a moonbeam that had fallen like a spotlight. His eyes glowed a silvery gray in the near dark.

"You're awake," he said. I noticed then he was wearing an orderly's white coat that looked a size too big for him. We made eye contact. "It's really you."

Though I felt my heartbeat pick up, my body still felt heavy and sluggish. I didn't move. There were a million things wrong with the fact that someone other than Vern was in my room at night. First and foremost, he was not an adult; he was a boy. He looked near my age, give or take a few months. Plus, White Coat night checks were strictly matched by gender to cut down on the chance for impropriety. Some inmates didn't have boundaries in that department.

Some White Coats didn't, either.

I watched the boy take a step closer. The hairs on my arms stood up, and everything in my body told me to be on guard. There was something about him, something *more* about him that demanded attention—period. He looked like he had stepped out of *The End of Almost.* How was it possible that someone who looked like this was in my room? This boy was almost aerodynamic, like a shiny sports car. Even wearing that oversize white coat, I could tell that there was no amount of flesh or muscle misused. He was just as thin as Bale, who had grown out of the skeleton boy he was as a child into something else entirely. But Bale's lines were softer because he was locked in his room most of the time.

I looked down and caught a peek at the boy's shoes. They were shiny and black, the kind you wear for an interview or to a party or a wedding—not to a crazy girl's room in the middle of the night.

I finally pushed myself up in bed.

"I didn't mean to scare you," he said in a whisper. "When I got a signal that magic was being used here, I had no idea it would lead me to you of all people."

Magic? Had he just said magic?

His hair fell over one of his eyes as he leaned into my personal space.

Most people at Whittaker—if they knew anything—knew not to get that close to me after the Hannibal incident with Vern.

But Sleepy had made my wits slow, and instead of biting him, I closed my eyes in a drawn-out blink.

"There you are. I see you under all those drugs. Don't you want to come out and play, Snow?"

Who was this guy? I stared off toward the wall and refocused, trying to shake off the drugs.

"Fine, just listen. The pills that Dr. Harris is giving you aren't helping you. They're hiding you from who you really are and what you're meant to be. They're hiding you from your destiny. Stop taking them. Start *feeling* everything. And when you are clean, come to me. I'll be waiting on the other side of the Tree." He stood up straight and crossed his arms. The room was still cloudy around him.

This guy I've never met wants me to leave and go where?

Bale used to talk about running away, and sometimes I would indulge the idea. But the truth was, deep down I was always worried that I would end up face-first in a mirror again. And Bale would burn down whatever house we were in. Now I regret never trying, for him. For us. If I were going to escape, it would be with Bale. Not for this stranger.

My lips and voice finally decided to work. "I could yell right now, and the White Coats would be here in sixty seconds," I said, thinking about the panic button behind my bed. There was one in every patient's room. I had never pushed it for a real emergency. I'd only used it once as a joke and asked for room service when Dr. Harris had briefly assigned me another orderly. Vern was back in a week.

The boy was undaunted by my challenge. He did not move a muscle.

"You could have called for help, but you haven't. Besides, I am the help."

"Who are you?" I asked.

"Who *you* are is what matters, Princess."

I had been called a lot of names at Whittaker. "Princess" was never one of them.

He saw that he had my full attention. A smile spread across his face. He was pleased. Then he bent down, closer. "You need to leave this place, Princess. It's breaking your spirit. The gate on the north corner will open for you. Head north until you see the Tree."

"The Tree?" I asked. I thought of the tree from my dreams. This had to be another dream. It was too coincidental.

"You'll know it when you see it. I promise. When you get to the other side of the Tree, I'll be waiting. And they will kneel for you."

"What are you talking about? And why do you keep calling me Princess? I am no one's princess."

"You really don't know, do you?" he said solemnly. "They've dulled your magic and your wits."

"What the hell?" I snapped. Sleepy's effects were starting to wane, and this guy's riddles were starting to piss me off. He clearly was a new patient off his meds.

"Just remember the Tree . . . "

I started to sit up farther, ready to show this guy just what kind of princess I really was. Then the boy abruptly turned around and walked toward the plastic mirror on my closet. And he did something that stopped me cold.

He stepped right through it.

I squeezed my eyes shut and pressed my palms into them. This was a dream. Yes, it would be my weirdest one yet, but still. A dream. Had to be.

I opened my eyes again. They adjusted to the dark quickly this time. The room looked normal. No strange boy to be seen. But when I stared into the mirror next to my desk, I swear I could see the silhouette of a boy in an oversize white coat, growing smaller and smaller . . . receding in the reflection. And in the background was the faint outline of a large tree, the Tree.

When I blinked again, the Tree and the boy were gone.

7

EVEN THOUGH I COULD barely see in the dark, I grabbed my sketchbook and began to draw the boy's face. I wanted to get it all down, every detail. Whether it was all in my head or not, I didn't want to forget him.

As the line of his jaw emerged from beneath my fingers, I shuddered. He called me "Princess." Whatever the reason why, I didn't like it.

I had been called worse, and I had earned every nickname with my words and my teeth. I looked down at the sketch again. Recording my dreams on paper was my own personal exorcism. Afterward, I always felt free of whatever it was that had haunted me the night before. But this time when I looked at the picture of the boy, I almost felt like his eyes were staring back at me.

I must have fallen asleep like that, gazing at my own handiwork, because the next thing I knew I was waking again to the sound of the door opening. Daylight was streaming through the barred windows. Vern was holding the pill tray. The boy from last night rushed to my mind, and I snapped the sketch pad shut. I had fallen asleep with the charcoal clutched in my hand. I didn't know if he was a patient or an orderly, or if Sleepy concocted him out of my imagination and put him into my dreams. Either way, I wasn't ready for Vern or anyone else to see the sketches of him.

"You're already up? That's a first."

"It was Grand Central Station in here last night," I said, thinking about the orderly again.

She raised an eyebrow.

"Dr. Harris stopped by. And a guy who dubbed me a princess."

"Princess, huh?" Vern snorted. "Yardley, you're as much royalty as I am." She said it almost affectionately, but then she held out the tray with the day's pills, and I thought about what the boy had said. Even if he was just a figment of my imagination, maybe my subconscious was telling me that enough was enough.

I knew each pill did something different. But eventually the effects wore off, and Dr. Harris would start something new. My medication changed more than most. We patients would compare sometimes. Chord and Wing were almost always on Sleepy. It kept them in place. For Wing, it kept her from flying. And for Chord, it kept him from blinking through time. Sometimes Dr. Harris added Happy, because there was a lot of depression involved with not getting to be exactly where he wanted to be.

I assumed that Dr. Harris was trying really hard to get the right combination that would level me off. Make me normal. Stop all the anger. Put my monster to sleep.

But what if what the boy said was true? What if the drugs were masking everything and not solving anything? The idea of giving up all the drugs terrified me. I hadn't been completely clean—not for as long as I could remember.

"Which of the seven dwarfs is it today?" I asked, assuming the answer had to be Dopey. Given my behavior yesterday, my mom's visit, and my Sleepy dose last night, I was sure rest was the continuing prescription of the day.

But this pill was new. It was black with little tiny dots. I wanted to recoil, to ask Vern what was in it, to refuse to take it. But if I did that, they would make me take it, or worse—they would give me a shot of it straight to my veins instead. So I hid my reaction and pretended everything was normal—well, at least normal for me. Instead of swallowing, I slipped the pill under my tongue and felt it threatening to melt. The plastic casing softened as I waited for Vern to check my mouth. She barely looked, either because she trusted me or because I had never skipped a pill before.

When she glanced out the window to exclaim, "Look at that! We weren't supposed to have snow today," I spit the pill into my palm. She looked back at me, expecting a response about the weather.

I just shrugged and felt a twinge of something—not guilt— but a shift in our dynamic. I had a secret. I hadn't said a word, but it was the first lie between me and Vern in a long time— maybe ever.

Hiding the pill in my pocket, I took my sketch pad, and we silently marched to the common room. It was time for *The End of Almost*.

Vern turned on the television and took a seat next to me.

We settled into watching her story, and I realized at some point it had become part of mine, too. The lives on-screen were a window to another world where anything could happen—even the impossible. Today the show was focused on the family's matriarch, Rebecca Gershon. She was like a chameleon and could make herself whoever she needed to be to get what she wanted. She had had as many careers as husbands, and she was currently working on Love #7. The characters vacillated between good and bad and back again. It was a world that wasn't real, but also one filled with forgiveness and second chances. By comparison, I hadn't even had my first job or been on an actual date.

"Why doesn't Rebecca just tell the soldier guy how she feels?"

I knew his name was Lucas. I liked to pretend that the stories meant more to Vern than they did to me. But I knew every detail, every subplot and history and twist and turn from Rebecca's first husband to her tenth, and I was pretty sure that Lucas was the one true love for Rebecca. He wasn't as handsome as her other lovers over the years. But he was the first to love her unconditionally. Only he could not actually say what was so completely obvious to me and to Vern.

"Sometimes saying something is harder than not saying it. You wouldn't know because you have no filter, but out there in the world people spend most of their lives afraid to say what's really on their minds."

It sounded like Vern was calling me brave . . . or crazy. Maybe they were the same thing.

I wondered about Vern's life outside this place. I knew she

had a husband and a kid who smiled at me from her smartphone. Tall, but not Vern tall. And the way Vern looked at Lucas and Rebecca on TV made me wonder if there was a lost love in her past—someone who would have altered the course of her everything. And just as the idea floated through my brain, another thought popped up: the boy. Not that he was going to really alter the course of my everything. He was just a new shade of crazy that I hadn't seen before.

I picked up my sketchbook and began to finish the drawing of the boy from last night.

"Who's that?" asked Vern during a commercial break.

"The new orderly." I was testing her for information.

"He's cute. But he doesn't work here. You didn't actually see him, did you?" Vern asked pointedly.

I shrugged. "I guess it was a dream."

♛

I was at home in my mother's room, staring into the full-length mirror by her dressing table. Suddenly Becky appeared. She smiled and shook her pigtails—but something was wrong. She was covered in blood. When I looked back at the mirror, it was broken and I was covered in blood, too. Beyond the shattered glass, I saw a giant tree glistening in the snow. Next to it was the boy from last night. Instead of wearing a stolen white coat, he had on a leather vest and bloodred tunic. A brown satchel was slung across his chest. He waved to me.

I pulled Becky's arm. "We have to go," I said, but she wouldn't budge. I pulled again and looked back at her, but then she was gone and Bale had taken her place.

"Bale," I breathed. It had been so long since I last saw him, since I touched him. I looked down at my hand around his wrist. He was covered in blood, too. "You're hurt." I turned to inspect him closer, but he took both of my hands then, intertwining his fingers in mine. He was okay.

He looked at me, really stared, his long lashes almost distracting me from the dark amber of his eyes. "I can't go with you," Bale finally said.

I turned back to the mirror and saw the orderly-boy still waving, the tree towering over him, and all around him on the ground people were kneeling, heads bowed in my direction. I wanted to go, but Bale wouldn't move.

"I can't," Bale said more firmly.

So I pulled him toward the mirror, as hard as I could, and he let go of my hands. I stumbled back, expecting to crash right into the cracked glass, but instead I felt only air. Cold air.

I found my footing again and looked to Bale, but when I turned around to face him, he was on fire.

I screamed myself awake and knew I had to see Bale. Tonight.

8

THAT NIGHT AFTER DINNER, Vern walked me back to my room.

When we turned the corner to the main hallway, we passed Wing and Sarah.

"Sno-o-o-o-w." Wing drew my name out and reached for me.

She was wearing a pink scrunchie today and had glitter on her cheeks. She loved colors, but the Whittaker uniform didn't allow for much else.

I brushed my fingertips against hers. "Hi, Wing."

"Got into the art supplies again today, Wing?" Vern scolded affectionately.

It was impossible not to love Wing, but sad, too. It was like being friends with a bird whose wings had been clipped. Her whole self was wrapped up in what she believed was her sole purpose in life. She could not think of anything else but flight.

"No, no, no, no, no." Wing shook her head rapidly. "No, no,

no. This is my Sparkle." She pointed to her cheeks. "I need my Sparkle."

Wing's "Sparkle" was like her magic dust. She said she needed it to grow her wings back so she could fly. We all had our dreams here, I guessed. I wished that there was a pill that could give her a different one.

"Come on now, hon." Sarah gently guided Wing into her room.

Wing reached for me again, and again I let her fingers brush mine. She smiled, and I did, too. But my smile turned quickly to a scowl when I heard another voice.

"Why are you still here?" Magpie hissed as she passed us. Cecilia immediately told her to "hush" and pulled her along faster.

Vern gave me the side-eye. Magpie was trying to get a rise out of me, and Vern didn't want another fight to break out. But I ignored them both. I was focused on my plan.

My mind and heartbeat both raced. It was happening. Tonight I was going to see Bale. We'd talk and leave this whole business of his breaking my wrist in the past. I had let too much time pass. The dream was my wake-up call. I had let what had happened after the kiss come between us. We were more than that moment. I would make him see that what happened had to have been a bad reaction to meds. It wasn't him. It wasn't me.

The heavy-duty duct tape Vern had hung my pictures with came in handy. While she was pulling out my nightclothes, I covertly stuck a piece against the lock of the door so that it wouldn't click shut.

"You okay, Yardley?" she asked as I dressed.

"Yeah," I lied. "Why?"

Vern just shook her head and held out my night's dose. It was the little black pill with the dots again. I didn't know what it was or why I should be taking it three times a day, but I didn't question it again. Instead I tossed it into my mouth and took a big gulp of water.

"Open up," said Vern. She examined my mouth a little closer than usual, but she still didn't see it hiding under the back of my tongue. "Okay then."

When I said good night, Vern paused in the doorway and looked back at me as if sensing that something was off. I held my breath, hoping that she wouldn't brush against the duct tape and pull it off onto her scrubs. Or worse yet, see it there.

"You're a good kid, Snow. Tough, but good," she said quietly.

I almost started crying then. All the anticipation and sneaking around had been building. I wasn't used to keeping secrets. Hell, my head wasn't usually clear enough to plan more than an hour in advance, let alone an elaborate scheme. Being off the meds only made all my feelings that much more intense. Vern was always so nice to me. More than nice. She was the only adult in my life who didn't treat me like I would crack at any moment.

"Thanks, Vern," I said quietly.

Vern just nodded, then let the door close behind her. I listened for the squeak of her sneakers to recede down the hall before checking to see if the door had locked shut. It hadn't. The duct tape had worked.

Then I got back into bed and waited an agonizing hour for

lights-out. It felt like an eternity, but finally all the orderlies left their wards one by one. When the coast was clear, I slipped out of my room and into the hall.

The doors of our rooms opened only from the outside, so I brought extra duct tape with me so I could get out. Getting into Bale's room was easy. What came next wasn't going to be. I didn't know how he was going to react to seeing me after what my kiss had made him do.

I watched him for a moment before waking him. Even with his arms and legs strapped to the bed—I could see the buckles peeking out from under the corners of the blankets—he looked at peace. His chest rose and fell in even intervals. He was beautiful. He was mine.

His red hair was matted, and the curls that I loved running my fingers through when the White Coats were out of sight were shaved near his temples. Vern had left that out when she told me how he was. I chastised her in my head for her omission before remembering my own deceit.

"Hey, where have you been, Snow?" Bale asked sleepily when I shook him awake.

I couldn't believe we were talking like it hadn't been a year since he spoke, like we hadn't kissed and he hadn't broken my wrist and my heart. I swallowed and spoke slowly. He was on the cocktail, and I wanted him to understand what I was about to say. "I know it doesn't seem like it, but you are the one who's been away."

"Where did I go?"

"It doesn't matter. What matters is that you're back now."

"It does matter. I remember," he said, his voice choking like he was struggling for the words. "I remember what I did to you after the kiss. I've ruined it. Us."

"How about I fracture your wrist and then we'll be even?" I joked, trying to make light of what was so heavy between us.

Bale flinched. He didn't know he'd injured me that badly. I'd said too much. I moved to squeeze his hand, but I wasn't sure if either one of us was ready yet. It was just good to talk to him, and for him to see me and not want to run away.

"I hurt you. We'll never get past that. It will always be between us," he said, sounding resolute and so sad. "I know who you are, Snow."

I could still remember the feeling of Bale's grip around my wrist and the look in his eyes when he said it the first time. *I see what you are now . . .* But I knew in my gut that what made Bale stop talking that day after the kiss had everything to do with Dr. Harris and this place and nothing to do with who we both were.

"And I know who you are, Bale. You're a good person." Tears welled up in my eyes. "I forgive you, okay?"

Bale wasn't listening, though. He was stuck reliving the moment of our kiss. I could see the guilt washing over him in waves, and I couldn't find a way to assuage it. But then just as suddenly he began to laugh as if he had finally understood a joke a little too late. His laugh was throaty and full of life.

I'd missed Bale's laugh.

And he had missed me, too. I could feel it.

I felt my cheeks stretch into a smile, something I hadn't done without sarcasm in forever. I put a finger up to my lips to warn him that we had to be quiet.

Bale's laughter faded away.

There was no forgetting.

"I don't have a choice, Snow," Bale said. His eyes took on a glassy stare.

"What are you talking about?"

"I have to burn it all down. It's the only way to make it stop."

"Make what stop?"

"We can't change who we are. We have to burn."

Bale wasn't okay. He wasn't anywhere near okay. "You're going to get better, Bale." I said it more for myself than for him.

I reached my hand out to touch him, but I hesitated again. I missed the hollow of his chest. That night a year ago, after the kiss and after the orderlies had taken him away, after I had had my wrist set in that awful air cast, I had sneaked into Bale's room and climbed into his bed with him. I curled up beside him and stroked his left arm softly. A mark had bloomed on his pale skin. It almost looked like a tattoo or a birthmark of a star with razor-sharp points inside a circle. I had never seen it before, and I thought I knew every inch of Bale's flesh that I had been allowed to see.

That night, I had put my head on his chest and listened to his heartbeat. It was my favorite sound in the whole world. The thumping was strong and solid against his rib cage. It reverberated through me, promising me that he would come back to me, promising me that we would be this close and closer someday in the future. Even though his arms were restrained. Even though his mind had gone somewhere that I could not follow. His heart was still here. And I was pretty sure that it still beat for me.

I was caught within minutes. A slice of bright light cut through the room from the open door. A White Coat stood, ready to pounce and punish. But every second was worth it. My head resting on his chest felt like the most intimate thing I'd ever done. More than kissing. Because there was absolutely no distance between us.

Now, back in Bale's room, I looked at his arms, restrained again. The circular mark on his left forearm was still there. I ran my fingers lightly across his arm just above the star. His skin was hot. Too hot. He was burning up with fever. Then he smiled a wicked grin, and for the first time ever, I was a little afraid of him. It killed me, but I had to look away.

Bale needed help. He was saying these awful things because he was sick. If he hadn't been restrained, he might have grabbed me then—and part of me wanted that more than anything. I wished for the right words to bring him back to me, but he was beyond my reach.

Should I kiss him again? Shame washed over me. I was selfish for thinking it, but I wanted to so badly. To feel his lips pressed against mine without meds thrumming through my body. If I was truly feeling everything for the first time now, I wanted to feel this, too.

Another thought came at me, jarring and random and wrong, like the ones I usually had on Dopey. *What if a kiss could cure him, un-break him and bring him back to me?*

"We have to burn," he said again, louder this time, pulling hard against his straps.

Bale, my Bale, was in trouble. This fire inside him wasn't just in his brain. His body was so hot.

I leaned over him, my face inches above his own. He stilled for a moment, looking up at me through those long, thick lashes.

"Snow." He sighed, his breath sweet and hot against my cheeks. I stayed there for a moment, stuck somewhere between desire and need. I wanted Bale back. But I needed him to be okay more.

"I love you," I whispered, leaning in. That was when I noticed something in the small barred window just above his bed.

Gone was the view of the Whittaker grounds, and in its place *was a mirror*. Its surface rippled and sparkled. Completely entrancing . . . but then a pair of stark white arms extended out of it. They reached for me.

"What the—?" I jumped back just before they made contact. From the liquid surface of the mirror, a cold gust of wind blew through the room. "Bale!" I screamed. I had to free him and get him out of there before this thing got into the room.

Bale was thrashing violently in his bed now, pulling at his restraints. When I tried to unbuckle his left wrist, I could barely get to it, he was moving so much. "Bale, please stop. We have to leave!" I finally was able to grab his wrist but had to yank my fingers back. Something stung, badly. I stared at them and noticed blisters were already forming. Almost as if they'd been burned.

The arms reached farther down from the mirror. They were

impossibly long. Two fingers touched Bale's forehead, causing him to cry out. As he screamed, his straps glowed, from yellow to a deep orange.

"Bale!" I screamed again and clawed at one of the arms, trying to pull it off him. I stumbled into the night table and hit the panic button hard.

"Help!" I screamed as loud as I could. I ran to the door and yanked it open, pulling the duct tape right off. "Help! It's Bale!" I yelled into the hall. Then I heard a tearing sound behind me, and a crack. When I looked back, Bale's restraints dangled off his wrists and ankles. His thrashing had stopped. He lay limp in the cold, white arms that were pulling him back toward the mirror.

I could hear commotion in the hallway, running footsteps, and the other patients awaking, moans and cries echoing in Ward D. I ran back to Bale's side, his door clicking shut behind me. I wrapped my arms around his body. Nobody was going to take him away from me. Not again.

Bale was slipping out of my grasp. "Bale, no!" I cried.

But the arms had a firm hold around his body and pulled him up until I couldn't hold on any longer. And in an instant, Bale and the mirror were gone.

My heart raced and my breathing deepened. I ran to the window, screaming his name. But I was all alone in his room when the White Coats answered my screams.

It couldn't be. But it was.

👑

Vern led me back to my room.

"We'll find him, sweetie. He's probably in the basement like last time."

No one had ever snuck out of Whittaker. Vern assumed wrongly that no one ever would.

"Hey, when did you become an escape artist?" she said almost gently, trying to deflect from what her hands were doing. Vern took out the syringe.

"Please, Vern," I begged, my eyes on the needle.

"Child, you need to sleep. Those bags under your eyes are so big, I could fit my scrubs into them. When you wake up, Bale will be back in his bed where he belongs."

I realized that she didn't believe me. She wouldn't believe me. The only thing I could do was stop her from dosing me so I could go out and find my Bale.

"I just wanted to see him again," I said, only telling her half the truth.

She pulled back the covers, and I crawled into bed, biting the inside of my cheek to keep calm, to keep from screaming. I heard myself whimper as the syringe went into my arm, right in the middle of all my scars that spread out like a spiderweb. Then my sobs died a quick death, and I was asleep in an instant.

But the pain of the needle wasn't why I was crying.

9

THE BOY APPEARED AGAIN that night, standing next to my bed. This time I was sure it was a dream. Everything felt sharper than usual, more surreal.

"You know where Bale is, don't you?"

The ceiling was gone. Glittery white snow fell from the darkness above and filled the room.

"You have him."

"I don't," he said with difficulty. The snow landed on him softly, but he flinched with each flake. Dots of blood formed on his skin where the snow pierced it.

I thought, *Maybe* I'm *hurting him*.

"What's happening?" I asked.

"You need to control yourself," he gritted. "I don't have Bale. If you come with me, I will help you find him. But you need to control your temper."

His saying that only made my temper flare, like a stoked coal.

"Please," he said with a grimace.

I believed him. Or at least I wanted to. And it was clear he was in pain, so I grabbed my sketch pad and started scribbling.

"What are you doing?" he asked.

I didn't look up. Not at the boy in my room. Not at the raining snow.

"I'm calming down," I said, breathing out through my nose slowly.

I would draw myself out of this mad dream.

Then the boy said the answer to everything.

"Bale is on the other side of the Tree."

When I woke a few hours later with dirty fingers and charcoal dust all over my bed, I knew two things: where Bale was and that I was going to follow.

I knew the boy was right. Because drawn over and over, page after page in my sketch pad, was the same image: the Tree with the carvings from my dreams.

I waited until the predawn room checks were done before trying to escape again. It was still dark out, but the moon was getting low in the sky. Luckily, Vern hadn't bothered to check the door on her way out, and the tape was still intact. There wouldn't be another sweep for at least an hour, so I slipped into the silent hall and made my way toward the exit.

"Again!" a familiar voice said behind me. I didn't want to turn around, but I did. "Sleepwalking is not part of your repertoire, Yardley. Let's get you back to bed," she said.

"I'm sorry, Vern. I have to go. I have to do this. I have to find Bale."

I took a hesitant step backward, just inches from the exit, but Vern knew my tricks and was by my side in an instant.

"Let our people find him," she said solemnly. "They'll bring him home."

"Only I can," I tried to explain. "He's somewhere only I can go. Please, Vern."

Her face crumpled. She wasn't disappointed. She was worried I was having a setback.

"I don't know what happened to him, but I won't let anything happen to you, too."

I wasn't sure if I could fight Vern. I knew I didn't want to. I knew that she was bigger than me—a lot bigger. But before she could drag me back to my room, there was a crash down the hall, followed by a rush of footsteps and voices.

"She's coding—"

"Vern!" another orderly yelled. "We need you!"

I stepped farther out of her reach while her head was turned in the direction of the commotion.

"Vern!" another voice called just as the alarms starting to ring in Ward D.

Vern grabbed me by both shoulders. "You're coming with me."

And then she galloped down the hall, pulling me along behind her.

The code had come from Magpie's room. As soon as we arrived, there was a flurry of activity and chaos. Orderlies filled the small area, shouting to one another, all trying to clear the floor around the center of the room where Magpie's prone form lay. In all the commotion, someone handed Vern the desk chair to get it out of the room and she let me go, giving me a stern look that said "stay put, or else."

I was mesmerized by the scene. Magpie was stark white. The kind of almost-transparent white when you're dead.

The orderlies were barking at one another while they hit her with the defibrillator. After a few tries, Magpie sprang back to life. She struggled and fought until they restrained her. That was when I saw the blood. It was all over her arms and her sheets. Magpie had cut herself badly.

"I want Vern!" she cried, which was odd because Cecilia was the White Coat assigned to her.

I couldn't imagine Magpie ever attempting to take her own life. Then I noticed a trail of things all along the floor. Magpie's treasures were out of their hiding place. A scrunchie like the ones Wing wore. One of my drawings of the Tree. Paper clips from Dr. Harris's office. A tube of lipstick. Some screws. This was her bounty. It was arranged in a semicircle around the bed.

Vern managed to wrap a bandage around Magpie's wrist and secure her to the gurney.

I took a step backward.

Magpie's eyes fluttered open and landed on me. She shared a look with me—one that said good-bye. Then she winked.

Maybe it was just an involuntary response to the trauma her body was going through. Maybe she really was trying to tell me something.

I didn't have time to process my surprise. I only had a few moments while Vern was still distracted by Magpie. Silently, I slipped out of the room and took off down the hall.

I hit the outer door release and felt the cool night air on my cheeks. The alarm for the door was drowned out from the alarm ringing inside. I was free.

There was nothing left to do but run.

Had Magpie cut herself on purpose? To create a distraction for me? I wouldn't know. I couldn't know. I just had to keep running.

The gate to the Whittaker grounds was open, thanks to the ambulance I watched rush through it from my hiding place in the bushes. Before it swung back shut, I slipped out. I had this strange feeling that more than just Magpie's distraction was in my favor that night. Something about the magic of everything working out lifted my spirits as I ran through the gateway and into the dark night. I felt like I really could make it to the other side of the mirror, to the Tree, and rescue Bale.

It was colder than I expected it to be, but adrenaline kept me warm. Soon, though, the biting air began to penetrate the thin Whittaker sweatpants and sweatshirt I was wearing. At least I'd remembered shoes.

10

BUILDINGS, STORES, AND OPEN spaces flew by as I raced away from Whittaker's north gates, away from Dr. Harris and Vern. My eyes caught on the Lyric Diner, where we'd taken field trips in my better days at Whittaker, back when we were in Ward A. The last time we were there we had to leave because Wing did a belly flop from the counter and Chord had freaked out the manager when he told him that "in the future his kids would all be dead from the war." That day Bale and I had shared a booth and a milk shake with two straws. We had to sit close to share, our shoulders touching.

I shook the memory away and pressed on.

I tried not to focus on how my legs felt like lead. I hadn't run or exercised much at all over the years, and each muscle was happy to remind me of it.

None of the other storefronts looked familiar, which wasn't surprising because I hadn't been this far from Whittaker in a

very long time. I was coming up on railroad tracks, and just
beyond them, a dirt road leading into the woods. I turned onto
it, partially because of what the boy-orderly had said and partially
because it would be easier to hide among the trees than out in
the open.

Before long, though, I was lost. I didn't know which way I
had come and which direction I should head in. All I saw were
trees and snow, and every tree looked exactly the same. I sank to
the ground. I could feel the snow through my clothes. What was
I thinking? Maybe I really was crazy. I'd followed the word of a
boy I didn't know to look for a Tree in the woods to save the life
of my boyfriend who had disappeared through a mirror. And, oh
yeah, supposedly I was a princess. When I thought about it, it
sounded totally insane. And now I was going to freeze to death.
I laughed out loud, my voice cackling through the woods. The
sound carried and echoed back, reminding me of how far I was
from everything I'd known and how screwed I really was.

The tears began to fall one after another. I was not a crier, no
matter which dwarf I took. The sensation was new. Like all the
sadness inside me was trying to get out. But instead of punching
and clawing . . . it was seeping out in a steady stream. My breath
was jagged; my nose was running. The drops were warm against
my impossibly cold skin. I was an idiot. I felt a wave of anger
surge—at myself, at my mom, and at that dream-boy-orderly for
leading me out here.

I wanted to go back, but I didn't know the way anymore. I
had run in circles too much, and there was almost no light out
here in the woods. Plus, there wasn't a real life to go back to. My

options were either bad or worse. So I cried until there were no more tears. And then I did the only thing left to do. I got up and started walking.

With every step, I scolded myself silently.

I should have packed food.

I should have taken a coat.

I should have grabbed a flashlight from the guard station.

The should-haves began to pile up, and the thought of giving up chased my every step.

And then I saw it: the Tree. It was unmistakable. Even in the dark, it stood out.

The Tree took up more space than I expected. It almost looked like it took up the entire sky. Above it, the darkness cracked open in a fury of lights, which reflected in its surface. Green chasing red chasing blue chasing yellow, encased in the blackest of clouds. The lights stopped moving and contorted into a face, which dipped down suddenly and seemed to be looking at me. I jumped backward and swallowed a laugh. What was I afraid of? They were just lights. They looked like the northern lights I had read about in books. But that would be difficult in upstate New York. Then again, so was the Tree.

I took a step closer to get a better look. The Tree was covered in some kind of fancy script and pictures. But the words weren't in any language I could understand, and the pictures looked like faces I had never seen. Not even in my dreams. What was this place? Who had etched them there, and what did they mean?

My arm stung suddenly. I pushed up my sleeves and saw a white light pulsing through the web of scars that ran along it. I pulled my sleeve back down, even though my arm was lit up like Christmas.

"Am I dreaming?" I thought out loud. It wouldn't be the first time my dreams had felt this real.

I stepped closer to the Tree and examined its surface, which was as smooth as glass. It looked totally iced over. But it also didn't look like there was any real bark under there. Either the etchings had happened ages ago and they became so smoothed down over time or the markings had actually grown as the tree had. I reached out to run my fingers over the carvings, but as soon as my fingers made contact, there was a creaking sound and my eyes were drawn to a fissure in the center of the Tree's trunk.

It broke apart with a sudden crack, proving my first instinct was right. There was no bark beneath the surface.

But I was wrong to stand so close. There was no escape. Thousands of ice shards dropped from the branches and headed in my direction all at once. Terrified, I hid my face in my elbow, protecting my skin.

But rather than pierce me, the icicles stopped a millimeter in front of me and dropped to the ground. Lifting my head fully once again, I saw the forest suddenly before me, bright as day. Which was impossible because it was nighttime. Or it had been. But this also didn't look like the woods I was just in. And the trees surrounding me didn't look like normal trees . . . They were tall, taller than I could crane my neck to see. And they were blue. The palest of periwinkle. Despite the color change, they seemed to be made of real wood. That was my first clue that I wasn't in New York anymore.

"Hey, Princess . . . ," a strong, familiar voice behind me said. "Sorry, I was a touch late."

I turned around to face the boy from my dreams. Gone was the white coat. Instead he wore a long black trench and a smile.

He raised his hand, and a tree dropped over the ice like a drawbridge. "Careful. It's beautiful, but it cuts deep."

The way he looked at me when he said it, I almost thought he was talking about me, too.

"Come on. We have to go."

I scrambled across his tree bridge, balancing myself a little self-consciously as he watched me, determined not to slip under his gaze. Behind me, I heard an eerie tearing sound, almost like a large canvas was being ripped apart. I glanced back and saw the Tree was there again, but this time it was blue like the others.

"The gateway sealed back up," was all the boy said. When I reached him, he offered his hand to help me down. I took it and felt a jolt because he was *real*.

"Welcome to Algid," he said with a smile.

"Algid?" I repeated the word, letting it roll over my tongue. There was something familiar about it. "Is that this place?"

He nodded.

"And Bale is somewhere here?"

He dipped his head again.

I didn't believe in coincidences. There was no way this boy had nothing to do with Bale's disappearance.

So I made a fist and decked him in the stomach. He jumped out of the way in time to miss the brunt of the blow, but I still got him pretty good.

"I guess I deserved that for saving you from a mental hospital and bringing you home," he said, not showing that my punch had affected him at all beyond an expression of surprise.

A smile crossed the orderly-who-wasn't-really-an-orderly's face as he stood taller. I resisted the urge to shake out my knuckles, which smarted from hitting the muscle beneath his coat. I didn't want to give him the satisfaction.

"You took me away from everything and everyone I know. Gee, thanks so much."

Sarcasm was always my first line of defense. And I was out of my depth, here in the middle of the woods, with this boy who I did not know. And who acted as if he knew so much about me.

"You came under your own speed," he attested, as if the distinction were important. "I can see that you're upset, Princess. I just wonder if all that anger is for me . . ."

"Where is he? Where is Bale? What did you do with him?" I yelled.

His face poorly hid a smirk. "If I could take Bale, then why wouldn't I have just taken you?"

He made a certain amount of sense, but I wasn't ready to trust him yet.

Relenting slightly, he leaned toward me and said, "I will tell you where Bale is, and I'll even help you get him back. But first you have to do something for us."

"'Us' who?"

"Not here. We have to get home first." He pulled a vial filled with a yellow liquid out of his satchel. "If you drink this—"

I smacked the vial out of his hand and it smashed against a tree, the contents dripping down the sides.

"Zads!" The boy looked genuinely exasperated. "That was my last one for home."

"This isn't my home! Now you better explain how you're going to help me, or I'm out of here."

The boy sighed with a little too much exaggeration. "Okay, look. I told you it's not safe to talk here. We'll help you with your man and tell you about the prophecies, but we need to leave first. And now that you just smashed the quickest way home, we need to walk. So follow me."

"Prophecies plural?"

"Both involve the King. And both involve you."

I digested the information. He took my silence as agreement and started to walk again.

"Do you really think I'm going anywhere with you?"

The boy was maddeningly confident, which was alluring and annoying at the same time.

"I do," he said simply. Unfortunately he was right this time. I didn't have any choice. So leaving the pieces of the Tree in our wake, we began to move.

"My name is Jagger, by the way," he said with a flourish and a bow.

"I didn't ask," I snapped. The name sounded as slippery as the boy it belonged to.

He laughed. "Yes, I noticed that." A village cropped up in front of us. I felt some part of me relax at the sight of houses. I was no longer alone with this guy. And some other part of me hoped that maybe Bale would be in one of those houses.

♛

Each house in the city was a different color, but they were also translucent. Light seemed to dance through them, though I couldn't make out the shapes inside. I walked by them, looking around for signs of life and skimming my fingers along the surfaces—all freezing cold and smooth. Ice.

"Where is everyone?"

"It's been a hard winter. It's lasted so much longer than anyone ever anticipated," he said quietly.

"How long?"

"Since the day you and your mother left Algid."

He kept moving as he talked. I followed the information he gave me like bread crumbs.

"This is how you live?" I asked, looking at the glorified igloos. They were nothing like Hamilton, the town closest to Whittaker.

"You haven't seen anything yet. Wait till you see mine," he said proudly, as if he had completely forgotten why I had agreed to come.

"Is that where you're keeping Bale?" I demanded. "Is that where you're taking me?"

He said nothing, continuing our walk in silence. If I wasn't so cold and hungry, I would have stormed off. Instead I swallowed my growing frustration and followed him.

After another ten minutes or so of silent walking, we spotted a man sitting on a bench. He was wearing a coat made out of something slick and black that made me think of penguins. Jagger followed my gaze, but his reaction was different from mine.

"Don't touch him. Don't touch anyone or anything," Jagger warned, his voice drained of its charm. I was focused on the man. He was too still. But something pulled me to him. Maybe he was hurt. I needed to know. I raced ahead.

"Excuse me," I said, relieved to finally see another living soul other than Jagger.

"No," Jagger growled.

I may have had to follow him to Bale, but there was no way I would obey his every order.

"Snow," he demanded.

I ignored him and touched the man's shoulder, anyway. Horrified, I realized he was frozen solid. He tipped over, and when his body hit the ground, his head disconnected from the rest of him and rolled away. I swallowed a scream.

"I told you not to touch him," Jagger said, catching up to me.

I looked up and down the street and noticed for the first time dozens of people frozen in place. There was a mother and daughter standing in front of a store window, admiring something that they would never purchase.

"Are they all . . . ," I began. I couldn't bring myself to say the word. *Dead*.

Jagger answered with a nod.

Their expressions were frozen, too. They were smiling. Like the man on the bench, they had not seen the attack coming.

"What happened to these people? A flash freeze? It doesn't make any sense."

"It doesn't matter how. It matters that we get out of here before the same thing happens to us."

Finally I understood Jagger's urgent need to leave this place. There was no one alive in the village. We needed to keep going.

But I couldn't move. I'd never seen a dead body before, let alone a frozen, headless one.

"Look, I'm sorry you had to see that. But you're going to see much worse if we're going to save your boy Bale. Now, we have to keep moving if we're going to get home by dark."

Bale. Just the sound of his name battled out the feeling that gnawed at me, telling me to go back, not to trust this boy.

Instead I charged on beside Jagger. I glared at his perfect profile. He had tried to spare me the horror. But still, he had brought me—no, lured me—to a place where whatever had happened to that headless man could happen to me.

Past the village, the landscape changed again. There were new trees—ones I'd never seen before. Their trunks were wide but not as wide as the Tree that had opened Algid to me. Their branches were twisty and had big white blossoms that were frozen as well.

I could see Jagger's breath floating up in tiny clouds. He trudged on, determined, his face so pretty and unmarred by what we had seen. Whatever he was thinking, he looked as though he had forgotten the village, while for me those dead, frozen faces kept coming back in flashes.

The questions and the silence and his relative calm were getting to be too much.

"You need to explain everything to me. Like how those people froze back there and how we're getting Bale back," I insisted, walking in front of him to halt his forward march.

"The key to finding Bale is to find the Enforcer. I will tell you everything," he said. "I promise, but I'm afraid I can't right now. You need to trust me."

"Well, why the hell would I do that?"

"Because right now we have to run."

Suddenly I heard a growl, low and guttural, behind us. The sound came from deep within the icy banks around where we stood. And then the ground started to take form, rising up on its own. Standing behind me was a wolf made completely of snow. Its legs and back muscles were hard-packed chunks of ice. The creature bared teeth made of sharp, pointy icicles.

Another Snow Wolf rose beside it, and then more beside them. Their glassy eyes tracked me as I took several steps backward.

"What are you standing there for? Run, Snow!" Jagger yanked me along behind him until I was finally running, too.

For the second time since leaving Whittaker, I was running, weaving in between the trees and following Jagger's graceful form. I was anything but graceful. My arms flailed, and I occasionally tripped over fallen branches, but I kept moving. I looked back, which was a mistake. The pack of Snow Wolves was gaining on me—and the time I took to glance behind me had allowed them to get that much closer.

Up ahead the trees thinned out, and I shot like a dart into the clearing, skidding to an abrupt stop at the edge of a high cliff. I'd run out of land. I looked down and saw a river flowing below. It was a ridiculously long drop. Looking back, I saw the lead Snow Wolf bearing down on me.

What should I do? Jump and risk drowning in the freezing water—that was assuming I didn't die on impact? Or be eaten by Snow Wolves? And where the hell did Jagger go?

They're not real. They're not real, I told myself. But my feet had other ideas, and I jumped. The free fall seemed to take forever.

My mind went back to Bale. I was doing this for him.

I took the deepest of breaths. I closed my eyes when my body hit the water. And then remembered I couldn't swim.

I think I heard Jagger splash into the water nearby but not near enough.

The water was ice-cold, and my body turned instantly numb. I tried to move my arms the way I'd seen people do on television, but they didn't cooperate. I was sinking amid the rushing water. The current dragged me down, and I could feel the pressure of the air I was holding in my nose and behind my eyes. I needed to get to the surface. I needed air. I felt myself give up.

As I sank farther down, I thought of Bale's face. I would never see it again. I would never see him again. Had I really come this far to die?

I exhaled air and inhaled water. A new kind of pressure filled my nose and lungs. I was suffocating. This was going to be the end of me.

Just when I had given up all hope, a light hovered above my head, followed by a shadow. I expected Jagger, but it looked like a woman. Her hair fanned out and swirled in the water. Long arms ending in tentacles reached for me.

The woman's face was wide, with big glowing green eyes. Slits that looked like gills lined each cheek. They gaped open and closed in the blue-green water.

I tried to push her away, but my body wasn't moving under its own power. Undeterred, she wrapped her tentacles around my waist and pulled me toward the surface. She was saving me.

This was my dream, my nightmare come to life. Only in this version, I was being rescued, not killed.

A few seconds later I was shaking like a leaf on the shore of the River, and the woman from the water was kneeling over me.

"We need to get you inside."

If liquid could be solid, that was what the woman looked like. She was completely made of water in the same way that the Snow Wolves had been made from icy flakes. Her skin wept water. Rivulets formed each individual strand of her hair.

"Snow." Her voice was sweet and even.

How did she know my name? All the impossible things that had happened to me since Whittaker piled up on top of one another. But the sound of my own name anchored me to the riverbed.

"Who are you? What are you?" I demanded.

"I am the River Witch," she said simply. "Nepenthe."

"What?" Despite what I'd seen in the village and woods, I wasn't ready to believe in witches. And I felt myself fading. Everything ached: my head, my limbs, my chest. I had been running and running since I'd left Whittaker, and now, in this moment lying on the shore, all my strength left me.

"The River Witch," she repeated out loud, just as the world went black.

The next few hours were a blur as I slipped in and out of consciousness. Blankets were heaped on top of me. A fire was set somewhere, and the witch forced a gross seaweedy porridge down my throat.

At one point I managed to ask, "Jagger? Did you find Jagger?"

A deep crease of confusion diverted the flow of water down her forehead.

"There was a boy with me. Did you find him?" I prompted.

"Do you mean the boy who was running in the other direction when I dragged you out and saved your life?" she said with a judgmental tone.

"I . . . guess?"

"Well, he's gone. He left you behind."

"Are you sure?" This made no sense. He was hell-bent on bringing me to this world. Why would he ditch me?

"I know the River, and the River said he left," she said gently.

The turn of phrase was odd. How does anyone know a river? I thought of that for a while as I faded back into oblivion. But not before I heard another voice, sweet and songlike.

"She's so cold . . . We have to warm her up."

When I woke again, my naked body was covered in what looked like thick leaves, though they felt like leeches. Where were my clothes? What the hell was going on?

I tried to sit up and pull at one of the leaves, but my body didn't comply. It was as if the weight of the water were still over me, holding me down.

Then I noticed a short girl standing next to me.

"Be still." The girl's voice was a song. It had more notes in it than mine. Than anyone I'd ever heard, really. It trilled with concern.

"What the hell?" I tried to say. But when I opened my mouth it was full of water.

This was a dream, I assumed. A really, really vivid, eyes-wide-open dream.

"They're scales," the girl explained, touching the leaflike things attached to me. "They draw off all the bad."

Great. I had been saved only to be tortured by wannabe witch people.

There's no way to draw off all the bad, I thought.

The girl picked up one of the scales and lit it on a nearby candle.

I tried to speak again, to scream, anything. Only now there was even more water in my mouth.

Then she touched the flame to the scales on my body. I would have jumped up, but I couldn't move. Something that looked like seaweed was wrapped tightly around my legs and arms.

I braced myself for the pain, but it didn't come. The flames raced over the scales on top of my skin, but I felt only a tickle. One by one, the tiny scales peeled off and floated to the ceiling.

As the fire receded, the seaweed retracted from my wrists and ankles. I ran my hands over my unburned skin, which was now warm to the touch.

The girl covered me with a rough, burlapy sheet and walked away as I tried to yell obscenities at her. But I didn't have the energy. I went back to sleep.

When I awoke, a boy was in the doorway, standing rod

straight. I hoped for a second that it was someone I'd know. But when he moved, I realized he was wiry and tall, not as graceful as Jagger. Not as solid as my Bale. He made me think of the toy soldier that Magpie had under her bed, but I couldn't focus long enough to find out who he was.

"The fever isn't breaking. There's something wrong," I heard the girl say, minutes or hours later.

Her hand hovered over my chest. "There's something not right in there," she assessed. "It's like something is stopping the magic from working."

"She's part witch and part snow. That's what's wrong," the boy countered, speaking for the first time.

Perhaps it was the fever, but his voice sounded distant and matter-of-fact, as if he thought the girl were overreacting. Or perhaps he didn't care whether my fever broke or soared.

"River Witch . . . Nepenthe . . . come quick," the girl called.

"Too hot or too cold. Make up your mind, dearie," the River Witch said, beside me again. There was concern in her voice.

She peered down at me, one of her scaly fingers pulling at the skin beneath my eye. "She's filled to the brim," she said. "We need to get the water out of her."

I felt panic grip me harder than that seaweed had. If fire was used to warm me, what exactly was the water removal method?

"You're going to feel this," the River Witch warned.

She put her hand over my heart. I felt my chest lift up toward it like a magnet. Water rushed out of every part of me, every pore. Even my eye sockets. And from my mouth a geyser spouted up toward the ceiling.

When the water stopped pouring out onto the floor, the girl approached me again. She touched my forehead and nodded to the witch. My fever had subsided. "You are going to be okay. You need to heal, and no one knows how long that is supposed to take. A normal person couldn't have survived that," the slip of a girl whispered.

I would have protested. Normal had been the unattainable goal for so very long at Whittaker. How was it possible that *not* being normal had saved me?

The next time I opened my eyes, the boy with the impossibly straight posture was staring at me. He was handsome. Not Bale handsome or Jagger-the-orderly-who-brought-me-to-the-Tree handsome. This boy was more innocent looking despite the deeply serious scowl on his face. The girl with the singsong voice was next to him. They were watching me as intently as Vern and I watched *The End of Almost*.

"I'm Gerde, and this is Kai," the girl explained.

I couldn't tell anything more about them. Were they brother and sister? Boyfriend and girlfriend? Husband and wife? They looked to be about the same age as me. She was obviously a witch, but was he a witch, too? So far, all he'd done was stand and stare while the River Witch and the girl worked their strange medicine on me.

"You were dead. It might take you a while to be completely alive again," Gerde explained.

What do you say to the girl who covered you in leaves

and set you on fire and the boy who probably saw you naked?

"Hi," I managed to eke out. If this had been Whittaker, I would have done or said something to mark my territory, to tell them not to mess with me. But we weren't there, and they had just saved my life.

The girl perked up, happy to see me awake.

"Who's Bale? You said the name like a million times. Also, Jagger. How many suitors do you have, Princess?" Gerde asked, her lilting voice filled with curiosity.

I couldn't explain who Bale was to me. We had never made a name for what we were, and we had never gotten past the first kiss. But he was more than her word "suitor" and more than a friend and more than any other person in my world or this strange one. And Jagger, this boy I had known for less than a heartbeat, was the boy of my dreams. Only my dreams were nightmares. I needed one boy to find the other, and now both were gone.

"Gerde . . . ," Kai warned.

I didn't understand why he stopped her. What harm were a few questions? He didn't know enough about me to want to respect my privacy.

"Right, you should rest," she singsonged again. She started to hum. I wasn't sure if it was coincidence or not, but the humming made me want to sleep. It pulled me like the tide under again into the blackness.

"Maybe the witch should have left her in the water," a voice said, chasing after me.

It sounded like the boy's.

11

"WELCOME BACK TO THE living, Snow," the River Witch said. She was standing in front of a large oval window when I awoke again. There were scales on her back that seemed to be part of a shiny, metallic cloak. I wondered what else besides her tentacles was underneath it.

Her long, thin feet were bare against the whitewashed wooden planks of the floor.

All the walls of the room were made of the same white wood, and thousands of drops of water dripped from every crevice of the structure. The result was cacophonous. The sound of water on wood hit my eardrums over and over. It was the constant kind of sound that could drive a person crazy. Other than the bed I was lying on, there was no other furniture in the place. Glancing around nervously, I could not see a way out. There was a rustling in one of the corners. Or rather a slithering. It was too dark to see what it was. But whatever it was, it was moving.

My bed lurched. It felt like we were on a boat, and I suddenly feared I was even more trapped. I looked around for Kai and Gerde. They were nowhere to be found.

I half remembered the boy saying that I should have been left in the River. But I wasn't sure if he'd said it or I'd dreamed it.

The River Witch turned and looked at me.

"What is wrong with you? How could you take a drowned girl on a boat?" I demanded.

She laughed. "It's the only way, my dear. Unless you prefer another swim in the River."

"What are you?"

"Oh, my dear, there are things above and below that no one has imagined or known about. I am one of those things for many people."

I sat up too quickly. My head screamed. I rested back on the rough pillow.

"You have more spunk than she did. That will serve you well," the River Witch said and laughed. "You will be on your way. All in due time. But not before I tell you a story."

"I don't need a story. I need to find my friend and go home," I said, feeling desperately close to whining.

"But that's the thing. You already are home. I have to say, you look so much like Ora. It's uncanny."

"You know my mother?"

"Know her? We are sisters."

I squinted hard at the River Witch.

Sisters? I had never met any other family outside my mom

and dad. And the entity standing in front of me had more in common with the water puddling on the floor around her than my very perfect, very human mother. "You think . . . You're my aunt?"

The River Witch laughed. "No, Snow. Ora and I belonged to the same coven."

Coven? The word thumped in my head. I'd recently discovered a lot about my mother. First and foremost, she was a liar. And now she was a person from another land. But somehow the idea of her being magical, of being the same as this mermaid-witch thing from the River, seemed inconceivable.

"You're saying my mother was . . . is a witch. Like you?"

"There are all kinds of witches, my dear."

"And what kind of witch is she?" I asked reflexively.

"Not the same kind," the River Witch answered cryptically. "But there is so much that you do not know. Shame on Ora."

I didn't like her insulting my mother even though I was mad at her myself. But I didn't have the energy to defend her. I could barely sit up.

The witch's cheek gills opened and closed with a sigh of annoyance. "Ora has not protected you and has kept you ignorant. If she really believes that is the best way to keep you safe, then she learned nothing from her time in Algid. You have missed years of preparing, years of training . . ."

"Preparing and training for what?" I asked, more confused by the moment.

The River Witch sighed, and a few drops of water splattered onto the floor as a result.

"Oh, dear. The first thing you should know is whoever you believe is your father is not."

"You're lying . . . ," I said. But some part of me stopped short. Some part of me wanted to hear her out. I barely knew my father. His visits were sporadic and always at the urging of my mother. I would have been sad about it if I hadn't been drugged up all the time.

"You don't believe me, but in time you will. Let's start from the beginning, then . . . with your *real* father, King Lazar."

As she spoke, I wanted to resist, but I leaned into her words like a five-year-old listening to a bedtime story.

"Algid wasn't always covered in snow," the River Witch said. "It used to have seasons. And then Prince Lazar was born, which would change the course of our world. Lazar was the first of the royal line to carry strong magic within him. Magic is usually reserved only for witches, so it created quite the stir. Some say his mother had an affair with a god. Others say she dabbled in dark magic herself. No one knows the truth, and we never will because when Lazar was born, he came into the world and froze his own mother to death. Not an auspicious start.

"Lazar's father feared for his own life and came to the coven for help. My sisters cast a protective spell on the boy, restraining his magic and putting a forgetting spell on all who knew of what he had done. And everything was fine for a time.

"But when the young prince came of age, he found an object that amplified his own powers so much that it broke the spell."

"An object?" I asked.

"A mirror. Even our coven believed that it was just a legend. But Lazar found it. Larger than life and more powerful than anything in Algid. Than anything everywhere. And in an instant Lazar's power was back with a vengeance."

A magical mirror sounded ridiculous. But then the memory of Bale going into the mirror that appeared in his room came flooding back to me.

"The King sought the coven's help once again. But instead of restraining his son's powers this time, the King could see only his own greed. He demanded that the coven teach Lazar how to wield his great power so that the King could use it for his own benefit."

I snorted at that. Witches training princes who wielded magical snow? That hadn't made it into any fairy tale I'd ever read. The River Witch ignored me and continued.

"Then something happened that the King did not expect. Lazar fell madly in love with one of the witches' nieces, and she loved him as well."

"My mother?"

The Witch blinked hard, interrupting the flow of water down her face, as if remembering. As if the idea of their being together were unnatural to her.

"Yes. And your father insisted on marrying her despite the law that said royalty can only marry other royalty. When his father refused to bless the marriage, Lazar lost control of his temper, and the King met an icy end. Prince Lazar became King Lazar. When he realized the extent of his powers, he froze over the lands of Algid so all would bend to his will. He took the throne and a wife on the same day, and you were born less than a year later."

"So what happened? Why did my mother run away from her icily ever after?" I smiled, proud of my pun.

The River Witch did not return the smile.

"She was still a witch. We believe in the Elements. In nature. It could not have been easy to see the whole world frozen in the name of their love. But she loved him deeply in return. And so they were happy for a time. Blissfully so."

Nothing says I love you like freezing the world, I thought. But this time I kept the words in.

"So what happened?"

"The oracle."

"Oracle?" I said, remembering a book of Greek myths I'd read from the Whittaker library. "Please tell me that this story does not involve a fortune-teller."

The River Witch ignored my comment and continued. "There was a prophecy spoken on your birth to the three most powerful witches in the land. Remember, you are the daughter of magic on both sides of your lineage. You have magic within you. Powerful magic, probably the strongest that Algid has ever seen. You can control snow. Thus, you were named. The prophecy said:

> When the Lights go out at century's turn,
> The progeny of the King will rise to power.
> She will either claim the throne herself . . . or she will give the King more
>   power than he has ever known.
> Only she can choose the path for Algid.
> But not every path is clear, and there are those who have the power to
>   change the course of fate:

the prince,
the thief,
the thinker,
the secret.

If they are destroyed, the King will surely fall. And should the sacrifice come exactly when the Lights are extinguished, whoever wears the crown will rule Algid forever.

"What does that mean?" I asked.

"One doesn't know the full meaning of a prophecy until it's fulfilled, but it likely involves the Eclipse of the North Lights and you."

"Do you mean the northern lights? How can they eclipse?"

The River Witch closed her eyes for a moment, as if my questions tired her. "It happens only once per century, and the next one should occur in just one month."

So basically I was supposed to fulfill some kind of major destiny in a month. And I had no idea this place even existed until now.

The River Witch continued, "But the three witches—the Witch of the Woods, the Fire Witch, and I—we wanted the seasons back. Our power was contained, boxed in by ice on all sides. So we decided to help fate along by destroying King Lazar's most prized possession."

"His family?" I asked.

"His mirror," she corrected, a look of surprise crossing her face as if she had underestimated the dark places my mind went. "Remember, all his power was amplified by it. He needed to be stopped. So the Three stole the mirror away and broke it, each sister hiding her piece somewhere that no one else would know about it. We thought we had saved Algid. But we were wrong."

Now the witch glided across the room. Her voice was mournful. "Somehow King Lazar heard about the prophecy. He had a choice: his crown or his progeny."

"That doesn't sound like much of a dilemma," I said.

"You don't know how power can poison, child. Imagine if the whole world trembled at a touch of your finger. Now imagine losing that power completely. What it means to know that your child will take your crown, to weigh your child's life against the thing that you think makes you . . . Well, it is no small thing."

The River Witch presented both sides as if they were equal— as if it were completely normal to consider killing a child, your child.

"King Lazar chose the crown."

I wanted her to stop talking. I wanted to close my eyes and open them back on the other side of the Tree. Because this witch was telling me my father wanted me dead.

I felt the floor rock underneath me, and for a moment I thought I was really losing it. But then I remembered we were on a boat.

"When your mother learned of your father's decision, she knew she had to save you," the River Witch pressed on. "So while the king was sleeping, Ora took you and carried you to the cliff above the River and jumped."

As the story unfolded, my old dream came back to me. She was telling me what I had already seen in my mind.

In my dream, I was standing on the edge of a cliff about to jump off, knowing the River was better than whatever was behind me. But what if it wasn't my vision? What if it was my mother's? It made sense, but it couldn't possibly be right.

How did the River Witch know about the dream? I pushed the thoughts aside and focused on the rest of her story.

"Your mother knew that I would be waiting for her in the water. When she took that leap, she knew that I would save you both. But still, I was surprised she had it in her."

My mother had saved me? If the River Witch was to be believed, she was still saving me.

"With the coven's help, your mother opened the door to another land—the land from whence you came—and she secreted you away where you've been all this time. Everyone in Algid thinks you're dead. Even we didn't know where she took you. She was supposed to come back when you were strong enough or when it was safe. It appears that neither is the case yet. But I can help you with that."

"And King Lazar? What happened to him?" I asked. I refused to call him my father.

"He has continued to rule Algid like a tyrant. It has been winter for fifteen years. And now that you have returned to us, you can help put an end to it."

"Right, so you're saying I am literally an ice princess?"

If what the River Witch was saying was true, I came from a long line of liars and monsters.

"Yes, Snow. Within you lies a great gift. You can control winter and have dominance over frost, over ice and snow. You are the heir to the throne and the one destined to take away your father's power . . . or to raise him to greater heights. Only you can choose your path."

My heartbeat quickened at that. I had a choice. I never had a choice. Every day of my life at Whittaker had been about other people making decisions for me: what to wear, to eat, to do, when to sleep. Even who I could talk to. Hell, the only reason I was here was because someone dragged Bale through a mirror, and I had *no choice* but to come here to get him back. "How did you destroy the mirror? Where are the pieces now?" I asked.

"What happened to the mirror pieces is a story for another time."

"And where is your piece . . . ?"

"I can't tell you that," the River Witch said.

"But—"

"I will not tell you!" Her voice was suddenly so loud, it shook the walls of the boat.

She had just unfolded every dark and dirty corner of my alleged history, but she couldn't tell me about mirror fragments? I didn't understand.

"And whatever you do, you must NOT let the King know you're alive and back in Algid. Or what your mother has done for you—what we all have done—will have been in vain."

I sat quietly—message received clearly. After a few moments the River Witch looked around her dripping houseboat with a critical eye. "You are like your mother in some ways. I hope not in all. Being a witch can be a dirty business, what with the things you have to collect and the things you have to sacrifice. Ora liked comforts. Being a queen appealed to her more than being one of us. Ora realized almost too late the value of what we were—and the power that we possessed."

Nepenthe looked at me for a long beat that told me that she was done with her story and was expecting some kind of response. I wondered if she expected gratitude for telling me her version of the truth. This moment was years in the making for her. Meeting me again. The one she thought would save her world.

I had no gratitude to give her. I did not know what to do with what she had given me. She had given me my mother as a hero, but the kind whose heroic act was keeping her daughter locked up her whole life and letting her believe she was crazy. Nepenthe had taken away the father who had disappointed me and replaced him with a new specter of a father who was possibly evil incarnate. And she was asking me to believe that the icy-cold anger I had felt my whole life could actually manifest itself as a physical thing, as a weapon.

"I don't believe I can control snow, but I . . . ," I began, sounding a little too much like Dr. Harris for my liking. He always approached the crazier patients with that tone.

"I believe that you believe that you can fly, Wing. That's what's important," he would say. His tone was gentle, but his meaning was unmistakable. He did not believe.

I sat there looking at the River Witch, watery proof that magic was real. But that did not mean that it was part of me— just because she said so.

The River Witch's face relaxed. "Time and the Lights will prove me right."

I didn't say anything at first. I couldn't convince her any more than Dr. Harris could convince Wing.

"Perhaps, but I want to thank you for saving me," I said, meaning it, as she turned to go.

The River Witch blinked hard at me, her eyes narrowing in confusion, and then she left without saying another word.

Was she drawing another comparison between my mother and me? Were thank-yous the domain of Ora as well, or had no one ever thanked the River Witch before? I was tired of people knowing things before me. Of knowing things about me. Destiny wasn't exciting or romantic or epic. It was annoying.

I could not stay in this strange place and learn whatever she thought I needed to learn. I had to find Bale. I would give her time to sleep or return to the water or whatever it was that witches did, and then I would make a run for it. She wanted me to make a choice? Damn the prophesies. That was my choice.

The next day, sunlight streamed through the oval window in my room. There was no sign of the River Witch. No sign of Kai or Gerde, either. My Whittaker wear was now dry and sitting in a pile on the table in the center of the room. Next to it was the witch's cloak. Perhaps it could offer me some protection from the forever winter that the River Witch had described.

I slipped it on. It felt exactly how it looked: scaly and slick, but there was something else, too. It felt warm. I felt half-guilty taking something from the witch who had helped me, but something told me that she could make another one. I looked around the place one last time, and just as I moved for the door, I heard the slithering sound again. The rustling was coming from every corner of the boat's room, both above and below. Slimy, scaly, larger-than-life tentacles came at me from the walls, floor, and ceiling. The hissing noise they made sounded like "Stay."

Turning the doorknob, I ignored the sound and made a break for it. My mind was cloudy. My stomach churned uneasily. I had no idea if I was making the right choice or not, and I had no idea where to go other than away from this boat and all the weirdness inside it.

The boat was moored. It was surrounded by giant chunks of ice at the River's end. There was no dock. The boat was held in place by two icebergs that were inexplicably anchored at the hull of the boat. I jumped down onto the ice and landed ungraciously on my butt. Worried, I looked up at the boat but saw no sign of the witch. My feet slid over the ice as I made my way back to the solid, snowy shore.

Back on my own again, I thought.

But I slipped and fell flat on my face. Feeling suddenly weaker, my chest constricted and I gasped for air. If I had been at Whittaker, Dr. Harris would have dosed me again. I was a wreck.

A pair of boots came into my view. I looked up and saw Kai, the boy from the boat.

He picked me up in his arms. I was so surprised I did not move a muscle. I found myself staring into his eyes a beat too long. They were big and blue and somehow distant. I didn't blink until he focused on me.

It wasn't like on TV. I didn't feel light as a feather in his arms.

It was almost an embrace. I could feel my weight against his chest, and the balancing act of his holding me up and pulling me into him.

"Your instinct to run was the right one," he said in a whisper as he cradled me in his arms and headed back onto the ice.

"What . . . what are you doing?"

"I'm taking you back."

"Why?" I asked as Kai went suddenly rigid.

He somehow belonged to the River Witch. Of course he was taking me back. I struggled against him.

"Let me down," I demanded. "Look, I appreciate your help. But I need to be on my way. Give my regards to the River Witch."

Was I being saved or kidnapped?

"You can give them to Nepenthe yourself," he said, not letting me down.

I considered kicking him or biting him. But since he had just saved me from the River, I wanted to resolve this with words, not teeth.

"Stop moving," he said in a whisper.

But I craned my neck in time to see a giant fissure in the ice coming from the direction of the boat. Kai took a deep breath and then jumped for the shore with me in his arms.

He managed to deposit me on solid ground, but he couldn't make it himself, slipping into the water and disappearing under the surface.

I screamed and rolled over and reached for him just as his hand came back grasping for land. His head popped up, eyes blinking hard and wildly searching for the way up and out.

I grabbed his hand. I would not let him go. Not like Bale. Not again.

"Hang on to me."

He managed to put his other hand on the shore, and I pulled back with all my might, hoisting him up.

He lay on the ground beside me for a moment breathing heavily. I watched his chest go up and down, concave and more concave. While I was making sure that he was still breathing, he opened his eyes suddenly and caught me staring at him. For the briefest of seconds his face wasn't scowling at me. Instead it was relaxed. He was almost smiling, just relieved to be alive. Then his face darkened again, but this time it wasn't at me—he was looking past me at the sky.

"We have to get inside. Now!" he said, leaping to his feet with energy I did not expect him to have so soon after his narrow escape from the River. He yanked me to my feet as well.

I looked at the River where the boat no longer had an ice path to get to it. "But how are we—"

He pulled me in the other direction, toward the tree line.

"What is it?" I demanded as I let myself be dragged along.

"There's a storm coming. And not just any storm. There is only one person I know who can create something with this much power: the King."

I didn't see anything. There wasn't a cloud or lights in the sky. It was perfectly clear and a pretty rosy pink.

Somewhere I heard the sound of a bird cawing. But I couldn't see it.

"Listen to that," he explained, still not making any sense to me.

"The birdcalls?" They were piercing and strange, but did he really think the bird was telling him that there was a storm?

He nodded, then began moving toward the blue woods next to the River.

"Hey, come back, Kai . . ."

He didn't stop. I had no choice but to catch up. What was it with the boys in this world? But unlike how I felt about Jagger, I actually think I trusted Kai. Maybe it was because he clearly didn't want me there, or maybe it was because he just saved my life. Either way, I had decided to follow him for now.

♔

In the next clearing, giant white sails sat atop a glass cube perched high in the trees. Colorful lights—which I can only assume were the North Lights—blazed brightly in the sky and were reflected on every surface as the house disappeared into the sky.

"Awesome . . . ," I gasped. "What is it?"

"Shelter."

But it was more than that.

"What are the sails for?"

"They capture the wind's and the sun's energy and run the house," Kai said.

"How far north are we?" I nodded toward the light show in the sky. "Where I'm from, lights like those are mostly near the poles . . ."

He shrugged. "You can see them from everywhere in our land. We just call them the Lights. The River Witch says there is a lady up there conducting an orchestra of light in the sky. But I think they're just lights."

So far nothing had been *just* anything since I got to Algid. Everything had a story, some hint of magic. And these lights were fated to go out. Time was up for whatever was going to happen.

"Come on," said an impatient Kai, already halfway up the stepladder to the front door. I was having a Goldilocks moment. I hadn't even stepped inside yet, but I knew it was perfect. It wasn't too big or too small, and it was up high and transparent. A place from which you would never feel hemmed in. You could see so much of Algid from there. If I could draw my ideal home, it would be exactly what stood in front of me now.

The inside of the house was compact and genius, though bigger than it looked from the outside. There were floor-to-ceiling windows for walls through a labyrinth of rooms. And the bones of the house were exposed within each wall. Metal braces were welded to the tree branches. The house, as modern as it was, wasn't just in the tree. It was part of it.

Kai said nothing as he handed me a blanket. He may not have wanted me there, but at least his manners had kicked in.

I handed the blanket back to him. I was chilled, but he was the one still sopping wet from the River. His lips even looked a little blue.

"You need to get warm."

He blinked and nodded, but when he tried to unbutton his shirt his fingers shook so hard that he couldn't do it.

"Hey, let me help you." I reached for his shirt, but he batted my hand away.

"I got it," he snapped. Then he turned away from me and pulled his shirt roughly over his head, tossing it to the ground. I stared at the muscles along his back for a moment before he wrapped the blanket around himself and faced me again.

I avoided his eyes as he made his way to a chair and sat down.

Outside, the strange birdcalls got louder, and then they were drowned out by a low whistling sound.

He was right. Something was coming. The trees bent like matchsticks.

"Kai?"

I looked through the icy wall of the cube structure, searching for the source of the noise. A giant wave of snow was coming right for the house. I started to tap my fingers, my go-to comfort move, but it did not help me. I needed to draw, but there was no paper in sight. I squatted down, bracing myself, but Kai, slowly warming up, moved about the house as if there weren't anything wrong.

"The house will hold," he assured me.

Seeing my distress, he joined me on the floor and sat next to me.

"The house will hold," he repeated, sounding sure.

The wave of white hurled toward us until I couldn't see its crest. The accompanying sound was that of a train.

I grabbed Kai's hand and held on to it, squeezing too hard as the glass wall in front of us whited-out. The house and tree bent backward with the whipping gusts of wind, but they did not break. They just swayed back again.

I let go of Kai's hand with an apology. "Sorry."

I never apologized.

"Don't get any ideas. I was just . . ."

"Scared," he completed my thought.

Scared was worse than sorry.

"I was not scared," I protested a little too much.

Mercifully, he shrugged and looked out the window.

"Was that a snow tsunami?"

"We call it a Snow Wave."

"Well, whatever it was, we should send the architect of this house a thank-you."

"You're welcome."

"You built this place?" I asked, surprised. "I thought you were an apprentice to the witch."

"Gerde's the apprentice. I am more of a caretaker. And I go to school in town."

He got up and moved to the glass hearth, the blanket still around him. My eyes followed his half-naked form. He was no longer shaking. Apparently, the effect of the River had worn off.

"Is this house magic?" I asked as Kai touched something near the tiny glass hearth and a fire sprang up.

Kai looked at me funny. I understood so little of this place.

"It's not magic. It's engineering. I don't do magic."

There was pride in his voice, and when he saw the relief in my face, his body language softened slightly. I felt the tension that had somehow built from the second we'd stepped inside the cube diffuse between us. But something else clicked into place.

"What do you mean, you can't do magic? You were with Gerde and the River Witch when they . . ." I remembered again that he hadn't actually had a hand in my revival; he was just an observer. Apparently, he was a reluctant one.

"No. It comes at too high a price."

"Do you mean it's expensive, or is it a selling-your-soul kind of thing?"

Kai blinked hard. Maybe the selling-your-soul idea wasn't in the Algid vernacular.

"It's both. It feels like a shortcut. If I want something, I'd rather work for it."

"Not everyone can do what you do, Kai. Not everyone can build this."

He blushed, not meeting my eyes. I guess he wasn't used to compliments.

"But the magic—how does it work?"

He sighed. "There is small magic and big magic. People can buy small magic for healing and cosmetic enhancements, for running the house. The King has big magic. So does Nepenthe. And the Witch of the Woods. And the Fire Witch. The Enforcer, though, does not have that power. Just brute force."

"Who's the Enforcer?"

"The Hand of the King. Some say he's the Eyes of the King, too."

"What does that even mean?"

"That the King can see through him and make him do whatever he wants. It's just a rumor. The Kingdom runs Algid on rumors and fear . . ."

Great, so my alleged ice daddy also has freaky mind-control powers.

"What about Gerde? What kind of magic does she have?"

"She's not a witch. Or at least she wasn't born a witch; I don't know what she is. She has always been this way."

"So what are you? Why do you live here?"

"I couldn't let Gerde do this alone."

"But you don't like it? And you don't like me because you think I have magic."

Looking away, he said softly, "I know you have magic."

"Even if that were true, it isn't something I can help. It isn't something I asked for. You can't hate me for what I am."

He shrugged. "I've seen what the witch can do. And you're supposed to be a million times more powerful."

"Look, what you think I can do . . . I can't. I am not like the River Witch, and I never will be."

"You will, after she teaches you. Like she's teaching Gerde. There's a price for what she does for you. You just don't see it yet."

"She saved my life. She and Gerde. How can that be bad?"

"When she helps you, you'll owe her. I just wonder if maybe all of us will pay for it."

I had thought the awkwardness that had descended between us had something to do with us being alone and him being half-naked, but it was more than that. He objected to me. I was used to people not liking me. But not until I had done something to warrant it. Kai objected to the very idea of me.

Maybe we should have left her in the water. I hadn't imagined it. He had really said it. I knew that now with near certainty.

"Then why didn't you just let me go?"

"There was a storm coming."

"Before that—you tried to stop me."

"You can't run away on Gerde's watch. I don't want to see her punished."

His concern for Gerde was the only thing so far that saved him from being a complete asshole. Well, that and the house. But my mind was caught on punishment. I wondered what that looked like in the hands or tentacles of the River Witch.

"Look, I should put something on. There's a room on the opposite side of that wall, up the stairs. There might be another wave. It's better that we stay here the night."

"You want me to spend the night here with you?" My voice dripped with incredulity. I suddenly would rather be with the River Witch.

"It's the last thing I want. But I didn't make that storm out there." He looked at me very pointedly when he said that.

"You think I did this? You think I wanted this?"

"You tell me! You don't have to want it. You were emotional. That's how it works. The snow responds to you. The Snow King can frown and cause a crevasse to fall all the way across Algid. The River Witch said you can control snow, even if you don't know you can."

"That's insane. I did not do this."

"I wish I was wrong. But everything I've seen tells me the opposite. I live with a witch who makes tsunamis when Gerde makes the dinner wrong, and Gerde herself, who . . ." He drifted off, stopping himself from saying more.

"Who what?"

He closed his eyes and gathered himself as if arguing with me were physically affecting him. He took a step back from me and said, "I'll see you in the morning."

The me from Whittaker, who would have taken a bite of him, considered the fleshy part of his arm. But a look at the whited-out windows stopped me. I turned my back on him as he retreated.

Before I climbed the stairs of the cube, I noticed another door. Curious, I opened it and found a loom with green wool sitting in a corner and a cage with bits of bone and fur on the floor around it. I closed it again, unsure of what to think.

As I climbed the stairs to the guest room, I wondered if I wanted to know any more about this house or its inhabitants. And where was Bale? From the second I had landed in the River I had been sidetracked. But no more, I promised myself. I promised him. Every person I met would be a step toward him. And if it turned out I did control the snow, which I doubted in my core, I would use every single particle of it to build a bridge to him.

The windows faced the woods. The view was not obscured by the Snow Wave. Outside, I could see the rainbow of the North Lights. It might have been a trick of the eye, or maybe I was just tired, but they seemed to be just a bit fainter than when I had arrived in Algid. Or maybe the prophecy was true. The Lights were going out. A storm bird's call rang out again, followed by another whistle. Another wave was coming. But after my talk with Kai, I felt like I'd already been knocked down by one.

I looked out the window and wondered how the strange, private boy downstairs had possibly done all this on his own. I'd never climbed a tree before, and from this vantage point it felt like I was standing on the tree's top branches.

I turned back to my little borrowed room. The last few days suddenly weighed heavily upon me.

What Kai and the River Witch had said was in my mind now, whether or not I wanted it to be. I did not think I brought on the Snow Waves. But could I really be the child of two enchanted beings? Could I really have magic?

There was only one way to find out.

I decided to see if I really had powers. I did all the things I'd seen witches do on TV. I wiggled my nose. I waved my arms around. I concentrated on lighting a candle with my mind. I tried to move a little deer statue on the bedside table without touching it. I tried to freeze something. But all that happened was I ended up frowning at the wall.

Feeling silly and frustrated, I picked up the little figurine, ready to throw it at the wall, but recalled at the last second that it did not belong to me. Dr. Harris would be proud. I put it back down on the bedside table and listened to the sound of the wind against the house. Vern said once that I was just a bull in a china shop, that one day I'd be fine in the open air. I felt suddenly aware of how far from home I really was. I knew the schedule at Whittaker: the sound of the doors locking and unlocking, the scuff of the orderlies' rubber soles coming down the hall. Here, I didn't know anything.

I was so very tired. But I couldn't sleep in Kai and Gerde's guest bed. It was pretty. It was soft. It just wasn't mine.

Eventually, I settled for underneath it. I took the blanket and pillow and curled up there.

12

WHEN I AWOKE THE next day, I opened my eyes to a gray metal wall. I stifled a scream before remembering that I was under the bed. The tree house . . . Gerde and Kai . . . It all came rushing back to me. I was staring at one of the brackets that connected the house to the tree.

I climbed out from under the little bed. My body ached from the cold, hard floor. Random thoughts scattered through my brain. Did Kai see me sleeping there? Would he say something if he had?

What did I care? He was a jerk. A talented jerk, but a jerk all the same. I heard the roaring sound again somewhere behind the tree house. *Another Snow Wave?* I wondered. But the sound was guttural. Alive somehow. I got dressed and went to investigate.

Following the sound, I showed myself into the greenhouse, which rivaled the house in its splendor. The flowers weren't like anything I'd ever seen. The pretty little tulips sprinkled across the grounds of Whittaker didn't hold a candle to these plants. The buds were enormous. And the color was an iridescent lavender. I had never seen a flower shimmer before.

There was a ton of food growing in the greenhouse, too. Neat rows of leafy greens and carrots and weird periwinkle fruit were ready to be picked.

I hoisted myself against a gate made of ice.

Continuing on to a clearing in the wood, I heard the sound again. There was another dome that looked identical to the greenhouse.

I could hear the animals before I could see them. There were two of everything. It was an underground menagerie.

The first creature I saw was a penguin with pale-pink wings. It wobbled around in its pastel tuxedo until it bumped into another one dressed in ecru. Another with blue wings joined in, making it a trio.

There were animals I was familiar with and animals I'd never seen before. There were sheep and cows and goats alongside penguins and polar bears separated by partitions made of ice. And at the very back of the menagerie, there was a pale-gray lion, the source of the roaring that had lured me there. The roof was a thin layer of ice through which the sun filtered in.

Maybe the cage inside the house was just for one of these creatures.

I wondered if the animals had always been different here. Or if these animals were here because they were different.

The ecru penguin opened its mouth, revealing a set of sharp teeth that did not belong.

I laughed seeing the adorable creature's weird adaptation. But the sound I made drew the attention of the other animals in their ice cages. They began to stir—clawing and biting and trying to get to me. The penguins advanced, and I took a step back, confident that the snow cages would hold and that I could close the door on the little fanged wobbly bird that Frankenstein-walked toward me, flapping its beige wings.

But beyond the penguins I saw something even more disconcerting. The top of each snow wall was suddenly covered in vultures. It was like that old Hitchcock movie that Vern made me watch, in which hundreds of birds descended on a town at once. Only these birds were going to descend on me.

I began to back out, but it was too late. The birds took flight with me in their sights. A black cloud of feathers and pointy beaks filled my vision.

The ice roof shook.

I shielded my face with my arms, then turned to run.

Gerde's singsongy voice broke out.

"Behave," she ordered, and the cloud of black parted.

The birds returned to their former perches. As their wings ruffled back into place, their caws died down into soft coos.

Gerde moved through the beasts that now were as tame as house pets.

"They don't always love new people," she said in apology.

I allowed myself to exhale. I felt my worry settle a few seconds behind the birds. I could have hugged Gerde. I was so glad to see her.

As we walked through, a vulture cocked its head and squawked at me as if to ask what I was staring at. Gerde whistled back at it, and it landed on her shoulder.

"Good girl, Zion," Gerde began sheepishly.

Zion made a sharp clucking noise, to which Gerde responded with a nod. She looked up at me as if remembering I was there.

"I know talking to birds makes me a little . . ."

"Nuts?" I wanted to tell her that where I came from people did much, much more outlandish things. "I think you just saved my life."

Gerde looked away from the vulture perched on her shoulder and back at me quizzically. I couldn't tell if she knew about my escape from the River Witch, but even if she did, she didn't ask about it.

"Kai built this for me," Gerde explained as we walked through the zoo. "We call it the Keep. I've always had a way with plants and animals."

"I've never had much of a way with anything or anyone. Except maybe a pencil," I countered.

And Bale.

"You draw? I bet Kai would lend you some of his supplies. He'll be thrilled. I can barely draw a stick figure."

My fingers twitched at the thought of a pencil. But I wasn't sure if I wanted to draw again. Everything I'd drawn had come true. What would I draw next?

Things were already so insane. I did not really want to see anything else come to life from my pages.

"I'm okay. Maybe later."

She nodded as we made our way through the animals. They all made happy noises in her presence.

"Please don't tell anyone about the Keep."

I wasn't quite sure if she and Kai really understood what a secret was. Having a hidden menagerie didn't seem like that big of a deal.

"I won't tell anyone," I assured her. "Who would I tell?"

Gerde clapped her hands together, pleased, but a flash of worry crossed her small face at the idea of my talking to other people. I was a stray she'd taken in. And like with her animal pets, she half wanted me not to remember where I belonged so she could keep me.

"Why is it a secret? Wouldn't people want to preserve all this?"

"Resources are limited. But because of what I can do, I can sustain them. Some would disagree with me for keeping them in the first place. They would think it was an indulgence in a time when we are not allowed many."

I looked at her closely. I could tell she loved these creatures more than she loved humans—except maybe Kai.

I wondered again about their relationship.

"You and Kai? What are you to each other?"

"We are like brother and sister," Gerde said, petting a polka-dotted pig.

My brain stuck on "like." The way she said the word bothered me.

"So you don't have the same parents?" I asked for clarification.

She shrugged.

"We were raised in the same home. But when winter first fell, things were chaotic. Mothers were separated from their children. Other mothers took them in. Even now, it still happens. There are a lot of orphaned kids in Algid."

"So you don't know for sure if you're brother and sister?"

"I just know he is my family. Now, do you want to help me feed something?" Gerde asked, putting an end to the topic.

I nodded and we moved on.

"I know this is going to sound odd. When I first got to Algid by the River, I was attacked by giant wolves. Only, they weren't made of flesh and bone . . ."

"Oh, the Snow Wolves." Gerde raised an eyebrow, her interest piquing even further. "Most people who meet the Snow Beasts don't live to tell the tale."

"What do you mean? What about you? I saw what you did with the birds just now . . . but does that mean . . . Can you control the Snow Beasts, too? And wait, SNOW BEASTS? There are more than just the wolves?"

Gerde nodded.

"There are Snow Lions, Tigers, and Bears . . . even insects. Snow Bees can sting a person to death in minutes . . ."

I shuddered at the thought as Gerde continued, clearly marveling at the Snow Beasts' prowess.

"Basically anything and everything King Lazar can dream up. They are not alive—not in the way my animals are. I don't know exactly how he does it, but they still move and breathe and obey."

"Could you survive them? Can you control them with your gift?" I asked again.

Gerde explained, "I can touch something in animals that reaches back to me. But in the Snow Beasts, that part is missing in each and every one of them. But maybe you can fight them with yours."

She still believed in my gift and in the prophecy. I didn't have any interest in going there again.

"I don't know about that. What about people? Can you reach people the same way?"

"To be honest, I don't always connect to people."

"That makes two of us." I reached down to pet a lamb. The soft wool gave me comfort. Bale was my best friend before he was more. I remembered a time when Bale caught me drawing him. We were twelve years old. I didn't let him see the drawing at first. Because it didn't do him justice. Somehow I'd captured the lines of him, but not the spirit.

"This is how you see me?" he'd asked.

"It's terrible. It doesn't capture you. It doesn't have your humor. Your heart . . . Your . . ."

He leaned in as if waiting for more compliments.

"You little . . ." I chose my favorite expletives and jumped on top of him, pummeling him.

He put up his hands. "I give up."

I relaxed my grip.

A second later, he flipped me over and pinned me down. We were suddenly out of breath and suddenly aware of how close we were. His eyes broke with mine and looked at my lips and back again. He didn't move, though. Like he was waiting for permission. And I didn't move because I didn't want to be asked. I wanted to be kissed like Kayla Blue on *The End of Almost*. She was never asked.

"You're getting a little old for wrestling . . . ," Vern's voice had cut through, breaking the moment.

Bale rolled off me. "Vern, you could stop clocks with that timing of yours," he said, hopping to his feet.

The memory stung a little.

"Now we have each other!" Gerde singsonged, bringing me back to the present.

I smiled but didn't agree or disagree with her. Instead I pointed to something pink through the ice walls and asked, "What's that?"

"Oh, it's the best part," she said excitedly. I quickly kept within a step of her as we made our way through the animals and back outside through the menagerie.

I gasped when I saw rows upon rows of pink wheat growing in snow.

"Is it magic?"

She shrugged. "It's botany. It's taken me months, but finally it took root."

As we wound our way through the pink wheat plants back to the house, I realized that this was the thing that Gerde wanted me to keep secret.

If the King found out about her magic with plants, his iron-clad grip on Algid's frozen, barren land would lessen forever.

On the way out, Gerde touched one of the flowers' buds. It responded like she was the sun. And maybe she was.

♕

"You showed her the Keep? Unbelievable." Kai stepped in line with us a bit later, looking less than thrilled to see me. I was guessing that he hoped I'd run away in the night.

"She found it. And who is she going to tell, anyway?" Gerde countered, using my words against Kai.

I shrugged and smiled at Kai, knowing that it would annoy him. I pretended that it didn't bother me when he behaved exactly as I now expected. Rude. Possibly a little cruel. The single moment in the house when he held my hand was the exception.

He scowled. This was who he chose to be. I could do the same.

"She's only here because I stopped her from escaping," Kai said.

Gerde looked struck. She had not known after all. Or if she had, she did not want confirmation.

"He's right. I'm only staying for the moment. I need to go out there and find my friend," I said, bracing myself for whatever was out there in the snow that stood between me and Bale.

"Well, I'm glad you decided to stay for now. And if anyone can help you figure it out, it's the River Witch," Gerde responded, looping an arm through mine. "Kai, let's not quarrel. She likes the cube. She thinks it's genius," Gerde said, apparently trying to bridge the gap between us even though clearly he did not want it to close.

Kai's blue eyes flickered briefly at the compliment before darkening again. He was proud of what he'd created. And it made me think of the last sixteen years that I had wasted. He had a true gift, and I was barely educated. My collection of knowledge was a hodgepodge at best from television and the set of encyclopedias that I'd read from *A* to *Z* in the Whittaker library.

"What's really genius is that map of Algid on your arm." Kai motioned to my left forearm.

"What?" I pulled my sleeve down self-consciously. He was pointing to my scars.

"You have a map of Algid on your body? How did I not notice?" Gerde clapped her hands excitedly.

"I don't," I said. "It's scar tissue."

Kai shook his head. "That's Algid. But if you don't want to believe me, take a look yourself." He walked out of the room and returned a few seconds later with a map.

As he unrolled the paper, familiar lines stared up at me. But instead of being etched onto my skin, they were right there on a map marked "Algid." I lifted my sleeve and put them side by side. How was this possible? Unless . . . unless the story about me walking through a mirror wasn't true, either? But I remembered it . . . I remembered all the blood. It was one of the few things that had stuck with me from my childhood. That mirror was the dividing line of my life. Between pre-Whittaker and Whittaker. Not-crazy and crazy. And Kai and his geography lesson had just called it into question.

"Incredible!" Gerde leaned over the map and my arm, her eyes wide with amazement.

I noted a mountain range in the top right corner of the map. Below it was a castle of some kind, and beneath it the words "Snow Palace" on Kai's map. On my arm the palace wasn't there, but the mountain range was.

"Where are we on this map?" I asked.

Gerde started to point to an area on the bottom left when Kai snapped the map shut again.

"Why'd you do that?" I said angrily.

It was the second time he'd done that. Kai had stopped Gerde from telling me something I wanted to know. He may have been protecting her, but he was pissing me off.

Kai said nothing. His face was a mask again, closing off me and Gerde. He walked back into the other room.

Gerde rolled her eyes. "Just ignore him. He's always so grumpy."

I nodded, even though I thought there was more to his attitude. And it likely had something to do with me.

"Do you believe what the River Witch said about me?" I asked as I traced a finger along the mountain ridge of my scar.

"The witch is tough, but fair. And I have learned much from her. She's changed my life. But if you let her teach you, you will change all of Algid."

"So you believe in the prophecy. Or prophecies. I heard there were two."

"I only know of one," she said, biting her lip. "But I think when the Eclipse of the Lights comes, the whole world will change. Or at least I hope so."

I looked around. I dropped my voice to a whisper. "I don't want to change all of Algid. I just want to bring my friend home."

Gerde blinked hard. "The boy from the water? You were calling his name and another when the River Witch brought you to the boat," she said, remembering.

I nodded.

"The boy from where I came from. His name is Bale."

Maybe it was because Gerde had shown me her top secret snow-growing crop, or maybe it was because I could see how much hope she had in me for the future of her land. I just couldn't let her continue to pin those on me, when I was not here to help her or Algid. I needed to be honest with her. And I needed to recite the story of Bale and Snow again out loud to keep it real for me. To keep me going. I left out the part about Bale being dragged into Algid through a mirror. And I left out the part about Jagger, too. "I need to find Bale."

Gerde was quiet, but her look was thoughtful. I was expecting her to be disappointed that I hadn't come here to save the world. But there was understanding in her gray eyes instead.

"You love him. You'll find him. If you let the River Witch train you, you'll be able to."

I hadn't really thought of it that way, but it did make sense. I needed to survive this world, and if I really possessed the powers everyone said I did, knowing how to use them might help. Gerde said there was a virtual army of beasts out there in the forest. I could not outrun them. But maybe I could defend myself. And if I was being honest, without Jagger I didn't have the first clue where to find Bale. Maybe I needed the River Witch after all.

"If I ask the River Witch for help, it has to be on my terms," I said hesitantly. "And there's no way I'm going back to her boat."

Gerde laughed heartily. "I think that can be arranged. Kai will bring her here. In the meantime, would you like some clothes that are a little bit more . . . a little less . . ."

"Less me?" I joked, pulling at my Whittaker pajamas.

Kai grunted disapprovingly. He had drifted back into the room. Kai didn't like me. But I wanted to dissect his dislike instead of punching him like I did Jagger. There was something about his attitude that was maddeningly interesting to me. Maybe it was because he wore his thoughts on his face, like I did, with no effort to hide them. Like right now, I couldn't help but notice the flash of his blue eyes even as his lips scowled.

"Don't mind him," Gerde said, turned on her heel, and returned with a green dress. "I made this. I promise that it will feel like you," she said with a small smile.

"To be honest, I don't know what *me* feels like," I said, taking the dress.

"I don't know what's gotten into Kai," Gerde said matter-of-factly. "When he gets his mind set on something, he doesn't budge easily. He'll warm to you in time."

"Why would he?" I blurted, and headed upstairs to change. I had a limited history meeting new people, but Kai's feelings about me seemed pretty intractable. It was dislike at first sight.

The dress Gerde had made was simple and pale green. She had used the wool that I'd seen on the loom in that strange room last night. I slipped it on. The material was soft to the touch. It clung to my torso before gently sloping out into a full skirt. Delicate buttons shaped like tiny sparrows and made out of what almost felt like bone dotted down the center of the dress. I twirled around, liking the way the fabric swirled around me.

When I got downstairs, Gerde was humming and there were literally birds in the kitchen chirping along with her. They'd flown inside and were perched along the top of the cabinets. My nose filled with the smell of her buttery batter frying up on the stovetop.

I felt jealousy well up in me. I had never had anything like this and would never be anything like Gerde. She hummed and sang, not to keep her anger down. She did it because she felt like it—because that happy noise needed to get out.

"The dress looks perfect on you," Gerde said brightly, complimenting herself and me in one breath.

"Thank you. I really . . . it's lovely," I said, an inexplicable lump forming in my throat as I got the words out. The gesture meant more apparently than I knew.

She turned mercifully back to the stovetop and said, "You're welcome. By the way, we eat a lot of greens and breakfast-for-lunch here. Sometimes we even eat it for dinner. I hope that's okay."

There was a pink porridge next to a leafy salad already on the table. A griddle full of bright-green pancakes sat on the tiny stovetop.

"On Tuesdays we have plain egg-white omelets. On Wednesdays we have cereal," I blurted, surprising myself. I was reciting the Whittaker menu. Days ran together there. However bland, sometimes the only way I knew the day of the week was by the food that Vern handed me on a plastic platter.

Gerde blinked at me, unsure what I was talking about, but played along. "Well, that sounds delicious, but I hope you don't mind trying something a little different."

"Everything's different here," I said, deflecting, as she plated a pancake for me and I took my first bite.

All of what Gerde had shown me back in the greenhouse was pretty mind-blowing, but I didn't know that food could actually make me feel things. As the green pancake melted in my mouth, I saw colors. I tasted colors. Technicolor ones. It was sweet and sour and spicy all at once. The flavors chased one another. It was a first, middle, and last course in one single bite. Maybe every surprise in Algid wasn't Snow Wolves coming out of the ground. Maybe there were good things for all the scary ones.

"How did you do that?"

Gerde shrugged and placed one of her tiny hands over my heart. "May I? I don't know how to explain. But I can feel that there's something . . . not right in there."

She took her hand away. "Never mind. I'm sorry. I'm still learning. Maybe I should stick to the animals in the menagerie."

I put a hand over my own heart. Gerde was still a novice, but maybe she sensed something that I knew for sure. My heart was still broken.

The next day I woke to find my arm hanging over the side of the bed, submerged in water. I was still reaching for Bale. The water lapped at my fingertips, and my eyes opened. This was not a dream. My bed was floating, and the ceiling was coming closer; the water was raising the bed farther and farther up.

I could still sit up. But if I didn't get out of the room soon, I was going to drown. Panic seized me, but I felt paralyzed, all while the water inched up. Faster and faster.

I didn't have much time. I tried to paddle toward the door. If I didn't do something, then I was going to drown for the second time in the same week.

"Help me, please!" I screamed.

"What is it now?" a disdainful voice said through the door.

It was Kai. A part of me wished that I didn't need his help right now so I could tell him where he could shove his "*what is it now.*" But my life depended on his opening the door.

"The room is flooding. Open the door—please!"

I could hear him trying to throw his weight against the door.

"It's stuck—"

"No shit, Sherlock," I blurted, realizing that Kai would not get the reference from my world.

"Kai, there's so much water . . ." I heard my voice change from its normal tone to the high-pitched range of fear.

"Use your snow! Save yourself. It's the only way!" he yelled.

This was not a fairy tale. No one was coming to save me. That's what he was saying. And I finally heard him.

Despite what he'd instructed, he hadn't given up trying. I could hear him making contact with the door again and again.

"I'll get the River Witch or Gerde."

"Don't leave me," I begged.

"Okay," he said, calling out for them instead of leaving the door.

I rocked back on the bed I might die in. I felt anger come again in waves. I did not want to end like this. But the fear and the panic that I'd felt in the River was back again, too.

"Think," I told myself as the bed rose higher and the ceiling grew even closer.

I started to hum like I used to back at Whittaker.

"Don't think. Freeze it—use your power and freeze it!" Kai yelled to me, his voice forceful and commanding.

"I don't know how."

"You do. You just haven't done it yet. The River Witch always says take what you are feeling and put it in the magic. You're angry and scared. Just take that and put it all in your snow."

He was trying to save me, but all I could think of was how easy it was for him to say that from the other side of the door.

I closed my eyes and tried to focus. This time something actually happened. I felt a flash of cold go all over my body like a shiver. Colder than cold. Like I'd reached my cold saturation point. Another shiver and the cold began to drain from me through my fingertips. A crystal formed on the surface of the water. It wasn't like the paper cutouts of snowflakes I remember making as a little kid when I was still allowed to use scissors. It was something like the graffitied Tree that let me into Algid, a strange language that I couldn't understand clustering on top of itself in a solid icy pattern on the surface of the water. Then one crystal split into two. And that crystal split again, multiplying over and over.

Suddenly my fingernails extended and resealed around metallically hard ice. The shards of ice were a few inches long and came to razor-sharp points. Like icicles. Like claws. My ice claws were out.

Somehow, within seconds, the entire room beneath me was frozen. My bed no longer moved. My head was an inch from the ceiling. I began to laugh, looking at the skating rink I'd made of Kai and Gerde's guest room. I looked at my hands that were now weapons.

What had been hidden from me in the other world my whole life, what was always there just beneath my skin, waiting for me to let it out all along, was proof that I was not crazy and that everyone in the world but Bale and maybe Vern had been completely and utterly wrong about me. My claws cut both ways.

The pain hurt, but it was good.

I had saved myself, just like Kai had ordered. And whatever else the River Witch had said, it turned out the part about me having the power of snow was true. For a girl who had spent the better part of her life stuck in a hospital for crimes against sanity, this was everything.

I felt my entire being wake up. I had a power I had only felt once before in my dreams, which allowed me to be sane and free and stronger than anyone or anything, except maybe the fabled Snow King, Lazar.

I heard the sound of the door creaking open, and the snow beneath me began to melt almost as quickly as it had frozen. The slushy mess flowed out the door as I and my bed's icy island descended back down to the floor. The River Witch stood in the doorway. Kai and Gerde were behind her.

Kai stepped forward. "Let's get you out of here," he said exasperatedly. He reached a hand out to me.

Did he not see what I had done? What I was capable of doing?

I reacted reflexively, swiping a claw at him and forcing him to step backward.

He was undaunted. He came forward again.

"Snow. It's okay. You're fine now." He didn't move again. Instead, his eyes were focused on me, as if his stare could somehow bring me back to myself.

For a second I thought it could. But I couldn't risk it.

I looked down at my ice claws, which were now shaking. But why? Was I going to freeze the world, or was I just coming down from what I'd done?

"Stay back!" I yelled.

The River Witch crossed the threshold and pushed past Kai.

"Stay back," I said, fear peeking through my anger. "I don't want to hurt you. Please don't make me hurt any of you."

"You can't hurt me, my child. You may be able to freeze me for a time, but I believe I can handle it."

The River Witch approached me and didn't hesitate. She grabbed my claws in her watery hands.

I tried to pull away, but she held firm. I watched with growing horror as her hands began to freeze and, instead of veins, flesh-colored scales began to rise from beneath her skin. The witch's face scowled down at me. I couldn't tell if her face was set in concentration or pain. I could suddenly feel the heat radiating off her and her hands. She was combating the ice with her water, which melted my snow faster than it could form again.

When she was done, when my claws were no longer, she pulled me to her and I let myself sink into her and begin to sob.

"I know. My child, I know. You're safe now. You must have been so scared. This was a test. And this is the feeling you need to remember to find Bale and to face the King. That day will come. It is your destiny. And mark my words, no matter what the outcome, it will take every ounce of strength you have."

"Help me," I said, clinging to her.

"You will help yourself," she replied, holding me closer.

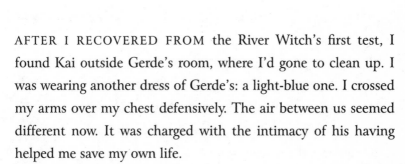

13

AFTER I RECOVERED FROM the River Witch's first test, I found Kai outside Gerde's room, where I'd gone to clean up. I was wearing another dress of Gerde's: a light-blue one. I crossed my arms over my chest defensively. The air between us seemed different now. It was charged with the intimacy of his having helped me save my own life.

I remembered the sureness of his voice through the door. There was no door between us now.

"Nepenthe wants to see you outside," he said curtly, walking away as he tossed the words behind him without bothering to turn around.

I followed him. He had just helped save my life, and now he'd turned colder than my ice claws. Maybe what he'd seen had made him afraid of me.

"Hey," I said a little more forcefully than I meant to.

He turned around.

"What you did before . . . talking me through it . . ." I held up my hands, which were just hands now.

He shrugged, not giving me anything.

Maybe the air between us wasn't different after all.

"It was just a test. I played my part. I would have done it for anyone," he corrected.

"You knew?" I demanded. Somehow it mattered to me if every minute of my pretended rescue had been pretend for him.

"No, of course not . . . I just meant . . . ," he began.

"Look, I know we got off to a bad start . . . But I just want you to know that I appreciate . . ."

"Snow, stop. I didn't do anything. That was all you. You have your powers now."

Right. I was not special in any way, shape, or form. Except for my snow superpowers, which he had no use for. And we had not been connected at all in the last few hours. He just gave me the same courtesy he would one of Gerde's farm animals.

"Long live the Snow Princess. I have to go." He moved off, leaving me reaching for more words.

Maybe Kai had carved out a life with his sister and had left no room for anyone else.

I'd spent my whole life trapped in Whittaker, but I had never felt fear on a day-to-day basis. Sure, I was afraid of Bale not getting better, and other people were afraid of me. But Kai lived with fear every day. He looked at me like I was an invitation to trouble, which I was if the King ever found out I was alive. Not a flesh-and-blood person, not someone who he could connect to. It occurred to me that Gerde was probably the only person he had let get close, and that made me want to knock down the wall around him even more. *If only he wasn't so hell-bent on getting rid of me*, I thought, but then I remembered I was supposed to already be gone.

I took the stairs and path all the way down to the water. There the River Witch was wrestling with some kind of sharklike creature. One tentacle was wrapped around its grayish purple body and another one extended down its throat.

I raised my hands. To do what exactly, I didn't know. To help? I could not produce those claws again if I wanted to . . . and the whole point of my coming down here was for her to teach me how to control it so I could NOT do it ever again.

"River Witch!" I yelled.

She dropped the shark back into the water. Her tentacle down its throat was triumphant. The dead animal floated to the surface, its blood eddying into the water around it. I began to look away, but something caught the light. She was also holding a piece of mirror. It was about the size of a hand. It wasn't just reflective; it was luminescent. It made me think of the mirror in Bale's room that took him away.

"People throw bits of mirror into the River. They are offerings to me. They think that I will grant their prayers and wishes."

"Mirror? As in *the Mirror*?"

The River Witch laughed at that. "If anyone had a piece of the King's mirror, they wouldn't be throwing it away just for a wish. It's much too powerful. These are just regular mirrors. But they represent the mirror and the power it holds. At least to the people making the wishes."

"And do you do that for them? Do you grant their wishes?"

In my head, I wondered if she would grant mine: to find Bale and go back home.

"If it amuses me. If it is a worthy wish."

It was like throwing pennies in a wishing well, only a witch with gills actually granted them.

"What constitutes a worthy wish?"

"Something that you can't get on your own. Something hard."

"Like making someone love you who doesn't?"

"Love is easy. It comes and goes like the River. Try power. That is much harder to find. And in short supply in Algid, save for a choice few."

I didn't want to hear any more about my father. Even though he was at the center of everything.

"What do you do with the mirrors you get?" I changed the subject.

"Mirrors reflect what we want to see, or sometimes they reveal what you really are or what you really want. You have to be very careful with a mirror."

She tossed the mirror piece up in the air, and it sank down into the water by her feet. Just below the surface were dozens of tiny pieces of mirror anchored on some kind of white coral. One of the mirrors caught the light, blinding me for a second.

A tentacled arm pulled me away from the edge.

"Look in the mirror only if you know exactly what you want."

"Okay . . ." I didn't know how to respond to the witch when she spoke in riddles. But it reminded me of Wing back home. "You said you could help me."

"Yes. But before you can wield your power, you need to understand it."

The witch became more watery as she said it, her rivulets becoming wider and their currents picking up. The effect made me want to both recoil and reach out and touch her at once.

"What I want is to find my friend." I decided to go for it. "He was taken from the Other World, and I believe he's in Algid somewhere." I left out the part about the strange mirror suddenly appearing in Bale's room in the asylum. I wasn't sure I could trust the River Witch enough yet.

She studied me for a moment. "If you want to find your friend, you need to survive in this world. And to survive, you need to learn."

"You think I can do that?"

She nodded.

"Because I froze the room?"

"And the Snow Waves you created."

She knew about the Snow Waves. She probably also knew about me spending the night in Kai's house with him. Which meant she also knew that I had tried to run. But from her unchanged expression, I assumed that she didn't care. After all, I was here now.

"But who's to say I made them?"

"Only the King makes Waves like that and he was nowhere

near here. I would have felt him. Snow, you can already wield a storm. In time, with practice, you can become one. And in the meantime you can do this—"

She mumbled some words under her breath I couldn't make out.

From the murky River, a person made of water emerged. She walked over to me and touched my face. Then she fell back down into a puddle.

"What is that?"

"My Champion. She can fight for me, but only where there is water and warmth. Out there," she said, gesturing across the frozen landscape, "she would not do much more than freeze. But yours could do whatever she wanted."

"You want me to make one of those. An ice person. But I don't want to hurt anyone."

"You can't get rid of your power, Snow. You can only learn how to control it."

This was not what I wanted to hear. But the witch didn't seem to know or care that I was upset.

"Then why train me? Why help me?" I demanded, confusion mounting.

"The same reason I help that girl up there," she said evenly.

She was talking about Gerde. But Gerde sews and maybe adjusts animal genomes. She doesn't make storms, I thought.

"You underestimate her. You can't see it through all the flowers. But she is not unlike me. And I know what it is to have power and not know what to do with it. I want you to reach your full power. You deserve that, and so does Algid," Nepenthe continued.

"I just want Bale back—" I said, overwhelmed.

Her curl of a smile dropped for the briefest of instants.

"Then we'll get him back. It's not an either-or proposition. But from where I'm standing, you need to get strong before you can do anything. Let me help you with that."

It was just like Gerde said, though there was something in her tone that I didn't quite trust. I thought I saw her face catch when I said the part about Bale. But I had to believe that she was going to help me. I had to, for Bale's sake.

"With practice, you could be stronger than either of your parents," she said.

I had always felt there was no one like me, but I hadn't ever seen that as a positive. The witch saw my value. In this world I was something that people wanted. That was new. For most of my life I'd only really mattered to a short list of people. And only one I was sure of: Bale. And I had to get him back at any cost.

"Okay," I said, making a deal with the witch. "I'll work with you, if you help me find Bale."

And so it was done.

14

THE RIVER WITCH DIDN'T waste any time. My "training" started immediately in the cold, early dawn, outside on the edge of a mountain far away from Kai and Gerde's cube house. If I didn't know any better, I could have sworn this was Mount Kilimanjaro or Mount Everest, or some equally ridiculously death-defying place. Places I had only seen when clicking through the channels on the TV in the common room or flipping through the encyclopedias in the library.

I didn't know how I got here, and part of me wanted this to be another dream. But the ice that kissed my face and the wind that picked up around me felt so very real.

When I had climbed down the ladder of the cube, instead of the final step leading to solid ground, my slippered feet touched down on top of the mountain.

I knew panic would seize me soon, so I allowed myself to take in the beauty of what was beneath me. I had lived most of my life in a locked room and had never seen anything like this. All of Algid stretched out in every direction. Pink, blue, and yellow trees dotted the floor of the land. Tiny houses sparkled in the distance. If I didn't know how messed up this land really was, I could almost believe this was paradise. Somewhere down there was the King, and roaming around those trees were more Snow Lions, Tigers, and Bears—oh my.

A strange fog rolled past me. I could feel its warmth before it settled above the nearest park. I gasped when the mist began to take shape. It looked almost like a woman. A face and a body began to articulate itself. The mist became solid. And the solid became the River Witch. Not a single drop of water dripped down her skin, and she was wearing a cape that reminded me of a creepy, scaled mermaid version of Little Red Riding Hood's. Even though she stood atop the next mountain over, her voice was in my ear as if she were right next to me. Her face was pretty. Dry, but pretty. But it was nowhere near as beautiful as the watery version. I could see why.

"You're . . . human."

"Let's not get carried away," she said, sounding disdainful. "But if you're so curious, come get a better look," she dared, nodding at the space between us. It was a challenge. It was, I assumed, my next lesson.

I raised my hand and tried to create a snow bridge between my mountain and hers. But nothing happened. It was like one of those wishes that the River Witch described as worthy, only I didn't know how to grant it. No matter how hard I tried.

"The snow is yours," she proclaimed.

"But it doesn't feel like mine," I said a little too loudly.

I wasn't sure if my voice was in her ear the way hers was in mine. My words echoed back to me, boomeranging with more confidence than they had had when they left me. The distance between us seemed insurmountable, and the drop down from where I stood was a ragged, brutal, sure drop to the death.

"You have spent your whole life locked up. You have spent your whole life ignorant of your rightful power. Because of your mother. Because of your father. They restrained you. Now you can do anything, be anything, you want. Claim your gift."

"Come to me, snow," I whispered, this time feeling like I had already failed before I had begun. The more I thought about my confinement, the further away from controlling my powers I felt.

"You aren't trying!" the witch snapped.

Was this lady kidding me? I was on top of a mountaintop trying not to fall off. Of course I was trying!

My eyes narrowed at the River Witch. My hands balled up reflexively. I knew what she was doing. She was trying to get a rise out of me in hopes that my anger would spark my snow. I knew the tactic from Magpie at the institute. Though Magpie's motives were not at all noble.

The River Witch tsked twice. "Algid has waited fifteen years for you. And look at you. So very disappointing. You're useless," she said. And then with a quick flash of her arms, an unseen force shoved me off the mountain and down into the chasm below.

I screamed as the cold air rushed by me, burning my ears and lips and teeth.

Use your snow! The witch's voice came from everywhere and nowhere. *You can control your fate. Use it!*

I let loose a string of expletives at the witch as I free-fell. She had actually done it. She had actually pushed me off a cliff as part of a lesson. I could see the rocky floor of the terrain getting closer and closer as I hurtled down to it.

I would not die like this. I felt a burning anger in my chest. I wasn't useless. I wasn't! I was not disappointing.

Kai's words from the flood came back to me. *You just haven't done it yet.*

I tried to whisper to the snow, but the air was moving too quickly around me, so instead I closed my eyes and concentrated.

Come to me, snow. I felt the slightest shift in the atmosphere as, degree by degree, I started to feel more attuned to the cold air and space around me. *Come to me, snow*, I ordered again, and I noticed that all around me snow was falling. Suddenly I wasn't afraid. Like the witch said, I owned the snow. It belonged to me, and I could make it take me where I wanted it to.

"River Witch," I whispered with newfound confidence.

For the briefest of seconds, I didn't feel cold anymore. I felt warm and whole. As if the emptiness left by Bale had filled up for the first time.

I felt myself lifted up off the ground, weightless, by a wave of snow. And in a white-out blink I was suddenly standing on the mountain next to the River Witch.

She was waiting for me. Her lips curled into a smile.

"I expected you only to stop your fall," she said, impressed. "But it could be beginner's luck, so don't get cocky."

I smiled. I knew I'd almost died, but I hadn't. I had done it. I had controlled my snow. Maybe it was good enough to get Bale back.

But when I asked this of the River Witch, she said, "You're nowhere near ready. Tomorrow we begin again."

After the River Witch deposited me in front of the cube house, I walked down to the River and looked at the mirrors in the water. I looked for my reflection, but instead I found Kai's. He appeared suddenly on the side of the boat.

He wasn't wearing a coat despite the cold. He was scrubbing down the hull of the boat.

"I just made a snow tornado. Aren't you going to congratulate me?"

I left out the part where the River Witch had pushed me. I assumed he would not approve.

"Bravo," he said, dumping fish off the side of the boat.

"What is your problem? The witch gets results."

"You think that the *how* doesn't matter. But it does. We don't always get what we want in this life. But we can control how we get there. She almost drowned you to get you to use your power. And I'm guessing you didn't just learn how to fly by closing your eyes and thinking happy thoughts."

"But it worked."

He turned away from me. When he returned, it was with more fish guts. The result of the River Witch's latest meal, probably.

I caught my reflection again at the bottom of the River in the mirrors. *So many fractured wishes. Did they get what they wanted?* I wondered before turning back toward the house.

15

WHEN THE RIVER WITCH pushed me off the mountain, I thought that she had gone as far as she could go. But the next day, she pitted me against Gerde. And Kai's warnings and words came back to me again as I stood at the side of the River, toe to toe with the girl who had served me the best omelet I'd ever had in my life only an hour before.

"She wants us to fight," Gerde explained in what was intended to be a whisper but instead echoed back to us.

I looked down at tiny Gerde. Even without magic, I could have broken her. Gerde may have been the more experienced witch, but she was all roses and healing and I was ice claws and a bringer of storms.

"I won't fight you," I said. "I don't want to hurt you."

"Don't be so sure you're the one in danger of causing harm," Gerde said.

This was not the sweet-as-pie Gerde I knew. There was an

edge to her that I hadn't seen before. I didn't know if I liked her more or less in that moment, but I did know that she had become a heck of a lot more interesting. I wondered what dark thing she was channeling her magic from.

"You don't even know who you are or what you can do," she taunted. "You have less than a snowball's chance in hell of getting your precious Bale back."

"Don't do this—" I warned. She was using what she knew about me to get me mad at her. Mad enough to push back. I knew what she was doing. Just like I always knew it when Magpie did it—and when the River Witch did it yesterday. But still I felt myself failing. I felt myself giving in to the reflexive anger. Giving in to my monster. And there was no pill to fight it now.

But this was Gerde in front of me. Not the River Witch, who could handle it. Not Magpie, who deserved it. Gerde was as innocent as the snow was white.

"Or what, you'll make me into a snowman?" she challenged.

Suddenly the surface of the River broke, and green, mucky seaweed oozed through the surface and coiled around itself a few feet from us.

It took me a few seconds to realize what was happening. The seaweed was forming a Champion to fight me. I got it now. That was Gerde's, and I was supposed to create something to fight hers. But when I concentrated on the water, nothing happened.

The seaweedy Champion inched toward me. Her slimy arms stretched out menacingly.

A new wave of frustration mounted in me as I tried to

summon my snow claws to cut at the seaweed that was winding its way around my ankles.

As it seized me, icicles shot out from under my fingertips. But they did not stop at claws like before. Instead the icicles shot from the tips of my fingers like arrows and arched toward Gerde.

They found their target all along her pretty dress, pinning her to a frozen tree. A trickle of blood ran down her face where an icicle had grazed her cheek.

The seaweed of Gerde's creation uncoiled herself and retreated back into the pond. Gerde struggled to break free. And then the most unexpected thing happened. Gerde's ears suddenly contorted into points, and her sharp, tiny features softened into lumpy cartilage, which was reconfiguring itself under her skin.

You underestimate her, the River Witch had said.

I winced as I watched. Her skin sprouted hair everywhere— from her face to her ears to her neck and on downward. Fur even grew on Gerde's once-delicate hands. Her shoulders increased in size, and thick muscles bulged through the silk of her blouse, while giant calves burst out from beneath her skirt's hem. And a catlike nose replaced her upturned cartoon-princess one. But one thing remained the same: Gerde's eyes, which seemed to be pleading for me to go. Or for me not to look at her.

"Gerde . . ." I said her name, but she didn't seem to hear it.

Did I make this happen somehow? I looked at my hands, which were already back to their normal non–icicle claw state. The out-of-control feeling had passed. But Gerde was still changing, becoming something else. Or had she been something else all along?

Gerde bared razor-sharp teeth, and I realized it didn't matter what I was in her eyes a moment before. She was coming for me and the witch.

The River Witch watched us both intently. She wanted me to stop Gerde. Would she let me hurt her, or would she let me be hurt?

"River Witch?" I pleaded as this new monster that was Gerde broke free from my icicles.

"Find your snow," Nepenthe commanded heartlessly.

Gerde charged.

I raised my hands in Gerde's direction. I would not hurt her. But could I let her maul me to death?

Out of the corner of my eye, I spotted Kai running toward us. He had a panicked look all over his normally stoic face. His handsome blue eyes pleaded with me.

"Kai! It's Gerde!" I screamed. He could stop her. He could bring her back.

"Gerde!" he joined me in calling her name.

She didn't stop. But she glanced in his direction for a split second.

That moment was all I needed. I held up my arms defensively and pushed her backward, knocking her off balance. I was going to make a run for it.

But Gerde was quickly back up on her feet again. I wasn't going to get far.

Kai called to Gerde, "This isn't you, Gerde. Come back to me, come back . . ."

In the center of the River, snow began to swirl in the water. I was brewing a storm.

"Focus," demanded the River Witch.

As Gerde ran at me again, I put my hand on the ground and a wall of ice sprang up between us.

Monstrous Gerde crashed against it and crumpled into a fetal position. She calmed down instantly, and let out a human cry.

"There you are . . . You always come back . . . ," Kai said.

He crouched down beside her, and Gerde shifted back to her previous small self in his arms. Her clothes were in tatters, and her face was full of tears. He wiped the shame away. I stood there shaking, still processing what just happened. Kai had been right. *How* mattered. Selfishly, I wanted his eyes to meet mine. I wanted him to know I understood that now. I wanted him to know that I was sorry to have been a part of what he'd just walked in on. But instead he was staring daggers. I followed his gaze.

Across the way the River Witch began to clap. Then she disappeared into mist.

A few hours later, after Kai had taken Gerde to her room, I went to see her.

She was back in human form, feeding her penguin in the corner of her room.

"You could have given me a heads-up," I said quietly.

"And ruin the surprise?" she said with a little laugh.

She looked at me, searching my face for judgment or pity. Finding neither, she smiled at me. I wanted to tell her that I was a monster, too, just not the kind with fur.

Then she shook her head and her eyes seemed even further away.

"You know what I remember most before the witch?" she said, her voice finding a little bit of its missing musical quality again.

"What?"

"Not the cage that Kai had to put me in every night. Not waking up in strange places with blood all over me. Not knowing what I'd done or who I'd done it to."

"What then?" I asked with growing dread.

"The hunger. It was constant. I wanted to gobble up the world. I know you don't approve of what the River Witch did back there," Gerde said. "And I know Kai doesn't approve of her in general. He won't even call her River Witch. It's always Nepenthe. He says that using her title gives her more power than she deserves . . . but her ends do justify the means. I am one of the ends. Because of the witch, I have my plants and my animals. I have peace."

After a beat she continued solemnly, "What do you feel when it happens? Your snow, I mean . . . or do you not feel anything at all?"

"I do feel something, but it's not cold. Or rather it's so cold, it's almost warm. I can't put it into words, exactly. It's just so cold that it isn't cold anymore . . ."

"Sounds nice."

Compared to the hunger she described, my snow sounded almost easy. Almost like a blessing.

♛

Kai was in his workshop, wearing a metal mask and a tank top that exposed his biceps, which I was completely surprised to find that he had. He was soldering a piece of metal.

"Never sneak up on someone when they're working with fire," he chastised, putting the equipment down on his workbench.

"What about when they're working with a . . ." I drifted off. "Monster" was the wrong word. "What is she, Kai? And how could you not tell me?"

"It was not my secret to tell."

"She could have killed me."

"You're the Snow Princess. I hear you're hard to kill."

"I could have killed her."

He turned away.

"So she's not your sister. She's a . . ."

"She's Gerde," he said simply. "I saved her and she saved me, and the River Witch saved both of us. I don't have to like the witch, but I owe her. And if you let her help you, you'll owe her, too."

I didn't know what to do with that information. "So that means that you and Gerde aren't biological brother and sister."

"She's my family!" he barked.

"Before the witch . . . you took care of her, didn't you? That's what the cage was for?"

"Why do you care?" he asked.

"I just like understanding you better than hating you." The words came out in a whisper.

He didn't respond. He let them hang there between us for another interminable instant before speaking again.

"There aren't many of Gerde's kind. She may be the only one. And if she had been caught . . . Let's just say she'd be a hide on someone's wall."

They'd traded their freedom for their personal safety. So that Gerde would not turn into a beast again.

I understood it even though I wasn't sure I would have made the same move.

But something seized me when I looked at Kai.

"Why did you treat me like shit for making the same compromise that you and Gerde have made a million times over?"

Kai didn't answer.

"Hypocrite," I blurted.

"I wanted you to find another way. Gerde remembers a time when she was hunted. She remembers that fear AND she channels that and she relives that over and over again. I didn't want that for you."

No wonder Gerde looks so faraway all the time, I thought.

"I hoped that it would be different for you."

"But it's not different. I don't like what happened today. But I need her to help me. Gerde understands that. She told me herself."

"Gerde said she would walk away once the witch taught her to control her beast. But we are still here. She got caught up in what else the witch can teach her. I don't know if she will ever want to leave. That could happen to you, too. Trust me, the River Witch wants more than just our thanks."

"That may be, but I'm only here to train, and then I'm gone. We made a deal." I looked around, thinking of the cage in Kai's house. Before the witch, he had been the one to put her there.

"I am sorry for what you and Gerde have gone through," I said, looking at him in a new light.

He saw the shift in me and almost flinched. "Don't pity us. I can't bear it. Not you."

He stood up straighter. If I could tell a story with my shrugs like Vern said I habitually did, he told them with his vertebrae. And right now he was trying to put a wall back up between us. I wasn't going to let him. Not until I understood what he meant.

"What do you mean, not me? You hate me. Why does it matter what I think?"

"Who says that I hate you?" He was looking at me intently. Like he wanted to say something else. But instead of saying something he closed the distance between us and in one strong, single-minded move, he kissed me. It wasn't tentative or sweet like with Bale. It didn't come out of a history of love and longing. It came out of a week of friction and misunderstanding and frustration that brought us to this moment. His lips were inhaling and hungry and challenging, and I felt myself responding.

And then I thought of Bale's lips against mine, our bodies pressing close. I pulled back, suddenly pushing Kai away. He looked confused, but he didn't stop me.

What had I done?

Why had he kissed me?

Why had I kissed him back?

It had taken me years to work up the courage to kiss the boy I loved. The boy I wasn't even sure I liked had closed his lips on mine within a week.

I had betrayed myself and Bale. My heart ached. But my lips

burned. The kiss had had its own inertia, as if it required a force equal and opposite to stop it. But it was the curse of my kiss that I thought of before I thought of Bale himself.

"Snow . . ." Kai opened his mouth to say something more, seeming unsure for maybe the first time since we met.

But the look in his eyes was unfocused. He leaned against his workbench.

I helped him sit down. When I leaned over him and touched his lips, they were cold.

"I'm fine. I just feel a little dizzy . . . Snow, I didn't mean to . . ."

I didn't let him say anything more.

I didn't, either . . . , I said in my head as I backed out of the doorway and ran to my room.

16

I WAS PACING MY room, contemplating the kiss when there was a knock on my door.

If it was Kai, what would he say? What would I do? *I'm sorry I might have frozen you a little. Good thing we stopped before I froze you to death* . . . Or maybe I just imagined the whole thing.

But when I opened the door, it was Gerde, not Kai, standing in front of me.

She slipped into the room, wearing a white low-cut dress I hadn't seen before and a hint of a smile. She was feeling better. Or doing her best impression of someone feeling better.

I, on the other hand, felt more confused by the minute. And guilty. The only explanation for kissing Kai was that I'd been too long without people being nice to me, and I didn't know how to handle it. Even before I'd come to Algid, it had been a year since I had really spoken to Bale, having only my mother, Vern, and Dr. Harris for company—when Magpie wasn't trying to make me miserable. My kiss with Kai had everything to do with my missing Bale and nothing to do with Kai. I was sure of it. But just almost.

What happened was all me. My kiss had done something to Kai. Not like Bale. But something. Maybe something. I wasn't sure. Dizzy wasn't frozen. Cold lips weren't definitive. But how had his lips turned cold, while mine felt like they were on fire?

I tried to refocus on Gerde.

"Let's get out of here," she said suddenly.

"What about the River Witch?"

"She still hasn't returned from the River. Sometimes she's gone for days."

"And Kai?" I said. His name felt different crossing my lips now that he'd kissed them.

"He's in his workshop. He might not come out for days, either. There's a little village not far from here. I think we could use a change in scenery."

Maybe having her secret out in the open had been a weight off Gerde. She seemed different somehow. Maybe it was all in the way I looked at her. But it seemed like more than that. She was not talking about being a beast. But she seemed freer somehow.

I wanted to tell her everything. I'd already told her about Bale. But I bit my lip. Kai and Gerde were so incredibly close. I had already disturbed their delicate ecosystem. And Kai had disturbed mine.

I hadn't been outside except to train since I first arrived days ago.

I got up to my feet and raced to get dressed.

♛

The town was really just a street of storefronts and tiny houses all made out of the same packed colored snow I'd seen right after the tree with Jagger. But this time nobody was frozen. There were people everywhere. And through the translucent houses, I could see families cooking and eating and kids playing.

There was a big bonfire in the center of the street, and people were gathered around it for warmth. A musician was strumming on a triangular stringed instrument that looked like a small harp, but the sound that came from it was deeper and sharper.

Gerde immediately began humming along. She twirled around, her dress creating its own wind. My spirits lifted, seeing her like this. I wished for the day that I could be that light, too. But that could not happen until Bale and I were reunited.

We stopped at a table to eat some savory meat pies. They were nowhere near as flavorful as Gerde's, but we were so very hungry. We washed them down with hot cinnamon milk in metal mugs.

"Kai is all business," Gerde said. "He comes here only to sell. But I like to look around."

Gerde had mentioned Kai about two hundred more times than usual today. Or at least that was what it felt like.

"Let's play a game. Imagine a story," I suggested, trying to change the subject. This was what I used to do with Bale. It was nice to have a friend again. "You pick someone, and you make up a whole life for them."

Gerde picked out a tall, slender couple whose hands were entwined. The man was slightly ahead of the woman and was waiting for her to catch up. Gerde pursed her thin lips together before saying, "I think this is their third date. Neither of them are being themselves yet . . ."

I hadn't expected anything quite as romantic from Gerde. I wondered if she thought of love at all. We'd talked about Bale, but not about her own love life. I wondered if perhaps her condition made it impossible to be with someone that way.

"Very sweet. I think she's a spy trying to extract information. She's getting close to him so that she can go in for the kill."

Gerde laughed. "Your turn, you pick."

"Her," I said, pointing to a woman sitting at a table.

Her face was round and pretty. Her clothes were made of thick wool in an inky color. Her expression was welcoming. In front of her was the most intricate set of cards I'd ever seen. They were hand painted. On the cards' faces were women holding hands in a circle, and there was a swirling symbol in the center. The images danced.

"She's a Land Witch, the lowest form of witch. She has some power but not enough to be considered a real force. There are lots of them in Algid. Some lead normal lives. Some sell their gifts," Gerde explained.

"Wait, I thought it was my turn," I said, assuming that the game continued.

"No, she really is a witch. She's a truth teller. Sorry," Gerde corrected. She had forgotten all about our game. And this woman was a real witch, however low she was in the witch hierarchy.

I glanced down at the cards on the witch's table. I wanted to know how they worked. I wanted to know what they'd say about me.

"Do you mean she has foresight? Like an oracle?"

"Do you mean *the* oracle?" she corrected, biting her lip as if considering. "Hardly. She probably can't tell you what happens much longer out than a fortnight, but she can give good advice about crops and small decisions. There are lots of different kinds of witches. There are the Three and everyone else."

"The Three?" I remembered the coven from the River Witch's original story.

"They are the most powerful. The River Witch, the Fire Witch, and the Witch of the Woods."

"And where does my mother fit in?"

"She left the coven to marry a prince. No one knows how powerful she would have become," Gerde said. Her tone was filled with disbelief, as if she could not quite understand ever giving up witchy power for love.

But to me, Mom wanting to be a pretty princess instead of part of the badass witch coven made a lot of sense.

"Can we see what she knows?" I said, turning to Gerde.

Gerde glanced at the witch again. "You know what, my brother has been such a cad to you, the least he can do is buy us a glimpse at our futures."

A few seconds later, Gerde placed coins that she'd taken from Kai's stash in front of the Land Witch.

"Hand or cards?" the witch asked.

Gerde stuck out her hand, and the witch examined it a long beat.

"You have a secret that has recently come into the light. Now that it is in the open, you are happier."

Gerde snatched her hand away. "Even a broken clock is right twice a day," she whispered to me.

I didn't think Gerde could ever be a snob, but I suppose the witch hit her where it hurt. She stepped back and nodded at me to go ahead.

"Hand or cards?"

I felt my scar glowing beneath my dress and chose cards.

"Pick six cards without looking at them. Each one tells part of your story, and together they make up your life."

I read each one as I put them down.

THE LOVER

THE THIEF

THE THINKER

THE KING

THE CROWN

THE JOKER

"What does the last one mean?"

"That you have a great surprise in store for you. It may be a betrayal. Or a victory."

I blinked hard at the witch. Did she know it was me? This was the River Witch's prophecy all over again.

The Lover was Bale. The Thief was Jagger. The Thinker was Kai. The King was my father. The crown was what was at stake, and the surprise was the prophecy.

"How does it end?"

"There are only six cards per reading," she said firmly.

"Tell me. Put down another card."

"I have no more to tell. The cards have finished their story. The rest is up to you. And the Fates."

I shook my head.

"Gerde, give her another coin."

I could feel my ire rising.

Gerde shot me a look. "Time to go, Sasha," Gerde said gently.

"Who's Sasha?" I began . . . then realized that of course she could not call me by my real name.

But I couldn't go. The witch's cards were telling my story. Maybe they could give me a clue to the rest, to my future, to my next move.

"I am not leaving until she tells me my future."

"Yes, you are. You both are," a voice behind us said stormily.

It was Kai. He tossed another coin at the witch and took us both by the elbows, steering us out of the village. His face was a mask of anger behind a tight smile.

When we got back to the boat, Kai laid into us.

"What the hell were you thinking?" he asked as we headed back to the cube. "You could have been caught. Someone could have recognized you. It was foolish and reckless . . ."

"And you're never either of those things," I countered.

Kai stopped talking and stormed off.

My cheeks burned, too.

17

IN THE END, KAI was right to be mad. The River Witch burst into the cube, looking as angry as a water creature could possibly look. Her tentacles were flailing, forming puddles in their wake. But it was more than the way she looked. The water outside was roiling—a storm was brewing within it. The current had stopped going downstream. Instead it was beginning a circular motion. And somewhere way too close to the cube, there was lightning over the River. I heard thunder in the distance.

"Your stunt in the village last night was ill advised. People are talking about a girl whose fortune matches the King's prophecy, and he's sent the Enforcer to seek you out. No doubt he has tasked the Snow Beasts and every other evil thing under his command to find you. There is no time left. The Lights will be out soon, and you are far from ready," she said coldly.

I have no intention of being here when the Eclipse happens! I wanted to shout back. But just as quickly as she had arrived, the River

Witch left. Thankfully, her storm left with her. And the sun and the Lights returned.

I looked at Kai reflexively, grateful for the storm's end. But then the memory of the kiss returned and along with it a flood of feeling. Embarrassment, mixed with fear, mixed with wonder. He acted as if it had never happened. I waited for some kind of acknowledgment. But I found none. And Gerde had not left us alone for even a moment. So I couldn't ask and I still didn't know what I would say if I could.

Kai returned my gaze with a half smile and announced that he needed some supplies. Kai usually did not smile. At least not at me.

Gerde broke our eye lock when she asked, "What about the witch?"

"I don't think she wants to come with us," Kai quipped defiantly. Last night he had been all over us for going out. But now that the witch forbade it, he had changed his mind. If the River Witch had said the sky was blue, he'd make an argument for any other color.

Gerde, apparently still undecided, was looking out the cube at the Lights. She said out loud what I was thinking: "Maybe it's just the fog from the River Witch, but they do look less bright today."

"We'll be careful, Gerde," I said.

Gerde nodded without looking away from the glass. Maybe she was feeling the pressure of the Lights. As much as she said she wanted change, maybe she wanted to lap up the way things were while she still could.

"You know, I haven't seen her that mad since that time I brought Gray on board the boat."

"Gray?"

"The lion," Kai offered.

I remembered him from the menagerie. I laughed a little too hard. I remembered this feeling from the institute. When someone laid down a new rule, the urge to break it was palpable. Something that you had never thought of doing was suddenly all you thought about.

Despite the witch's warning or maybe because of it, we were going to the market, somewhere I hadn't been in a city so big we would go unnoticed, via something called a Hopper.

The Hopper turned out to be part motorcycle, part car, and part snowmobile. Gerde and I took the seat beside Kai, and a glass dome covered us like the roof of a convertible sports car. Our seat was meant for one. But Gerde was small, and we fit easily. I wore the River Witch's cloak again for warmth. I'd left it in my room at the cube after that night with Kai, and the River Witch had never retrieved it. Now its slick surface brushed against Gerde in our tiny seat.

"Just wait till you see the market. They sell magic in Stygian." Gerde was bouncing with excitement.

I thought back to the vial that Jagger had pulled out of his satchel when we were being chased. Maybe I could buy more of that at the market. That kind of thing could prove useful if Bale and I needed a quick escape.

"Flimflammers," Kai said in response, not turning around. "That's what they are. Stay away from them."

Gerde just rolled her eyes, and I couldn't help but laugh a little at their comfortable banter. She had an interest in all magic, no matter the size. It was her savior. And Kai made no secret of his complete disapproval of it. Of course, he didn't make a secret of his disapproval of most things. If Gerde felt slighted, I didn't see it on her smiling face.

"So you never buy magic?" I asked Kai, trying to make small talk.

I wanted him to look at me. To answer me. I wondered if last night had changed anything, but if it had, he wasn't showing it. It was as if he had Snow-proof blinders on. He wouldn't even glance at me.

Perhaps a kiss was just a kiss to him. Even if it was a cold one. But it wasn't just a kiss to me. Before that kiss, the only person I had ever thought of that way was Bale. Now I didn't know what to think.

Kai kicked on his machine, and it purred like a cat. We began to accelerate over the ice, speeding away from the cube.

👑

We took the Hopper to the outskirts of the city they called Stygian. Once we got within reach of the city's border, Kai killed the Hopper's lights and stopped.

"It's not much farther, but we should go the rest of the way on foot," Gerde said brightly as if she were having fun.

Kai shot her a "dial back the enthusiasm" look, but she ignored him.

Gerde brought us to a tunnel that led to the city, and we entered.

She produced a glow-in-the-dark plant from one of the pockets of her dress. Kai brought out a much more effective battery-operated light from the Hopper. I stood close to Kai, feeling a tinge guilty for abandoning Gerde's little plant light.

"What is this place?" I asked.

"Shh!" Kai said sharply. I was about to slam him for his rudeness, but he pointed the torch toward the low ceiling. I heard the sound of fluttering wings and thought about Gerde's creepy birds.

"Look up."

There were bats hanging down from the ceiling of the tunnel. Hundreds of them.

Kai pushed me against the wall and pushed Gerde forward, as if she were supposed to protect us. And even stranger still was Gerde's reaction.

"Please let us pass," she said to the bats.

The bats gave a collective shriek as if they were answering her. A week ago I would have thought this was ridiculous. Now I was getting used to magic.

Gerde nodded at Kai and took his hand. He took mine.

The bats were clearly annoyed we had disturbed them, but they just beat their wings together and left us alone.

When we reached the end of the tunnel, it was getting darker out.

"The tunnels are usually used for royalty," Gerde explained. "Every public space has an exit route for the King."

When we emerged from the tunnel, we found ourselves just outside the city. Kai didn't let my hand go right away. He held it and turned his palm down to show me a deep scar on the back of his hand before he let go.

Gerde raced ahead, not noticing us.

"I got this from Gerde when we were kids. She turned, and I couldn't get her in the cage in time."

"Why are you showing me this?" I asked as an image of poor little Gerde came to mind. Behind the bars of the cage in the tree house.

"She didn't mean it. She didn't mean to hurt me. Just like you didn't mean to last night. Gerde, you, and the River Witch believe it's magic. But it's also biology. Maybe magic's just the temporary cure."

"Why are you telling me this?"

"Because someone should. Because you shouldn't have to carry this with you wherever you go. Whenever you go. Whoever you kiss. You should know."

I didn't know what to say. But Kai didn't seem to want or need me to say anything. He strode ahead and I followed. I still didn't know if the kiss mattered to him. Or what it meant to me. But he was right. Freezing him with the kiss was no different from my paralyzing Magpie back at Whittaker. I'd lost control. The kiss with Bale was another story. One I still questioned.

A monolithic gate stood at the entrance to the city. Buildings black and mat as coal were stacked high behind it. The place looked nothing like the quaint frozen village I'd passed or the village I'd visited with Gerde.

The buildings themselves looked like tides, frozen at their crests. Only the glass windows that perforated them made it clear that they were man-made and not some freak of nature. I remembered that dark colors absorb heat. Maybe they were designed to absorb the heat from the sun? Perhaps the whole city was.

A low wall encircled the city. There were caldrons of fire set about a foot apart atop it. The gate was pushed wide open, and a steady stream of people entered and exited. The men flanking the entrance wore stiff, light-blue uniforms. The city women wore pants and elaborate corsets decorated with circular disks. The city men wore a mesh of the same over their torsos like armor—armor against the cold.

I wondered if the ring of fire around town was to keep everything awful in the woods out.

We crept closer and saw an enormous town square that wasn't actually a square at all. It was a series of interlocked circles, each devoted to a different sphere of activity. Kids played on a complicated jungle gym made of ice, its slide extending dangerously high in the circle.

The ground inside the gates was free of snow. A shock of red stone formed a circular pattern around a stage.

As we got even closer, I debated whether or not this was a good idea or a terrible one.

And as it turned out, the witch's cloak hid me well, even though it reeked of river water. No one noticed us. I began to wonder if maybe the cloak had some magic in it, some bit of invisibility.

The town was kinetic. Every person was in motion. They all had places to go. My days had always been structured around one-on-one therapy and group meals and recreation. I had never been around this many people before. They were too close. They were moving too fast. I suddenly felt dizzy, and a strong desire to shrink to the ground and pull my knees into my chest overtook me.

I began to hum, as quietly as I could. Someone's elbow made contact with the cloak and then pulled quickly away. There was a mumble of an apology. I was not invisible, after all.

Mercifully, there was a gap in the crowd and I escaped into it, happily reclaiming the air around me.

Maybe it was the weird buildings, but the sounds of the children seemed to be absorbed somehow by the black buildings, too.

Where were these people going? What did they do? Would I be safe here?

A wooden carriage painted black made its way through the circle. A horse decorated in the town's colors labored under the weight of its load.

Along the side of the square, market stalls offered edibles I had never seen before. I eyed a strange blue-gray fruit in the baskets. They were apple shaped but almost periwinkle in color, like the trees. Next to them were similarly colored banana-like and cherry-like fruits. Gerde looked at the fruit appraisingly. Her nose turned up the tiniest bit. She knew that hers were better.

There were other wares, too. Some stands displayed clothing, while others showed off wrought-iron jewelry.

One of the booths was unlike the others. It was gilded and covered in real jewels. More people were gathered around this booth than any other, and I moved closer to get a better look.

Kai looked down at me and warned, "Ignore them. They're flimflammers."

The merchant was handing out small glass bottles of every color in exchange for silver coins.

The girls working the booth wore dresses made out of feathers. I locked eyes with the girl whose face was more painted than her outfit. Her pale-green hair made me want to reach out and touch it and made me want to change my own washed-out shade. I wondered what she thought of me; I had no makeup and wore a witch's cloak made out of scales. I wondered if a girl who looked like that had any thoughts about me at all.

The girl with the mermaid hair produced a wilted orchid-like flower that looked like it was dying. She took a green bottle and poured a drop from it into the soil. The other girls sighed impatiently. Then suddenly the flower perked up. Its petals looked radiant and fresh. In fact, I could have sworn I could see it growing.

Nobody seemed as taken with the performance as I was. It was magic.

Magic. The word rattled around in my head, shaking loose the possible from the impossible.

I'd seen big magic by the River Witch. I had never expected magic in the hands of normal people. I wasn't sure if this was real or a trick like Kai thought it was.

The man in front of the table was barely impressed with the revived flower. He argued over the price.

"But will it heal her?" he demanded to know.

"It will do whatever you want it to do," the girl said, but as the words came out of her mouth I saw one of her fingers twitch.

When the man cast his head down, digging in his pockets for money, the girl winked at me.

No part of me wanted to see the outcome of this transaction. If it wasn't real I didn't want to know. And if that girl was taking advantage of this man's desperation, I didn't need to see it.

Before I turned away, the girl caught my eye again.

"Anything you want to buy?" the girl asked, taunting from a distance.

I walked away without replying.

My hunger gnawed at me. I found myself returning to the fruit stall. Its owner, a burly woman, was distracted by the still-growing orchid that now reached the top of the booth.

I reached out for one of the tiny blue apples. I nodded at Gerde for coins. She reached into her dress pocket. A loud whistle from a high-pitched instrument sounded. I turned, sure I was caught. Someone had recognized me. Gerde must have thought the same thing, because she stepped closer to me protectively.

But no one was looking at me. Or Gerde. The commotion was at the center of the market square, up on a podium.

All eyes were focused there.

A guard in blue held a small boy by his wrist. A woman ran to the boy's side, her face full of alarm.

What had he done? I glanced back at the stall owner, who was staring at the guard and the boy.

Just then, a handsome, stoic man joined the woman on the dais. The family tableau paralyzed me for a second and reminded me of the River Witch's story about my mother and father.

"He didn't mean it. Please," the woman begged the guard.

"Isn't there something we can do?" the man asked. He stuck

a hand in his pocket as if he were considering whether or not to offer a bribe. "Punish us instead," he bargained.

"He's just a little boy," the woman added.

The boy looked from parent to parent with growing awareness that he was in real trouble.

What did he do?

He couldn't have been more than ten. I could feel his fear even from a distance.

I thought about the feeling I got in my gut when I did something wrong at Whittaker. I knew there would be punishment, but ultimately the orderlies were more at risk than I was. From the look on this boy's face, whatever was coming must be much, much worse.

"You should have thought of that before you told him that story," the soldier said again.

"You're right. It's my fault. I should be punished," the mother offered again, trying to move in front of her son.

"Please," the father said beneath his breath.

"He was spreading the story to the other children, and he told them she has returned. You know the King's Law. No one can speak of the Princess. To say that she is alive and well is treason."

My heart fluttered in my chest at the words "Princess" and "treason."

"It's just a story children tell one another—like the boogeyman," the man reasoned again, trying to make the guard relate to his son.

A shadow crossed the guard's face.

From beyond the crowd came the sound of armor moving quickly.

Everyone turned and parted as one.

A man clad in reflective black armor strode confidently through the gap left in the crowd. It was impossible to see the color of his eyes through the slits in his helmet, but they seemed black.

"It's the Enforcer," Gerde answered when I tugged at her sleeve. "They say the King can see through his eyes."

I pulled my hood up on the witch's cloak. I didn't know if that was even possible, but I did not like the idea of the Enforcer laying those eyes on me.

"Sing your little song for the Enforcer," the guard demanded as the man in black made his way to the platform.

The boy whimpered.

"It's not a request, boy," the guard said. He shook the child roughly, which caused his mother to sob, turning into her husband's shoulder. The entire market square that was loud and bustling just moments ago was now silent, everyone watching.

The boy cleared his throat and began,

She brings the snow with her touch,
They think she's gone, but we know
She will come again,
She will reign in his stead,
She will bring down the world on his head.
Oh come, Snow, come . . .

The boy's voice quavered as he sang.

And then for the umpteenth time since I had left Whittaker, I felt fear seize me. The boy was singing about *me*, and he was about to be killed for it!

"We should go." Kai breathed into my ear. "Now."

But I was mesmerized by the scene before me. The Enforcer's sword caught the light in the circle. Silently, he looked from the boy to the soldier.

"We will make it so that the boy never speaks again. That is the punishment," the guard declared. "Your child will learn his lesson. And so will you." The guard laughed, but the armored figure at his side showed no emotion.

My fear doubled—for the boy and for myself.

I closed my eyes and tried to wish it away. Somewhere in my chest I felt a burning feeling grow.

"Snow," Kai hissed.

There was an urgency and an edge in his voice. He was protecting Gerde again and maybe me. But how could he do that when what we were seeing was beyond me?

"We need to get out of here."

But I was fixated on the little boy's terrified face. Anger could will out fear. They were going to hurt that boy, and everyone was going to stand by and watch. I didn't care who the Enforcer was in that pile of weird metal. He could not do this. *I would not let him do this*.

I took a step forward . . . and someone in front of me screamed.

The crowd went wild. People ran off in all directions, pushing and shoving one another to get away from me. Something was clearly wrong. I looked down at the ground and saw a spiky needle-sharp frost spreading across in a circle around me. I had done this. Without thinking. Without knowing. I wasn't sorry though.

"He's here! He's here . . . The Snow King is here!" someone screeched.

But it was me.

The once-organized crowd devolved further into chaos in seconds.

Kai grabbed my arm. "No more arguments. We leave."

"But the boy!" I protested.

"Nothing will happen to the boy now," Gerde said pragmatically, nodding to the market podium. But there was emotion in her voice. She was not immune to how close he'd come to the blade.

The boy and his family saw their opportunity to escape. The mother pushed her son gently and whispered something in his ear.

The boy hesitated for an instant and then broke away into the chaos.

"Get him!" the soldier ordered.

I expected the Enforcer to chase the boy, but he was rooted to the spot. Instead he cocked his head and looked in my direction. Clearly he had noticed I was the one who had created the frost. The jig was up.

"Kai's right," Gerde said, sounding frightened for the first time.

Kai studied me a beat and then took the lead. "This way . . ."

I shook my head, my eyes still on the Enforcer, who was now staring at me and was getting down from the platform.

Gerde's eyes opened wide. "You can't."

"Can't what?" Kai demanded.

Gerde moved in front of me, blocking my path and ignoring Kai. "It's too dangerous. You won't find him this way. You'll be killed."

"Find who?" Kai said. He sounded different.

I put my hands on Gerde's shoulders. "You know I need to go. I might not have another chance." I pleaded with her silently to understand.

"Will someone clue me in to what's happening, or are we just going to stand here and get trampled?" Kai snapped. "Or worse, captured?"

"The River Witch will not be pleased. You know that." She looked at Kai for backup, but he just glowered at her. Around us people were still running in all directions, crying for mercy as snow poured from the sky. "She's here to find the boy she loves. His name is Bale, and we think the Snow King has him."

Kai was unreadable. He looked from me to Gerde and back again. Then his face fell, just enough for me to see it there: humiliation, pain. It hurt me to see it, but time was running out. I didn't want to leave Kai like this, but I had to move. Now. Before people started to notice where all the swirling snow was coming from.

"The Enforcer can lead me straight to Bale. That's what Jagger told me."

"But the River Witch promised to help you with Bale," Gerde argued.

The circle of snow at my feet began to pile up. I was getting upset. The Enforcer was striding closer.

"The witch promises a lot of things," Kai said, putting a hand on her shoulder. He wouldn't look at me, but I was grateful for his help just the same. Or maybe he was just helping himself and Gerde. I would finally be out of the way.

Was he helping me because of the kiss? Did he want me gone because he didn't feel anything for me? Or because he did?

"I won't run," I said with gritty determination. "Not now. So either stay and fight or save yourselves."

"I can't let you do this," Kai argued as we both watched the Enforcer grow nearer.

Gerde's eyes met his for the briefest of seconds. They had sacrificed so much for her secret.

"Gerde, no . . . ," he said, reading her.

"I won't let you fight him alone," Gerde cut in—and in a flash, she had transformed from girl to beast. Fur and feathers ripped through her dress, and she crouched on all fours, her back arched like a cat's. With a blood-curdling snarl, she leaped toward the Enforcer, blocking his path to us.

18

THE ENFORCER DREW HIS ax and swung it at Gerde, but she easily jumped out of the way. She landed on all fours, teeth bared and muscles taut.

Kai ran toward the Hopper, the only weapon at his disposal. Unlike Gerde and me, magic wouldn't save him.

The Enforcer gave me a steely gaze. He was completely undeterred by Gerde and strode mechanically toward me, crushing the snow under each heavy footfall.

I remembered what Gerde had said about the Snow King seeing through his eyes. And I remembered the River Witch's and Gerde's Champions. Was the Enforcer human? Or was he the King's Champion, an ice man held together by armor?

There was nothing left to do but summon the snow. I closed my eyes, slowed my mind, and let loose a burst of icy cannonballs. A dusting of frost fell softly down around me as each blast hit its mark.

I watched as the Enforcer stumbled back, but I was surprised to see him regain his balance and continue toward me. Gerde attacked him again, but the Enforcer merely deflected her advances as if she were made of tissue paper. She fell in a heap in the snow. She let out a quiet whimper, and her body shifted back into human form. She was naked and shivering atop the pile of snow. He had hurt Gerde.

I raced to her side. She stirred. In the distance I heard the Hopper approaching. Kai was coming.

In order for the Enforcer to lead me to Bale, I had to defeat him first. But now I wanted to kill him.

Gerde's eyes fluttered open and then closed again. She was only half-conscious, but alive. Relief and guilt washed over me. *Have I made a mistake? Can I really do this?* I wondered if the Enforcer was cold underneath that armor. I wondered if he felt anything at all.

I let loose a series of icicle spears, pinning the Enforcer to a nearby tree. Just as I let my guard down, of course, that's when all hell broke loose.

An army of Snow Beasts surrounded Gerde and me. Their teeth gnashed, and their giant paws scraped the ground in anticipation.

"Gerde, get up," I ordered.

But she didn't respond.

I sent an avalanche at the beasts, and it seemed to wipe them out. The wave of snow rose and crashed over them. Bone and ice and debris fanned out as the wave crested behind where they had stood.

I let out a sigh of relief, but it was too soon.

Pieces of the beasts unearthed themselves and dragged themselves toward one another in slow motion, like drops of mercury pooling back together. And then I heard the sound of metal crashing against ice. It was the Enforcer. He had freed himself from the tree.

He moved fast. Faster than the armor should have allowed. His speed couldn't be natural. It had to be magic.

Using a gust of icy wind, I knocked over a tree in his path and ran away from him, the River Witch's cloak trailing behind me in the snow. I was outnumbered and possibly outmagicked.

I could hear the sound of the metal blade against the wood. The Enforcer was breaking through. I didn't turn back. I picked up my pace.

Within seconds, he was a few feet behind me, reaching for me with a black-gloved hand. Behind him I could hear the growls rising again. The Snow Beasts had re-formed. But I also heard the crunch of the Hopper as it crushed one or more of the Snow Beasts.

"Thank you, Kai," I whispered.

I could hear the Hopper's engine. But I still couldn't see what had happened to Kai. Was he being crushed or was he crushing something else?

I strained to see, but the Enforcer was blocking my way. His hand was close enough to grab me. I inched away, but he was too fast. He grabbed me and I kicked him, but the kick knocked me off balance more than it did him. An echo of pain reverberated in the bones of my foot where I had made contact. The Enforcer held firm and turned me to face him.

The Enforcer's eyes were dark pits. It was as if there was only blackness inside his suit of armor.

I spit at him and wrestled away from him. I didn't know how, but somehow I slipped through his grasp. A soft blanket of snow came up to greet me as I landed on my back.

I raised my hands and attacked with a sharp snow-cicle projectile. The Enforcer lifted his weapon and deftly sliced it in two. The pieces fell dumbly to the ground.

He will not win! I thought, and concentrated on the ground behind him. The air began to kick up and cyclone.

The Enforcer struggled against the wind, holding tighter to his ax, which he raised in my direction. But as he raised it, my wind caught hold. His battle-ax flew from his hand, swallowed up behind him by the vortex I had created. He followed a second after. His armored figure bent at the waist as my storm sucked him backward and he disappeared into a whirl of white.

I shook myself off and stood up in the snow, my feet sinking into it.

I could have used a tornado to get away immediately instead of facing the Enforcer. I should have. But I needed to know that I could defend myself. I needed to know because when I finally found Bale, the Enforcer would be the one standing in my way.

I heard the sound of boots against ice. This was not over yet. I knew the Enforcer was coming back even before I saw him. It was just like the superhero movies on television. The bad guys never died. They always lived to fight again. It was the same in *The End of Almost.* A character could drop off a cliff and be resurrected in a coma.

I pushed another cyclone in his direction, but his dark silhouette advanced through my storm.

And this time, inexplicably, my snow did not make contact with his armor. It should have leveled him, but the ice fell away from him as if he were surrounded by a force field.

I threw daggers of ice at him, but they, too, did not make contact.

Suddenly, instead of feet there were mere inches between us.

The Enforcer reached his hand up, and his battle-ax came tumbling toward him, landing in his grip like a boomerang.

His hand squeezed the handle.

I felt my ice claws come out. I swiped at him. I clawed at his metal shell with icy nails. I was unable to penetrate the hard metal exterior, but I left a mark. Five jagged lines rippled down his arm where I'd tried to gain traction.

I kicked him again. But he stepped aside, and I lost my balance.

This time, he was on top of me. He dropped the ax and pinned me down with his chain-mailed hands, keeping my arms against the snow so I couldn't use them against him.

I saw what he was doing. But he was bigger and stronger.

I looked into the deep black pools of his eyes and wondered if the King could actually see me now. The Eyes of the King . . .

"Can you see me, Lazar?" I said. "You can't face me yourself, so you send this thing to get me? You're a coward . . ."

There was no response from the Enforcer. His hands were crushing me into the ice.

"And you . . . You're just a minion of the King. You don't even know me . . . You just do whatever he tells you to do . . . That boy in the square . . . and now me . . . You are the worst kind of coward . . ."

Is there any thought, feeling, or free will inside there? I wondered. I had stared into the eyes of a lot of vacant kids at Whittaker who were too drugged up on the cocktail to care, but there was always something . . . that flash of something underneath the dark.

I searched for that now in the Enforcer, but I came up empty. Still, I felt his grip loosen just a fraction.

He wasn't human. He couldn't be. But whatever he was, he couldn't or wouldn't die.

With every ounce of energy I had left, I ripped one hand free and sliced at his face. My ice claws made an impression on the hood of his armor: four lines tracked across the surface of the magical metal. The Enforcer had my wrist secured again in a half second.

He was a soulless monster, a pawn of the King.

"Do you enjoy this? Do you get your kicks doing this? Do you feel anything at all? Or do you just do what he wants?"

He tilted his head like he was contemplating my words. And then he brought his ax down. I kept my eyes open.

I ordered my snow to freeze him, but nothing happened.

I focused on the eyeholes of his armored hood again. I ordered my snow to freeze whatever was inside. The blade continued to fall and fall.

I do not end like this, I told myself, willing my snow to come to my aid. Frost crept up his armor, but it melted away. And the blade didn't stop.

I didn't believe in the prophecy. But I also didn't believe that I was going to die here. That I was never going to see Bale again.

I didn't blink. I wouldn't blink. Blinking was giving up. Giving in.

I do not end like this, I told myself again.

"Bale, I will come for you. No matter what. I will find a way," I whispered, my breath making wispy clouds in the cold air.

And a hair's breadth from my face, the ax finally came to a halt.

But I wasn't the one who had stopped it. My snow hadn't stopped it.

The Enforcer had.

With a guttural growl, the Enforcer buried his ax in a tree. He looked from me to the tree and then pulled the ax out.

His head tilted to the side. Was he deciding whether or not to kill me?

I closed my eyes and tornadoed myself away.

19

WHILE I WAS SPINNING away from the Enforcer—my ice and snow hurling around me, keeping me above the changing landscape—I closed my eyes and saw the River Witch again.

I was standing on the River's edge, and she was beckoning me from underwater. She said something I couldn't quite make out. And even though everything in my body warned me not to, for some reason I was desperate to hear what she had said. I leaned farther over the water just as the River Witch leaped up. Her tentacles wrapped around my arms and legs and pulled me underwater. I could hear her clearly now, even though she was whispering.

"I knew you'd come back to me."

And then the snowstorm released me, depositing me on the cold, hard ground. I shook my head clear. I was somewhere in the woods. Lost. But at least there was no sign of the Enforcer.

The pale-blue trees seemed to wink at me. The North Lights

overhead had turned gloomy and mauve as if they had witnessed our fight below.

I let out a string of curses more colorful than the Lights and found a tree to lean against. As I inspected myself for injuries, I admonished myself. What was I thinking, fighting the guy whose main mission in life was to kill me? And now I was screwed. He was the key to finding Bale. I had no idea which way led back to the city or which way led to the King's palace. I was alone.

I could call on the River Witch. I could call a snow tornado and take myself back to her and Gerde and Kai.

"Bale, how am I supposed to find you now?" I said out loud.

My arm twitched. When I lifted up the witch's cloak, I saw that the scars across my arm—what Kai had said was a map of Algid—were lit up again. I recognized the city by the terrain surrounding it. And then I remembered Kai had said the King's palace was at the top right corner of the map. I could do this. I could figure this out. I didn't need the Enforcer anymore.

I pushed my sleeve down and started walking.

I'm coming for you, Bale.

I walked for hours in the snow. Hunger began to gnaw at me even though the cold did not.

When I finally thought I could not go on any farther, the palace came into view.

I looked at the fortress for signs of where the dungeon might be. If the Enforcer had Bale captive, that's where he'd be. My scars were lit up just above my wrist. I had found my way here, and no matter where I was in Algid, I knew I could find my way back.

I examined the castle. Through the window I could see one of the drawing rooms, where an ornately dressed man played chess with the Enforcer, who was inexplicably still in complete armor.

I could not see the man's face, as his back was to me. But I guessed it was the King. The man everyone in this land claimed was my father.

I suddenly couldn't catch my breath. And there was a twinge of pain in my heart. I had to look away. I pressed myself against the side of the castle and closed my eyes. When I opened them, I saw the last person in the world I thought I'd ever see again: Jagger.

"Where have you been?" I asked, reaching out to touch his face to make sure that he was real and not a snow exposure–addled daydream. His skin was cold but smooth.

"Around. I have my ways . . . ," he boasted. "You missed me?"

I realized that my hand had lingered, and I pulled it away.

"Why did you leave me? How did you find me?"

"I watched you with the River Witch, but I couldn't get to you."

A desire to punch him again hit me with the familiar wave of trust that accompanied his magnetic smile. The pull of his charm I had felt a moment ago made me want to flee even more.

"I thought you ran away! But you were spying on me? Who does that?"

"Someone who doesn't want to get drowned by the River

Witch. Nice work giving her minions the slip. And getting to the castle on your own."

I slid down my sleeve where my scars were probably still lit up like Christmas. "Bale's in there somewhere. We have to get him out."

"No, we have to leave. Now."

"What are you talking about? You told me the key to Bale is the Enforcer. He's in there. I'm going to get him out. With or without you."

"I know the River Witch helped you get in touch with your snow. But how do you think you're going to play this? Level the whole castle and somehow miraculously spare Bale's life?"

He had a point. The Enforcer had come this close to killing me. My body still ached from the battle, but my pride hurt more. But I didn't admit that. Instead I said, "Exactly how long were you spying on me?"

"That is of no consequence. I will help you get in there—me and my people. I promise. And we will break Bale out. But right this second, we need to get out of here."

I could feel anger whirl inside me. Had this been Jagger's plan all along?

Had the King really taken Bale or had Jagger and his people? I suddenly needed proof of life—proof of Bale.

"You can go back to doubting me as soon as we get clear of the King's army."

"What are you talking about?" But just as I said it, the snow behind Jagger sprang into an army of Snow Beasts. There were thousands of them.

I had walked right up to the castle and not seen a single guard. He didn't need them. The snow itself contained all the protection he needed.

My claws extended the tiniest bit in my palms, drawing my own blood. There was a Whittaker pill for the feeling I was feeling. I called it Boring. But it was really Dulling. It counteracted the jumpy feeling of anxiety that was gnawing inside me at the moment. The feeling that said there was no way out of Whittaker. And now there was no way through to what I wanted to—what I needed to—do; there were thousands of beasts in my way. It was an improbable, impossible path to Bale. The pill didn't make things possible. It just dulled the wanting and the needing.

Then I got a flash of something. My eyes were open, but they were not seeing Jagger. Instead I got a flash of a dark room with a triangle of light pouring through.

"Bale . . . I don't know how . . . I saw Bale . . ."

"Snow! We have to go now. Before this gets messy."

Jagger pulled out a small yellow vial like the magic ones I'd seen the girls peddle in the square.

"Don't smash it this time," he suggested, holding it out to me. "Drink."

I didn't move a muscle. I looked from the bottle to the Snow Beasts. I didn't have enough control of my snow to take out all of them and spare Bale. Coming back to fight another day made sense.

"It's a transporting potion. All it takes is a sip," Jagger urged.

I had never tornadoed out with someone. I didn't know what

would happen if I tried to take him with me. I considered the bottle again. Another possibility occurred to me immediately. I felt myself light up with hope.

"Will one of those take me and Bale back to New York?"

"No, there isn't enough magic in the world to transport someone to another world. For that you need a gateway."

The Tree? I thought.

He shook the vial in his hand. "This will take you to my home."

I shook my head. "What do you know about the King's mirror?"

I wanted to see how he'd react. I thought I saw his eyes widen slightly, but I couldn't tell for sure in the dark. "And do you really think that I am going to drink anything that you give me?" I balked. There was no way I was going home with him.

The things in the snow had other ideas. While I had been talking, they had been getting closer. I heard a rustle of snow too close beside us.

"Sometimes it's easier to ask forgiveness than permission," he said as he downed the vial himself—and suddenly put an arm around my waist.

Then in a blink, before I could twist away, we were someplace else.

👑

"Welcome to the Claret," Jagger said as he let go of my waist.

I shoved him not so gently away. My head was full of questions—but they would have to wait because all my brain cells were currently trying to comprehend the building before me. This wasn't one of my dreams, but it very well could have been.

It was hard to tell if the castle was English or Russian, but it looked like a chimera, a mythical creature composed of part man and part lion. I half expected to see part of a pyramid on the other side of the Claret.

The combination of building materials was seamless. Wavy glass met the bottom of the highly decorative Russian palace, which in turn flowed into the English battlement wall's stones, which led into a pointy cone steeple that connected to a set of Roman columns topped with a triangle of marble filled with tiny sculptures. And on either side of the castle was a dense forest unlike any I had ever seen. The trees, the thicket, and the grass were all red. The Lights in the sky were dimmer than even the night before, their colors fading into the dark sky, making the red all that more stark in contrast.

Something told me that Jagger really, really wanted to show off this view.

"Come on," he said, and began to move toward it.

"You live here?" I asked, processing. "You said I was a princess. Are you some kind of a prince? Because I have no intention of getting married anytime soon . . . "

I had read too many fairy tales, but even so, I was pretty sure happily ever after wasn't how my story ended.

"Relax, Princess, I'm not that kind of prince," he countered lightly, still walking toward the castle and staring at the facade as if he, too, were still fascinated by its existence.

"What other kind of prince is there?"

I stood my ground for a beat. Some part of me did not want to follow until I had answers. But when the wind picked up, I could see him shiver. I could stay outside forever. But maybe Jagger would be more talkative inside.

When we got to the castle's giant wrought-iron double doors, they opened automatically. I hesitated. He glanced at me, as if to say it was only a few more steps after coming all this way.

I stepped over the threshold and into the Claret. The anteroom was as eclectic as the facade, in contrast to Kai's home, which was economical and perfect. Jagger's was massive and the opposite of organized. Every style of decor from modern to baroque was represented.

A trio of sculptures greeted us, each in a different style and material, depicting the same woman wearing a crown. I looked at the faces of the gold, silver, and bronze statues, looking for a likeness of my mother. The River Witch had said she was a queen, after all. But she was not the one depicted here. In every incarnation, the woman's hair was wild, her smile was broad, and the expression more spirited than royal.

The floor of the anteroom glittered with a mosaic of colorful stone. The walls of the anteroom were covered in tapestries, each with a different crest. *Does this place represent more than one kingdom?* I wondered, trying to make sense of it.

The giant doors closed and locked behind me with a wave of Jagger's hand. *Is this a trap?* I thought a second too late.

I looked at him hard. The desire to punch him again rose.

"How did you do that?" I demanded.

"I'm a borrower. A Robber. I am not like you, or a real witch. My gifts come from without, not within. I wasn't so lucky."

A thief. Was everything here borrowed? Even the facade?

"I don't have any magic," I argued, thinking that magic wasn't what I would call it. A runaway, unwanted force of nature, maybe?

"You know you do," Jagger said. "You just don't know how to use it fully. I can help you with that . . . Maybe we can help you with that."

We?

I already had a teacher in the River Witch. It was the Bale part that interested me. If he could help me get back to Bale, it didn't really matter what he or his friends stole.

Turning back was not an option. Curiosity won out over my growing sense of dread. I walked with Jagger through the anteroom and into another room, ready to find out who "we" really were and how they would help me rescue Bale from the King.

20

THE "WE" TURNED OUT to be the girls from Stygian, the ones selling bits of magic in colorful bottles. When Jagger and I entered the Throne Room, I saw twenty or so girls lounging on velvet sofas. I searched for the one with green hair who had winked at me, but I could not find her among them. I had no idea who these people were or what was going on. If this was supposed to help me understand the truth, it wasn't working.

Every single one of the girls was beautiful. In fact, they were a whole other level of pretty that surpassed what I saw on TV back at Whittaker. They were different sizes and shapes and colors. I had never seen skin like that before. Each girl's skin shared a mysterious glow with the aurora borealis, which had no business being above wherever the heck we were.

As we approached, I felt twenty pairs of eyes following us.

"That is Margot," Jagger whispered, pointing to a platinum blonde with an angular, brown face.

She was sitting on a throne decorated with gems. Hers was the face that I had seen cast in metal.

"She considers herself a queen, and us her subjects."

"Back at Whittaker, I knew people who considered themselves all sorts of things," I whispered.

Even if I hadn't recognized her image, I would have known she was their leader. She was holding court. The girls were busy talking and laughing, but they were stealing glances at her for approval. And judging from her smile and her posture, she was enjoying every second of it.

Jagger stuck close to my side, and I wasn't sure if he was being protective or territorial. The stares from the girls ranged from daggers to curiosity.

"Queen Margot, may I present Princess Snow of Algid," Jagger said with a flourish and a bow when we finally reached her.

I was suddenly embarrassed by my simple pale-green dress. The clothes that Gerde had made me were a marked improvement over my gray Whittaker wear, but these girls took fashion to another level in the same way Kai had taken architecture. They were vibrant flowers, and standing in their presence, I felt like a common weed.

Jagger rose, meeting Queen Margot's gaze with a humility I hadn't seen in any of our previous encounters. It was clear that she had sent him to get me. But to what end?

I bowed my head to her, too—not out of deference, but a tactical decision that I hoped would pay off. A bow from who she thought was a real princess should count for something.

"You honor me, Princess Snow," Margot said with a tight

smile that seemed to cover the giddiness that my gesture sparked. "It's not every day we are graced with true royalty. And by someone as infamous as you, to boot. The King is looking for you. It's not safe for you out there, wandering the woods of Algid alone. I'm glad you chose to seek asylum within the walls of the Claret."

Jagger shot me a sideways glance and a toothy grin that said he was impressed.

"Everyone, welcome Princess Snow," Queen Margot instructed, her voice formal and lilting.

There was a shift in the crowd, which instantly came to attention. The girls scrambled to their feet within seconds.

One, if possible even prettier than the rest, stumbled forward and curtsied. Her hair was deep red, and she had medium-brown skin. Her eyes were also brown, but rimmed with gold.

"We're not used to being around actual royalty," the girl said. Her voice was filled to the brim with sarcasm. She bent into another exaggerated curtsy but was unsteady on her feet and ended up falling on her perfect bum.

"Enough, Fathom," Queen Margot warned.

The red-haired girl retreated to her overstuffed chaise, still laughing. There was something in the way she looked at me that felt familiar.

Margot gave me a sympathetic look. "Jagger, why don't you show the Princess to her room? She can get acquainted with the girls in the morning."

I'm pretty sure "acquainted" isn't what Margot means, I thought, feeling very unwelcome in the crowd. At least in this place, my cage would be a gilded one. I just hoped it had a lock to keep Fathom out. I didn't know her, but I suspected she would be trouble. I could feel it.

I didn't have time for the drama. I was here for a purpose. I needed us both to just get to it, despite Jagger's look that told me to hold back and play it out at Margot's pace.

"Did Jagger tell you what I require?" I asked. "He said you could help me get my friend back from the King's castle."

"Did he, now?" she said with a laugh that denoted that Jagger might have made a promise that he could not deliver.

"I will give you whatever you want in exchange. But time is not on my side."

Margot laughed again.

"If you are not interested, I will retrieve him myself," I said, prepared to walk away.

"With your snowflakes, my dear?"

"Yes," I said, feeling my cheeks begin to burn.

My knuckles began to itch; my claws about to stretch out.

I felt a surge of anger rise from within, but tried to tamp it down. I didn't know what would happen if I couldn't control my temper here. Would I bring on another ice storm? Or freeze the room solid? Or worse?

If they didn't let me out of this room soon, it wouldn't be my choice anymore.

I looked up at the ceiling. Giant icicles had formed on the tile, razor sharp and shaking.

The icicles fell with a thundering crash. I shielded my eyes, not wanting to see what the ice guillotine had done to Margot.

When the room grew deathly cold and quiet, I dropped my hands, afraid to see the possibly bloody aftermath of my snow. I heard clapping and saw that the ice had fallen in a circle around me—but also around Margot, who stood before me unscathed.

Margot let out a gleeful yelp.

"So marvelous. But you will need to do better than that to extract a boy from the King's clutches without impaling him. I can help you."

With that, she downed a vial of liquid and disappeared.

"Come on," Jagger said, steering me toward the room's giant double doors again.

As I let him lead me away, the other girls inspected my icy handiwork. It wasn't panic that I had inspired. It was curiosity. When I glanced back, I saw the mermaid-haired girl pick up one of my icicles.

As we made our way down the hall, Jagger tried to explain the Queen's behavior.

"She's not a real queen. Margot was born without royal or magical blood. She came from nothing and nowhere, and she built all of this."

I feigned interest in the wallpaper as we walked. I did not want to talk about what had happened back there. I had thought I had come so far with Nepenthe. But it was luck instead of intent that stopped me from slicing Margot in half with my icicles.

"It's not you. Well, it is," Jagger continued.

The walls were adorned with a variety of sconces—each one unique—and tapestries from different time periods.

"We . . . spent a lot of magic in the Other World," he explained. "I was sent there to find someone."

"And I'm not what they expected?"

"You're not *who* they expected. I was supposed to bring back Margot's daughter, a girl who had gotten lost. But I found you instead."

"Lucky me."

"Hopefully, lucky for all of us," he said ruefully. "I'd used a locator spell to find Margot's daughter. Only magic's a little more imprecise once you get to the other side of the Tree. Or at least it's supposed to be. I felt a surge of magic when I was looking for her. Unlike anything I'd ever felt. And it turned out to be you."

I thought of the time I'd pushed Magpie and she wound up paralyzed on the floor of the Whittaker drawing room. I didn't know it then, or maybe I did deep down. I remembered how cold she was and the blue of her lips. Her accident must have been caused by my snow. By me. It had to be that.

"And how did you know who I was?"

"You look just like your mother."

Jagger took a coin from his pocket and flipped it in my direction. I caught it—to my surprise. I was never much of an athlete. On one side of the coin was my face staring back at me. Only, it wasn't me. It was Mom.

"Your mother was the only royalty anyone ever believed in. At least in my lifetime."

"Why?"

"Even though she was a witch, she was really just a common person like the rest of us. Lazar married her anyway, and it gave people hope, even after he froze our lands over."

I felt my eyes go wide in disbelief. My mother was a lot of things. Now, I could even buy that she turned out to be a magical being from another land. But one of the people? My mother was always above . . . apart.

"Did you know her?" I demanded, annoyed at him suddenly. This bit of information seemed like something he should have mentioned before now.

"I don't remember her, but the elders do. She died young, saving her child. Your mother was the stuff that legends are made of—except the story turns out to be only half-true. She is alive, and so are you."

"Who is Margot's daughter?" I asked.

"It doesn't matter."

"I bet it matters to the other girls here. It's Magpie, isn't it? Magpie is Margot's daughter? You saw her at Whittaker. You had to have."

Jagger didn't confirm or deny. He remained infuriatingly noncommittal, which made me more sure. I had finally taken something from Magpie. I had taken her place in Algid.

"I could take only one of you back. You were the better find. Margot understands. We'll find another way for Magpie. Robber Rules: we are not allowed to be sentimental," Jagger said finally.

I highly doubted that Margot really thought this trade was okay. But I held my tongue.

When we stopped in front of a silver door, I didn't know what to expect. But I knew the room wouldn't have the simplicity of Whittaker or the stark beauty of Kai and Gerde's cube house. Jagger pushed open the door with a soft touch.

Every inch of the round red room was decorated—even the wall—with tufted fabric. The floor was carpeted. A canopy bed hung from ribbon-covered wires that stretched up to the ceiling. Next to the oval window stood a dressing screen and a wardrobe adorned in floral cloth. Through the window I could see a red forest against white snow.

"I'm staying in a padded room," I said under my breath. The irony wasn't lost on me. "I won't stay here without answers. Why am I here? What do you want from me? What is this place? I know you steal things, but what do you want me for?"

"This place holds magic—magic we've stolen from the King and anywhere else we can find it. But not only that, the Claret runs on magic," Jagger explained, "and we need more of it. You have magic. From where we're sitting, you're the mother lode. You will become one of us, a Robber, and you will give us magic."

"And in exchange, you will help me get Bale."

"Yes, we will."

"It doesn't work like that. You can't bottle what I have." I was still figuring out my snow, but given my lack of control, I was more likely to freeze him to death than "give" him my gift of snow.

"You'd be surprised. Not all magic requires bottles."

He produced an old-fashioned watch on a chain from one of

his pockets and clicked open the top. On one half of the case, there was a clock, and on the opposite side, a pill case.

Jagger held up the timepiece, put a pill under his tongue, and muttered something under his breath. My insides protested. The mere sight of a pill, any pill, made me knee-jerk to my own seven dwarfs. But as he took this one, it was immediately apparent that it wasn't a Whittaker cocktail. His features began to shift, and I heard the sound of bones cracking underneath his skin. I watched his nose flatten with a crush before building up again, more pronounced and somehow familiar. His eyes clouded over and changed from silvery gray to blondish brown to red and then from emerald green to amber. Before I knew it, I was staring into the one face I had been longing to see.

"Bale! My Bale?" I shouted in disbelief.

Jagger examined himself in the pocket watch's sliver of a mirror. "I saw him in the Other World. No offense meant, but there was nothing special I could see. What did he do to make such an impression on you? To make you come from one world to another for him? To put yourself in such incredible peril?"

His look was insecure, as if he did not know that in one breath he had insulted Bale—and me, for choosing him.

"You should know. You were spying on us, right? For how long? How much did you see?"

I was mad, but seeing Bale's face again made my anger melt away. I reached out and touched Bale's face—Jagger's face. I wanted Jagger to shut up, if only for a few more seconds so I could pretend that this was real, that magic didn't exist, that Bale was here with me.

But Jagger was no more capable of being quiet than I was capable of controlling my temper.

"I meant no harm," he said. "I was just curious. No one's ever crossed worlds for me . . ."

Looking at his impossibly perfect face, I almost said that I was surprised.

"Don't fret about it, Snow. It's all water under the bridge. Now, let's see who you want to be—"

Jagger began to mutter a new spell. He handed me the timepiece, but I wouldn't take it.

"No, please, I don't want it."

I couldn't explain to Jagger that I didn't want to be someone else looking at Bale—even though I knew that Bale wasn't really here. It was all a trick, magic.

He put the watch away—and then Bale's face rearranged itself into its original configuration: Jagger. My heart fell.

"All of us in the Claret take on new faces. It's the Robber Rule."

"So you never show your real faces? Why?"

"You can't betray a person whose face you don't know. Think of us as a family. But we don't pretend to trust one another."

"How progressive of you."

"I think it's liberating."

"And what about Margot's daughter? Wasn't she family? It's okay to just leave Robbers behind in other worlds when you see a better score?"

"Margot's daughter ran away of her own volition. But you're

right. Our code does not lend itself to rescues. We often steal as a group. But if you get caught, you're on your own."

"Some family," I said under my breath. But remembering my mother who had me committed and my father who apparently wanted me dead, who was I to judge?

"Is there a list of these rules?"

"More of an oral tradition, I'm afraid. But you'll catch on."

I accepted this for now, but my mind reeled from what I had seen. Something clicked about the redheaded Robber girl in the Throne Room.

"The girl out there who curtsied? I had this weird feeling when I saw her. Like déjà vu. I think I saw her in the circle in town. But she had green hair and a different face then. Was it her?"

He nodded. "It's the eyes. You can change the color and the size. And even the shape. But if you look closely enough, whoever you are is still there. Luckily no one looks that closely."

Ironically, he was looking at me closely, as if he were memorizing my eyes for later, in case I ever took him up on the new face thing. At Whittaker, I was the queen of staring contests, but I looked away.

"You should watch out for Fathom. You should watch out for everyone, really . . ."

"Except you?"

"Especially me," he said. "Margot will give you a spell tomorrow. You don't have to use it, but you should take it. You don't want to offend her."

He turned as if ready to go.

I fought an urge to ask him to stay. Jagger was a liar and a thief, but I wasn't ready to be alone in this strange new space yet.

"Good night, Princess," he said, and disappeared into thin air. I chalked it up to leftover magic from his transporting spell. Even so, it felt like Jagger was showing off for me.

21

WHEN I WOKE IN the morning, it took me a moment to orient myself in the round red room. Glancing out the window didn't help matters much. The red trees that had surrounded the palace last night were gone. In their place was a field of unblemished snow and a dark-purple range of mountains in the distance.

I blinked hard at the glass. Had the castle moved in the night?

"Snow?" Jagger knocked on the door and pushed it open before I could answer.

My pulse raced at the sound of his voice. I knew I shouldn't trust him, but a very small part of me wanted to. Even though he had told me not to.

"What's wrong, Snow?" he asked when he saw the look on my face.

"What happened to the trees?" I asked him. "There was a whole forest of red trees. Did we . . . Does the Claret move?"

I waited for confirmation. I waited for him to tell me that he was seeing the same thing I was. I waited to know that I wasn't losing it.

"Fear not, Princess. The castle didn't move."

"Then what?"

"It's a cloaking spell. We change the surrounding of the Claret so that no one will find it. Margot tried to move the castle once, but apparently there isn't enough magic in all of Algid to do that. This is the next best thing."

I turned away from the window, relieved.

"I brought you some things," Jagger said, and nodded toward the wardrobe.

A scarlet red dress hung in the wardrobe. It was beautiful and the same style as the dresses the other Robber girls wore.

I remembered the joy I'd felt when I'd gotten my first dress from Gerde. But I liked this one, too.

I changed behind the room's dressing screen. The garment didn't fit. The arms were too long and the gaping bustline reminded me that I was just south of a B-cup.

"I think I need something a little less . . ."

"Just give it a minute," Jagger said almost impatiently.

I looked down as the fabric began to move on its own. The sleeves of the dress shortened. The bust was ruched in and lifted and separated and made things look a little larger than they actually were. The excess fabric cinched itself along my waist, and the material that grazed the floor hemmed itself up.

Astounded, I exited from behind the screen.

"See? A perfect fit."

"This dress is amazing!"

"You're overdue for a little surprise after all those years in Whittaker," he said in jest.

But he was wrong. I'd had enough surprises in the last week to last my whole life. I didn't want any more. But I guessed that was not something I could prevent.

Jagger led me through a couple of corridors. We crossed a glass bridge that looked over an indoor greenhouse that was every bit as lush and thriving as Gerde's. Then we started across a rope bridge suspended over a small pond.

Jagger didn't look down, and for a split second I wondered if he was afraid of heights. I quickly shook off the idea, thinking he was probably not afraid of anything.

Fluorescent scales slid under the surface of the water. They made me think of the River Witch. Distracted, I bumped into Jagger halfway across the bridge.

"Careful," he warned, his voice sharp, "and hang on."

Just then one of the fish leaped out of the water. It had pointy teeth.

"Why do you have piranhas?"

"Believe it or not, they are a delicacy. They also provide an added layer of protection. We have magic, and we don't want to lose it. We have been hiding our magic from your father. Everyone who uses magic in Algid has to be careful and secretive. It's a dangerous thing, magic. And mirrors—even more so."

"Wait, are you talking about the pieces of the King's mirror?"

"Yes, I am. We know who has one of the three pieces, and we

want to steal it. The Duchess has it hidden away. You know, the Duchess Temperly. She's your cousin."

"The Duchess?" I asked, remembering that the River Witch had said the coven protected the pieces of the mirror. How did the Duchess get a piece? And my brain was confused doing the family tree math, too.

"Yes, your cousin. She has a piece of the King's mirror, and we need it. In fact we need them all. I hope that won't be a conflict of interest for you," Jagger said, stepping off the bridge.

"I have a cousin? The River Witch never told me," I commented, following Jagger.

"She's the King's niece."

"Is she evil? What's she like?"

"She always wears a mask. Always. It's rumored nobody's ever seen her face. She's pretty smart but dull."

A masked Duchess? She sounded pretty glamorous and mysterious to me. Not even *The End of Almost* had one of those.

"Um, how can you be both those things at once?"

"She doesn't have any magic of her own."

"But neither do you."

"I steal mine. Your mission, my dear, is to steal something very important from her. She keeps the mirror under lock and key. We need it. In return for that, we will help you rescue your sweet Bale."

"What do you need it for?"

"To keep doing what we do here. We need magic for that. And for something else."

I knew there was more to this. I might be the ultimate score for the Robbers. But why not just trade me to the King?

"Like what?"

"The King did something to all of us. And the only way to make him pay is to take what he holds most dear."

"What did he do to all of you?"

Jagger didn't answer.

We crossed into a rectangular room as I processed the idea that I had a cousin and I was going to rob her. And that for all the Robbers said, there was much more to their story than they were telling or were willing to tell.

Secrets were everywhere in Algid, it seemed. The River Witch wouldn't tell me where the three pieces were. *Whose piece is this?* I wondered. *Which of the Three? And how did the Duchess get it?* My mind swirled with questions. I thought about asking Jagger but wasn't sure he actually knew the answers.

Jagger interrupted my thoughts when we got to the Bottle Room. It had a domed ceiling, and the walls were covered with bottles of every size and color. There were hundreds, maybe thousands, of them, and they illuminated the darkness with a bright glow. These were the magic potions the girls sold in the square.

"It looks like you have enough magic," I commented.

Jagger shook his head. "There's only the tiniest bit in most of the bottles. It's not enough."

Enough for what? I wanted to ask. But even if I did, I wasn't sure I would get a straight answer.

"How do you know which is which?"

"By the colors."

The bottles made me think of Vern and the seven dwarfs. Each bottle did something different, just like each pill had.

I picked up a golden bottle. It was similar to the one I saw Fathom use on the orchid in the circle.

"Can this magic heal people?"

"It's magic—not the All High."

I could not imagine Jagger worshipping anything other than himself.

"But you sell it and say it does."

"I've heard that sometimes the act of believing can help heal someone," Jagger said simply.

The idea reminded me of Whittaker. I shook my head and wondered if things were different for other people.

Jagger swept his arm across the walls. "This bottle lets you know what people are thinking. This one lets you be invisible, but only for a little while. This one makes you a good dancer. This one lets you read minds, but only for a few minutes. This one makes people tell the truth. We spell the magic before we bottle it. That way it can't be used against us."

His eyes went back to the dancing potion. "Do you want you try it?"

"No, thanks."

"You have to," he dared and took a sip.

I liked dares. I thought of all the years and all the times Vern came into my room with her silver tray and paper cups filled with the seven-dwarf pills. I took them not knowing that what was wrong with me could not be cured with a pill—and perhaps did not need curing at all.

I pushed Jagger's hand away with a little too much force and the bottle tumbled to the ground, making a tiny crash. The spilled magic on the floor evaporated into a glittery dust.

Jagger looked up at me, confusion across his brow. "How can you throw magic away like that? I can't make sense of you, Snow."

"Well, that's not a first," I quipped—but I ached, too. I was closer to the truth about myself than ever before, but the closer I got, the further I felt I was from everything and everyone else. I was not like Jagger. Or those girls out there.

"Well, we can't let that bottle go to waste. You'll just have to experience it from my magic, then."

"What? No."

But Jagger ignored me. He held up his hands in a waltzing stance.

I had never danced before, and I didn't want to use magic to do it. It felt like a shortcut—and I was done with shortcuts. But Jagger had other ideas.

He took my hand and wrapped his other around my waist. As soon as he did, we rose off the floor. Jagger held me close, and I could feel his heart beating against my chest. There was no music, but our bodies moved together to a silent rhythm.

"You've got to be kidding me."

"Margot would kill me if she knew I was using this potion. We're supposed to save it for a mission."

"A mission that involves dancing?"

"You never know."

"Since this is my first dance with a boy, I wouldn't have minded having my feet on the ground," I blurted.

"Then why not make it extraordinary?"

What Jagger didn't know, what I didn't tell him, was that the dance *was* extraordinary. It was the strangest thing dancing on air. It was the prom that Bale and I had never had and would never have . . . and I was in the wrong person's arms.

"You're thinking about him again, aren't you?" Jagger asked, his question breaking the moment.

Which him? I wondered. *Bale or Kai?* I didn't answer Jagger. Luckily for me, whenever I felt too close to him, Jagger did me the favor of blinking first and creating distance with his words.

A flash of anger rose in me, and we crashed suddenly to the ground, our feet coming down hard where the spilled potion used to be.

"I guess I didn't pay attention. I guess the magic ran out," he lied, studying me for a beat, uncertain.

Jagger didn't let go, though, and we continued to dance. His eyes held mine, and this time it was my turn to blink.

I stopped moving, and we finally broke apart.

"Does everyone here lie?" I asked.

"Everyone lies everywhere. I saw your world, too, Princess. Not much of it. But enough."

I hadn't seen much of my world, either. And definitely not enough.

That night Queen Margot held a party at the Claret in my honor. The drawing room was filled with girls. A girl was playing a harp, and a couple sat at a piano playing in tandem. There was another girl hanging from a trapeze suspended from the ceiling, and yet another doing ballet at a bar in the corner.

Jagger took me around the room to meet everyone. The girls' names were even prettier than their faces: Dover, Garland, and others that flitted right out of my brain.

I wondered if they named themselves when they took on new appearances or if those were their real names. Maybe I wasn't so different from them, after all. Gerde had given me a fake name in the village.

I had so many questions. Were these girls hiding from something or just choosing a new life? I wasn't sure if they were lying to one another or to themselves—or if this magic menu that let you be whoever you wanted was the most incredible, empowering thing ever. But at the same time, if you changed your identity over and over and never stood still, how did you ever know anyone?

I wanted the girls to tell me everything. But who was I to demand their secrets when I had no desire to share my own?

Suddenly a girl left her perch on the couch next to Fathom and made her way atop a table. She had a tattoo on her cheek that looked like lightning. She began to sing. Her voice was deep and strong and full of spite. At first I didn't recognize the tune, but I soon realized that she was singing about me. It was the song the boy had sung in the circle.

The other girls joined in, too, with a melody full of venom.

She brings the snow with her touch,
They think she's gone, but we know

She will come again,
She will reign in his stead,
She will bring down the world on his head.
Oh come, Snow, come . . .

I beat a hasty exit for the door, eliciting laughter from the girls and a little frost on my palms.

Jagger caught up with me in the hall as I wiped my hands on my dress. "Ignore Howl. She gets a little carried away. Believe it or not, that was not a bad welcome."

The girl's name was Howl. And this was how she and the others had chosen to greet me. They might need me for something, but they wanted me to know they didn't want me.

"I'm not afraid of them. They are a means to an end," I said finally, not liking the pitying look that Jagger was giving me.

"In the end, you're afraid of what you'll do to them."

I looked up at him, surprised. It wasn't pity; it was understanding. The girls were doing what they did to any new guest. But I wasn't just anyone, not anymore. I nodded and let him walk me back to my room. He was uncharacteristically silent. I took that as a kindness.

👑

There was magic here.

My mind kept returning to the Bottle Room. I still didn't know so many things. I needed to hear the rest of the story, didn't I? Everyone in Algid had their own agenda. I suppose the same was true of my world. I just never looked beyond

Whittaker's walls. What I did know was I needed to get Bale and get home.

Jagger had come to my world, to Whittaker, using magic. What if that yellow bottle could take us all the way home? Or at least to the Tree? That was where all this started. Perhaps it could end there, too. If it could, I could get away from Algid, from my father, and from everything I didn't understand. I could forget about this place forever.

I stole out of my room and made my way over the two bridges to the room where Jagger and I had danced. But when I opened the door, there were no bottles. Instead I saw Margot standing in front of a large silver basin that hovered in the air. There were a gazillion shards of mirror floating around her. The room was lit by candles that had been arranged in a peculiar sequence on the floor.

The room was hot. I assumed it was another test of some sort.

The walls themselves began to glow with a warm white light. It felt a little like I imagined the inside of a microwave would feel.

Streams of white light roped from her hands.

They danced around me. I could feel the heat emanating from them. I felt power. The force behind it was strong.

I remembered what Jagger had said about the Robbers having a history with the King. One which called for reparations.

I felt my snow rise up within me as her heat circled closer. As I tamped it down I wondered if maybe the Robbers weren't just robbing. Maybe they were working on a weapon against the King.

"Were you . . . are you part of the prophecy? Did you help my mother escape Algid?"

Margot looked at me sharply. But the dancing ropes distanced themselves from me and began to fade.

"I knew Ora. Whether I helped her or not still remains to be seen. When I was very young, I met the Witch of the Woods and I apprenticed with her. Ora was there. I didn't have your natural gifts or hers. So my stay with the coven was not to be. But when the coven broke the King's mirror, there was more magic in the world. Magic that anyone can hold in the palm of his or her hand."

The Witch of the Woods. The River Witch had said she was one of the witches in the coven. Queen Margot had once been an apprentice like Gerde was now. I suddenly wanted to bring Gerde here. I wondered if Margot could help her find her magic through the light—instead of through the darkness, like the River Witch. Gerde relived her pain and shame to keep control. Maybe Margot had another method.

"Did the Witch of the Woods give you her piece of the King's mirror?" I asked bluntly.

Queen Margot produced a vial and turned it over in her hand before she continued.

"The Witch of the Woods gave me many things," Margot replied craftily. "I used what I learned. I practice a little magic to hide our home. To maintain our lives, it takes a lot of power. But I am not a witch. You, on the other hand, are the most powerful thing in Algid since the Snow King. We are honored to have your presence."

"You want to use my power. But the joke's on you. What I have can't be contained or tamed. I am at best a storm. Only, I can now determine the time and place."

"You can do much more than that. I understand why you would lie to me. But do not lie to yourself, Your Highness. Yes, you are a force of nature. But nature is where most magic comes from. It's a conversation between the Witch and the River. Or the Witch and the Woods. Or the Witch and the Fire. When the prophecy comes true, it is believed that you will be able to talk to all the Elements—that you will have all their power. Or at least that's my interpretation. But for now, you need to focus on the one that you were born with: your snow. In time you will learn to thread that force like a needle."

"I never was much of a seamstress."

"Perhaps you did not have the right teacher."

I focused on the walls, and suddenly they were once again lined with bottles of every shape, color, and size. Their contents reflected hazily on the multiple surfaces of the mirror shards.

"Then, if you were not born with this power, how do you have so much of it?" I asked.

"You flatter me. Magic likes poetry and sacrifice. Pretty words over an open wound. And poof! You have magic."

She picked up a vial and opened it. A stream of vapor left the vial and wrapped itself around her arm. She closed her eyes, and the vapor became solid. It slithered up her arm. A tiny garden snake. She opened her eyes, and it became a pretty, metal arm bracelet.

"There is magic in nature just waiting to be tapped. You are attuned to snow. There are others who are attuned to water, like the River Witch, and still others to fire. Like the mirror, water can reflect power," Queen Margot explained. "With the right words and sacrifice, water can also be infused with power. I wish I had more potions. I wish I could crack them all open and drink them all up. That is who I am. That is who we all are. Moderation is really the only curse, but it is a necessary one for now."

Looking at Margot, I realized that she would trade everything—the Claret and every bottle in her arsenal—to have the River Witch's natural gifts or mine.

Power trumped beauty. And then there was the matter of her real daughter. What was her daughter worth to her? Would she give up magic and power? It was a calculation I hoped was true, but I wasn't so sure.

I thought about telling her about Magpie. But the story wouldn't necessarily endear me to her.

"How did you learn the spells?" I asked, pushing the mystery of Margot's daughter aside for the moment.

"I was lucky enough to learn from a great witch, like I said before."

"And what kind of sacrifice do the potions require?"

"That's where you come in, my dear."

Finally, we get to the heart of the matter, I thought, my brain ahead of my body for once. But unlike before, I wasn't afraid of the answer. I needed to know.

"I don't want to hurt you. I just want a little blood. Your blood. That's what the magic requires. You will give me your blood. Then you will help us steal the piece of the King's mirror at the Duchess's palace, and in return you will have our assistance in retrieving the boy you love."

Blood? Jagger had shown me Algid's magic, but not where it came from. Nor its cost.

"Before I agree to anything, I must know if you possess what I need. I'd prefer to ask rather than take. It's much more polite that way," said Queen Margot, taking a step closer to me.

"That's not creepy at all," I blurted, remembering what the River Witch had said about magic. She was right. It was a dirty business filled with sacrifice and, I assumed, blood.

"There are much greater sacrifices," Queen Margot said evenly, although her tone carried the edge of a threat. Margot may not have been a witch, but when her eyes caught the light I saw something that reminded me of the River Witch. Something that made me want to run in the other direction as fast as I could.

But I didn't run. Like it or not, we were in this together. I needed Queen Margot as much as she needed me. She was the key to getting Bale back and returning to my world. I had no choice but to agree. I was careful to choose my right arm. The one without the map of Algid on it. Taking a deep breath, I held out my arm and pulled back my sleeve, revealing the faded puncture marks of hundreds of Whittaker needles.

Margot unsheathed a deadly-looking, bejeweled knife—but she hesitated for the briefest of moments at the sight of the needle marks. Whatever she was thinking, it was only a short pause before she slid the blade across my palm.

The cut wasn't deep, but it still hurt. The pain was physical and tangible—not the swarm of conflicting emotions and confusion that had been circling me since I stepped through the Tree.

What was I doing? How much blood did she need?

I pulled my arm back, putting pressure on my palm to stop the flow of blood. It was my turn.

"You want Jagger to take another trip to my world to find your daughter, right?" I asked.

Margot looked up sharply. "Jagger told you that? Jagger talks a lot, but he so rarely gives as much information as he takes. One would think being surrounded by pretty girls all the time he would eventually become immune to their wiles, but you must have had quite the effect on him," she said.

"Let Jagger take me and Bale with him when he goes, and you can have as much of my blood as you want," I offered.

"Dear, do you think this is a negotiation? I think I could have every last drop of your blood if I wanted."

It was clear that Queen Margot felt she had the upper hand despite my lineage and where I had come from.

"And I could level this place," I countered, almost biting back the words as I said it. I had failed to defeat the Enforcer. How did I expect to defeat the King alone?

"Could you? You admitted yourself that you do not have control. Something tells me that you'd rather not rip apart my palace if it means killing all those innocent girls and my Jagger."

I answered with an icy, silent stare, and Queen Margot continued her examination of me by candlelight.

"How does it feel knowing that a whole world was destroyed because of your existence?" Margot asked, a hint of excitement in her voice.

"No different than not knowing."

It was a lie. But I could not wrap myself around her claim, or the River Witch's, even after what I'd seen. Everything in my life had taken place in the tiny Whittaker snow globe, and now they were spinning some epic tale with me in the starring role. I did not want to be Algid's savior, and I did not want to be its curse. I wanted to go home.

"Jagger told me about your life in the Other World. Dreadful conditions for a princess. What happens when you go back? Do you really think Queen Ora is going to let you go home to her? Do you really want to spend the rest of your life trapped in that place?"

"I'll confront her with the truth," I challenged back.

"And then what? She'll pretend you're crazy and give you the cocktail again? Keep you drugged and safe until the prophecy passes?"

The cocktail? Jagger had more than told her. He'd gone into every detail. And hearing about it from Margot's lips brought it back all over again.

"I don't know, but I'd rather take my chances there than here."

"But don't you see? Once the prophecy passes and the Lights are extinguished, you will have no choices left. There will be one moment when you can ascend the throne. After that, the world belongs to him, and everyone in it will suffer."

"This is not my world."

"So you would leave us and not look back? You're just like your mother."

"She was saving me."

"But what of her land? What of Algid? She was our queen. She put your life above all others, and you are doing the same with yours now."

"I am, and I cannot care about a place that doesn't care for me. I don't know this place. I don't need this place. And from what I've seen of it, it's not worth saving. It's filled with liars and robbers and bad people all around."

Another lie. Gerde had gotten hurt and tried to save me. And Kai had used his Hopper. Even the River Witch in her twisted way had tried to help me. But I wanted Margot to stop talking, and this was a much better way than the icy alternative.

"Your Highness . . . ," Queen Margot began, and then quieted, reconsidering. "Very well. Once I have your blood and its magic and the mirror, your fate is up to you. I will grant your request."

I had been convincing. I had effectively lied to the queen of thieves. I had shoved aside everything I felt for the good people of Algid, and then I held out my arm again. My blood pooled into a silver chalice that appeared from out of nowhere in Queen Margot's hand. Margot smiled and held it up to the light. It did not look special to me, but she looked at it like she'd found the answer to everything.

For her sake and for mine, I hoped that she was right. Some tiny part of me twinged, though. If I indeed had that much power, should I have given it away? Should I have asked what she intended to do with it? I didn't trust Margot or anyone here. Would she ultimately hold up her end of the bargain?

It was done, though. No use crying over spilled blood. I

leaned forward as I watched her. Her green eyes glowed with anticipation.

"I know you don't believe, child. Contrary to popular belief, it doesn't matter. Magic is not a matter of belief. It's of sheer will and science—and I have enough for both of us."

"What is the blood for?" I demanded, too late. I should have asked first. I'd told myself that I didn't care what it was for. That all that mattered was Bale. But as she swilled the blood around in the chalice, I had a wild thought that she was going to drink it. Or somehow make a weapon out of it. The idea sounded like something Chord would have believed back at Whittaker, but after the things I'd seen in the last few days, the impossible was outweighing the possible more times than not.

"Telling you why was not part of our bargain. But I don't see the harm in your knowing."

Another wave of her hand and some kind of medieval-looking ring of knives appeared in the center of the room, hovering in midair in front of me.

"What is that?"

"The last time we were at the Duchess's palace, we found out she had a piece of the mirror. It was only a matter of time before we tracked down the architect who designed her safe, and he was kind enough to make a replica of the lock for us. The knives are part of the lock.

"This device is identical to the one that guards the safe," she continued. "Only royal blood will open the safe. We can't replicate whatever trap lies behind the safe wall. But this will get us past the first obstacle."

She took the chalice and carefully placed a drop of my blood on one of the knives. Nothing happened at first. Then the knives slowly turned their points in Margot's direction.

Margot whispered some words I could not hear, and the knives fell to the ground.

"So I'm guessing that was not supposed to happen? It didn't work?" I asked.

Queen Margot held up a crystal from around her neck. It glowed a scarlet red.

"This reacts in the presence of magic. It proves that you have magic in you. It should have worked. I don't understand. You have your blood to take, entrance you must make." This time she spoke louder, but nothing else happened. "I was sure it would be in your blood. I was sure it would be enough . . ." She drifted off, confused.

The knives rattled on the floor again. Their blades pointed toward me.

"Leave!" Queen Margot ordered.

As I rushed out of the room, I heard a crash of crystal landing on the floor.

22

A SNOW TORNADO WAS forming outside the window of my room. I had tried the front door of the Claret and found it spelled shut. I had to find another way.

"I can't stay here. I need to leave," I said to Jagger. "Will you help me? Or do I have to do it by myself?"

"I can't help you."

"Of course, you can't. Robber Rules, right? Then you might want to get the hell out of my way. It's not going to be pretty."

He stood in my way. He knew I wouldn't send a tornado through him.

"What happened, Snow?"

"Margot tried my blood in that lock of hers, and when it didn't work she threw a temper tantrum with knives, Jagger," I said, pacing away from him. "I may have snow, but I am not impervious to sharp, pointy things," I finished.

He studied me a beat, considering.

"It doesn't matter if you go. You made a deal. Margot has your blood. She can do a locator spell. There isn't anywhere that you go that she can't find you. And if Queen Margot doesn't give you up, there is a roomful of Robbers out there wondering what you're worth. There's an Enforcer scouring all of Algid in the hopes of finding you for the King. Do you know how much the King's offering to pay for your head?" Jagger said bluntly.

I was in danger again. These girls were not my friends, and neither was Jagger. Convincing anyone to help me get home, to find the mirror and to get my life back, was a long shot.

I suddenly felt tired. Like every muscle in my body that had been holding me up was sagging. For the first time ever in my life, I longed for my cage at Whittaker. For my quiet. For my Bale.

"I thought I was doing you a favor in bringing you here," Jagger continued.

"Because you thought I'd repay you with my blood."

He shrugged nonchalantly. "Even so, I promise I will protect you."

"You're the reason why things are happening to me." He wasn't completely. My father had started this. It just felt better to blame Jagger, because he was there.

"I won't apologize for giving you a way out of Whittaker. For giving you a way to save Bale."

"Let me guess. Robber Rules."

"I know you have no reason to believe me. But I don't want anything bad to happen to you. I want to honor my promise."

"I don't know that. I can't trust you to save the one person in the world that I do trust. I don't know who you are. You hide your real faces from one another. How is that living? I don't want to hide my scars, I wish I didn't have magic, and I'd rather dance with my feet on the ground! I don't want to live in a dream—I just want to live. Like a normal person. And I want to feel things for real."

"Well, you're not going to like what I have to say next," Jagger added quietly.

I wasn't sure if he had really heard me. But his eyes softened with what looked like hurt, as if my each and every word were a body blow.

"There's more?" I asked, incredulous.

"I know a way to make sure that Margot and the other Robbers will have to keep you safe, too."

"What could that possibly be?"

"Become one of us. We're down a Robber."

"But that's . . ." Insane? Ridiculous?

Before I could say anything more, my field of vision went black, and then all I could see was the inside of a house.

It was small, and the walls were white. The furniture was sparse but didn't look like anything in Algid or Whittaker. I didn't understand the dream—especially because I felt completely awake. But the house looked familiar.

I'd seen it before. Bale had showed me pictures. This was his house. The one that he burned down.

Dr. Harris had talked about how the mind creates a safe place where you can go when things were too hard in the real world. Bale had taken himself to his childhood home, the one he'd burned down. And he was setting it on fire again and again.

Little boy Bale pacing the house. Little boy Bale outside watching it burn.

But why was I seeing Bale's safe place? Then I saw a flash of somewhere else. Another place I'd never been. A triangular room that seemed to have a steeple.

"Snow." Bale said my name.

Wherever he was, he was thinking about me.

♔

"Snow . . . ," another voice called.

Jagger's voice took me out of it and back to the shadow of the Claret. I needed another minute and another second more. I needed a few more seconds with Bale. A few more seconds to pinpoint exactly where he was.

"Snow," Jagger said again, his arms on mine, shaking me gently.

It took me a second to focus on him.

"What just happened?" he asked, studying me closely.

"Just seeing through my missing boyfriend's eyes. Or at least I think that's what was happening."

"Where was he?" Jagger asked.

"A dark room. I think he was in pain. There was a triangular room like this."

I drew the image into the frosty air, excited that my control over my powers was progressing. Worst-case scenario, it was a cool party trick.

"The King's dungeons," Jagger said almost proudly, taking this as proof that he was right about where Bale was. The fact that he didn't care what shape Bale was in made my fingers twitch, with snow.

Stuffing down the urge to freeze his mouth shut, I asked, "Do you really not care about anyone?"

"Everyone cares for someone," he said, sounding sincere for a moment. "If you're lucky, more than one someone," he added, as if remembering that sincerity was not what he wanted me to see.

I sighed heavily. I was tired of his charm. I was tired of the Claret's shabby beauty.

"You're probably marked," he said as if he could sense that I had reached another in a series of breaking points. "That's why you and Bale are connected. Why you can see him."

"Is this part of the prophecy?" I asked.

"No, it's part of Algid. When you love someone—really love someone—and you have magic, it's possible to imprint each other. But it's just a legend. Then again, you were just a legend until I met you."

Imprint? I'd seen a movie once where a teen werewolf had fallen in love with a girl and he imprinted on her, linking them forever. Were Bale and I imprinted?

I ignored what I thought was a compliment and tried to unravel the point. "Like in fairy tales? Like when princes wake up princesses with kisses from magically induced comas—like that?"

Jagger looked at me as if the idea was completely foreign to him. He was not familiar with Sleeping Beauty, apparently.

"Of course, it might not be the mark at all. Maybe you're more like your father than you want to admit."

"What is that supposed to mean?"

"King Lazar claims to be able to use his snow to get inside the good people of Algid's heads. Or at least that's the rumor. I think it's just bull-thorn, personally. Just another way of making the people fear him . . ."

"If I had mind control powers, you would not be talking anymore," I said evenly.

He considered this with a smile and went back to his first theory.

"Usually, the imprint is accompanied by some kind of physical marking."

I drew the mark I'd seen on Bale's arm in the air. The image hung there for what seemed like an eternity.

"Like I said, I've never seen an imprint before, but I think that the legend says it's specific to the giver. Every one is supposed to be different."

"Like a snowflake," I finished, sarcasm dripping from the word.

He shook his head. "I was going to say like every love is different. But your metaphor works, too."

"The symbol—it looks like something on the Tree, Jagger."

"Your mom and the other witches made the Tree to get you and her out of Algid. It's probably your rune."

"Rune?"

"I hate to say that I have never been much for symbols—Fathom's the one you should talk to—but the witches carve them into things for all sorts of reasons, mainly protection."

"And I carve them into people?"

"You are special, Snow. You're the product of a King and a witch . . . Like the prophecy says, you might just be the most powerful thing ever. Why wouldn't you love more powerfully, too?"

Jagger's words hung between us like my drawing had. I fought the urge to look away from his unrelenting stare.

"So either I am tied to Bale in my mind, or I have freaky mind-control powers over everything . . ."

"I kind of hope it's neither," he said.

"Huh?"

"I hope that you aren't channeling your boyfriend. That you aren't capable of freaky mind-control things, as you call it."

"You would prefer that I have lost my sanity and I am just having waking dreams of my kidnapped boyfriend? Why?"

"Two reasons: One, I don't love the idea of your being psychically hitched to Fire Boy."

"What's it to you who I'm psychically hitched to?" I interrupted.

"Which brings me to reason number two: I don't love the idea of your getting into my head and figuring out what I was really thinking."

"Why don't you just tell me what you're thinking?"

"Where's the fun in that?" he answered.

"When I first kissed Bale and he melted down, I was so drugged up. I thought . . . I thought the kiss . . . I thought I had actually made him crazy . . . ," I blurted without looking at Jagger.

He reached up and took my chin and made me face him.

"You are a force, Snow. But I would never believe that."

He released me.

I looked away again, more grateful than I wanted to be. And more affected by his touch than I liked. Especially with Bale's consciousness so close to my own.

Perhaps I had for once penetrated through the layers of Jagger's charm, and then he said something that stunned me.

"The connection would go both ways, Snow. Bale can see you, too. If he's in the King's dungeons, maybe this will give him hope. Keep him going until . . ."

"Until we get him out? I'm in. Whatever you want, I'll do it. You want me to be a Robber? I'm a Robber."

Margot appeared suddenly beside Jagger.

"I couldn't have said it better myself," she said with a smile.

I didn't know how much she had heard. But I still needed to negotiate terms.

"You're spying on me now?" I demanded, squaring my shoulders for once. My ire was up. Outside the window, I could hear my little snow tornado knocking down a few of those trees.

"I have done my duty for the Claret," I said. "You promised me that you would help me get Bale back and that I could go home if I gave you my blood, and I have."

"Snow, you were to give me blood imparted with magic. Your blood has secrets that elude me. So, no, you have not held up your end of the bargain entirely. I will not help you until I hold the Duchess's mirror in my hand. We thought we could transport your blood and take it with us, but for the spell to work, you might have to be present. The blood might have to come directly from your body. Or at least that's what Fathom hopes. Of course, first we need to know that your blood works."

"Fathom's the resident blood expert?" I asked.

She nodded. She wanted me to stick my hand into the trap for real this time. No chalice.

She rolled on, as if I had already agreed.

"And so it seems, Jagger is right. We must turn you into one of us or you will never get past the Duchess. Contrary to what my children think, you could drink every drop in every bottle and steal a thousand mirrors and *still* not be a good Robber. It will take hard work. But you are the Snow Princess. I have no doubt you will be up to the challenge."

"There's something else that I want," I said, an idea forming.

"Robber Rules: you must learn that there are no gifts, my dear."

I knew that before I got here, I thought. I thought of the mittens my mother had given me the day before I left for Algid. They now represented a lifetime of guilt and secrets on her part.

"I just want to know one thing. I have spent most of my life not knowing anything. I don't want to be in the dark anymore."

"What are you asking, exactly?" she said.

"I want to know how it works. How I work. Teach me. Teach me how to wield my magic," I said, standing in front of Margot.

Margot leaned against the doorframe and said, "I wish I could. But I can't. I don't know how."

"Then I want something else. I want anyone other than Jagger to teach me. Keep him the hell away from me."

Jagger looked at me, surprised. Margot just laughed and said a single word: "No."

23

A FEW MINUTES LATER I sealed my deal with the Robber Queen. We went back to the vial room, and this time I stuck my hand inside the lock. It drew my blood, and the knives clattered to the ground.

"Of course, there is a rumor that the lock changes on a daily basis."

"And the lock maker couldn't confirm this?" I asked, suspicion rising.

"Unfortunately, the lock maker died before he could share that information."

She disappeared with a satisfied smile. I walked back to my room, wondering if I had made the right choice.

I had agreed to become a Robber. It was the only way I could protect myself. And the first step to becoming a Robber was finding out exactly what that meant and what I would have to do. It was time to make peace with the Robber girls.

I found Fathom in a cold, fluorescent-lit room that reminded me of the medical or scientific labs I had seen on TV.

"You shouldn't be here," Fathom dared.

"What is this place?" I asked, taking it all in.

Something growled from the corner of the room. I swiveled around to see a Snow Wolf trapped inside a glass box. The animal was strangely alluring. I had only seen Snow Wolves when they were chasing after me and there wasn't enough time then to get a good look. I couldn't help myself. I walked over to the box.

When I got closer, the Snow Wolf lunged at the glass and disintegrated into a gazillion flurries, which fell onto the floor of the cage. After a second, the flurries came back together again, re-forming the Snow Wolf. It lunged at me again, repeating the process.

"I've never seen it do that before," Fathom said, wrinkling her nose. She looked from the glass case to me and back again, trying to figure out the connection.

"Why do you have a Snow Wolf?" I demanded.

"It's a hobby. Nothing in the Claret is free. Margot allows me my hobby in exchange for my services."

"What services?"

Fathom flicked a switch, which turned on a light at the far end of the room. There were bodies of women laid out on wooden slabs.

"Did you ever wonder how we get the faces?" Fathom asked.

Stunned, I looked from her to one of the corpses. It had the same face as Fathom.

"I never really . . ." I hadn't thought about the faces they borrowed. I just assumed that each Robber made one up.

"We steal the faces," she boasted. "You have to have some part of them, like hair or blood, in order for the magic to work." She walked over to her face twin. I remembered how Jagger had borrowed Bale's face. That meant he had taken something from Bale. But when? How?

"Do you kill them?" I asked, fearing Fathom's response. What the River Witch had said about sacrifice came back again. It seemed that perhaps the less magic you came by naturally, the more sacrifice you had to make.

"Not usually. Think of it this way: after they die, some part of them gets to live on. That's something, right?"

"But where do you find the bodies?" I asked, hoping and assuming she was joking about the killing part. Finding dead bodies was creepy enough.

She sighed. "Grave robbing, of course."

That's better than the alternative, I thought. But I felt the already slippery world of the Robbers turn on its axis toward an even darker reality than I'd imagined.

"You can come with me if you'd like. We can pick out something pretty for you," she dared, almost sweetly.

What had I gotten myself into? I shook my head and walked out of the weird morgue. Once I got out the door, though, I began to run.

24

WHEN I GOT BACK to my room, there was a dress laid out for me on the bed. It was prettier than the collection of day dresses that had appeared in my closet after my first night at the Claret. It had feathers all over it. And it was a stunning silvery lavender color that reminded me of the trees tonight.

I touched the dress.

"Wear me and come to the roof," a voice whispered in my ear.

The door slammed shut a second later. The voice belonged to Howl, the girl who was singing in the Throne Room.

She must have used an invisibility spell. But to what end? Would the dress suffocate me to death when I put it on? Was it a trick? Was it a trap?

I stared at the dress for a few minutes before I slipped it on and headed up the stairs. With every step I took, I reasoned that I was doing the right thing. But the truth was I couldn't sit alone with that dress a minute longer. Maybe it was all that time at Whittaker not being able to do things that other kids did. But a ball gown and an invitation to mystery could not go unanswered.

When I got to the roof, all the Robbers, save Margot, were standing in a circle around a strange symbol scrawled on the rooftop. It reminded me of the markings on the Tree.

The girls wore feather dresses like mine, only theirs were in iridescent pastel colors. A couple of the girls stepped aside, and I spotted Jagger just outside the circle. He dragged his hand through his hair, messing it into tousled perfection, and smoothed down his suit, which was covered in feathers, too: black ones. The fashion statement shouldn't have worked for anyone, but Jagger's good looks had a magic all their own. He could wear anything. And he still looked good, even when I was mad at him.

Each Robber held an unlit candle.

I realized this was some kind of initiation. All this was for me.

"You can't be serious?" I asked.

"When you first arrived, we didn't get to properly welcome you into the Robber fold," Fathom said.

She was clearly in charge of the girls in Margot's absence.

"So what happens now?" I said impatiently.

"Tomorrow you train. Tonight we welcome you," Fathom said with a flourish.

I was more than a little surprised. These girls had made it pretty clear they didn't want much to do with me, and I had made it pretty clear that I didn't want anything to do with

Jagger. I hadn't even bothered to get to know all their names, because I thought I wouldn't be staying long enough for them to matter.

Despite what I thought of him, I watched Jagger as he took his place at the symbol on the floor. I wondered if he actually knew what the symbol meant, after all. Was that another lie on top of all the others?

Light some candles, say some poetry. Dance around a bonfire. I could do this. Howl handed me a candle, and I walked to the center of the symbol. I turned my back to Jagger.

Fathom blew on her candle and it lit.

The flame jumped through the air from one candle to the next. Another magic trick. Finally the candle in my hand lit.

"Welcome, Robber Princess. Your life is yours. Your spoils are ours. We will see you on the other side."

Fathom put down the candle and grabbed my hand.

Was that it? That was less painful than a group therapy session back at Whittaker. But no. It wasn't so easy. Fathom pulled me to the edge of the roof.

She took a step up and expected me to follow.

She wanted me to jump off the roof.

It was another test. I was supposed to tornado down or something. I wasn't sure if I could do it without tearing the Claret apart.

"You want me to use my snow . . ."

"No, I want you to a take a leap of faith. Trust in us. Trust in the Robbers. And when you land, you will be part of us."

"But I am not a real—" I began, but I stopped myself before saying the last word: *Robber*.

"You don't have to do this," Jagger offered.

I scowled at him. I was still not ready to talk to him.

"We've all done it," countered Howl, a lot less gently.

The girls looked on, waiting to see what I would do.

I would have to be a real Robber to get to Bale. I knew I would have to take this step no matter what.

When I was in group therapy in Ward A at the institute, we used to do trust falls in the shared rec room. It was a comedic disaster. Wing did not want to be caught, and Chord believed he would fall into another century. I had not much more faith in the Robbers as my toes curled around the edge of the roof.

But then I remembered Margot and the way that the Robber girls looked at her. I remembered my snow and how I thought it might just save me even if I didn't direct it to. And I thought of Bale, who was out there somewhere under the Lights, dreaming of me and waiting for me to find him.

The other girls joined me on the ledge. And then I stepped off the roof.

The other girls followed, a line of us falling in the dark.

Gravity took hold faster than I thought it would. The sensation of being pulled downward filled me with a new kind of panic. I looked below and began calculating the distance and time to the ground. How many seconds would it take for my snow to pick me up, if it came to that?

I waited and watched, feeling like I was both inside and outside myself as the Claret whizzed by on the left, the now-purple trees on the right.

The other girls looked happy, as if they were exhilarated by the fall.

Maybe they were all a little off. Maybe this was just a game of chicken and I was supposed to pull my snow like a rip cord. Maybe I was supposed to save them all.

The ground was coming up fast to greet me. I closed my eyes and called on my snow. Perhaps I could sweep us all into a tornado. Maybe it would work if we all joined hands and held on tight enough.

Just when I had hit the serious-wishing-and-hoping-for-a-miracle stage, I heard a flapping sound. My eyes opened. It was the feathers on my dress. They were flapping.

I was pulled upward by the feathers, and so were the other girls. It was the strangest sensation. Relief washed over me, and I could feel myself smiling in the few seconds of flight as we ascended and then descended again, landing softly on the ground in front of the Claret.

Howl let out a noise befitting her name. Girls stretched and laughed, then began to file back inside.

"You want to go again?" Howl asked as she approached me, pushing her feathers down.

"Maybe in a minute."

She shrugged and headed inside.

I leaned back against the Claret and looked up.

A few minutes later, I watched as the girls floated down from the roof again. Each in a different dress, feathers flying. I wished Wing could see this. I had really come so far from my tiny room at Whittaker. Tonight I could fly.

25

THE NEXT MORNING I found Jagger sitting on Margot's throne.

"What the hell? Where's Margot?"

"She's in her lab. No doubt still trying to find a way to use your blood without having to use you. Now, shall we begin your Robber education?"

"No!"

"There are two tenets to robbing, Snow," Jagger said, ignoring me, "the physical and the mental. And then there's the seduction . . ."

"I told Margot I didn't want you to teach me."

"First rule of being a Robber. No one gives you what you want. You have to take it."

I felt myself coming to a boil, but I didn't want him to see it.

"Fine."

"If you're going to be a thief, you're going to have to be phys-ical. And I don't mean using your magic," Jagger continued. "Until you get a handle on your power—until you can use your power in big ways—it's not going to help us in a heist. A Robber is physically and mentally faster than their marks, and you spent a long time drugged up in Whittaker."

"And what about seduction?" I asked, raising an eyebrow.

"It's not what you think," he said with a knowing smile. "You just have to figure out what people want and then give it to them. And while they're busy being happy, you pick their pockets. The idea is to get in and get out without anyone noticing until much later. So that hours from now the mark will get home and wonder if maybe the fault was their own. Maybe the thing they're missing was lost and not stolen."

"You make it sound so easy," I said.

My mind went to Magpie, the look of secret joy that she wore a lot of the time. It wasn't the stuff that she had under her bed. It was the pride in taking. It was the game itself. Magpie wasn't born evil. The tools that she had used against me in Whittaker she had learned here at the Claret. How could I ever really trust the place and the people that had made her?

Jagger smiled. "Robbers sometimes work by themselves, but actually collaborating in couples or in groups is the norm. In some ways it minimizes the risk. But relying on another person can also increase it."

My heart was racing at the future and maybe also a little at Jagger. It was both exhilarating and frightening at the same time. I was going to be his Robber girl.

A few hours later, Jagger was close. Too close. Kissing close. He was leaning into me. I was pressed against the stone wall of the Claret. We had taken our lesson outside, just in case I got frustrated and decided to freeze something.

But heist training had been a little more intimate than I'd anticipated.

He smelled like a girl. Like a heady mix of roses and orchids. I just couldn't pinpoint which one. Which Robber girl had been close enough to him to leave a lingering scent on his clothes? Underneath there was something else, coffee and something more masculine, something clean and soapy and all Jagger. Despite the fact that he probably had been equally close to one of the Robber girls some time today, I felt myself tempted to lean into him in return.

Being with Jagger was like a constant game of chicken, and I somehow always managed to blush first.

I ducked under his arm and took a few steps away from him.

"Now check your pocket," he demanded.

I already knew that it was his timepiece.

I fished it out and tossed it back to him with a sigh.

"Your turn," he said, slipping it back into his pocket.

He wanted me to take it from him again.

We had been at it for hours; perfecting a lift meant hours of staring into Jagger's silvery-gray eyes while trying to keep him from seeing what my hands were doing.

Snow formed between my fingers, and I threw an icicle at the tree line.

He stepped in front of me.

"You saw what I did there. Now you do it."

"You want me to kiss every mark . . . there must be some other way . . ."

"Sometimes it's not the thing you want. It's the promise of the thing you want . . . I want you to think about me and nothing else for just a second. And in that second, I'll rob you blind."

For a moment, I wasn't sure if we were still talking about robbing, and while I was wondering just that he pressed me suddenly and without warning into the side of the Claret.

"Jagger . . . ," I said breathlessly. I knew I was supposed to push him away. I knew that this was probably a more advanced part of our lesson. And I was probably failing spectacularly. I was supposed to control the moment. The attention. Get his eyes on me while I stole something from him. But somehow even when I took the timepiece from him, it felt like I was the one who had given something away.

"Don't move until I tell you to," he said, his silvery eyes lighting on something on the horizon that I didn't see. I followed his gaze and found nothing.

The stone wall dug into my back. And I didn't care. I didn't want to move.

I reached out one of my hands, experimenting with a web of ice between two of my fingers, considering how I could use it against him.

But he pressed my hand closed with his own and dragged me along the building's side as if he were running from something.

This wasn't the game. This wasn't the training anymore. There was something out there. Something big and bad enough to cause Jagger to lose his cool.

"Quiet, Princess," he said, his voice urgent, devoid of its usual charm.

When we got to the front door, the other Robbers were there, weapons drawn. There were daggers and vials at the ready. They were still dressed in their Robber dresses and heels. If it weren't for their weapons and their crouching positions, ready to pounce, they looked like they should have been waiting for a music video shoot. Not for whatever threat was coming.

I heard the rustling in the snow at the green tree line. Snow Beasts shook themselves out of the snow.

They were here for me.

I half expected the girls to offer me up—or for Margot to. She was standing behind the line of girls, looking at me almost pityingly.

"Hush, child," she warned.

Then she began to chant something under her breath.

Jagger whispered to me, "Cloaking spell."

The other girls chanted, too, all the while prepping for battle. Shields appeared out of thin air. Two girls wheeled out a catapult.

The Enforcer emerged from behind the Snow Beasts.

The girls stood frozen-statue still, their eyes scanning the moving beasts and their Enforcer, who shepherded them.

"He can't see us," Howl whispered with confidence.

But the Enforcer was looking in my direction. Just as he had in the square back in Stygian.

Part of me wanted another shot at the Enforcer. I also wanted to hide behind the Robber girls. I had never lost a fight before, not counting the few times Vern had to restrain me.

I inched a step in his direction.

Howl stepped beside me and grabbed my hand. Jagger did the same on the other side of me. One by one, we all held hands, forming a line. It was as if every Robber were letting me know they stood with me against the Enforcer.

But the Enforcer came right up to me, inches from my face, just like he had during our fight.

This is not my end, I reminded myself. And despite the line of those who were ready to fight for me, who I knew I should stay quiet for, I felt myself tempted to take another punishing stab at the Enforcer.

Jagger squeezed my hand tighter. Either he had taken a mind-reading potion or he could see it in my face.

The Enforcer looked to the right and moved on, his Snow Beasts trailing after him.

Jagger released my hand. The other girls put down their weapons and began going back inside the Claret.

"Does this happen all the time? Or was that just for me?"

Howl spoke first. "The King leaves us alone, mostly. He has a history of underestimating us."

The Enforcer was here for me. I had put them all in danger. I half expected her to volunteer to give me up to the King. To say that I was too much of a risk.

But all she said was, "If you don't know how already, you're going to need to know how to fight."

We stood there watching the diminishing North Lights until there was nothing left to do but go back into the Claret.

26

AT DAWN, I got up and went outside. Watching the sun rise, I practiced my snow. I sent wave after wave of snow against the tree line, thinking about the Enforcer in my face the day before and imagining eviscerating him with every wave. When he found me, I had a taste of power for the first time in my life, and he had shown me that it wasn't enough. At least not yet.

I noticed a couple of snow angels on the ground. Leftover from some of the Robbers, I assumed. I filled up the outlines with snow and tried to animate them.

The winged snow figures were halfway up when I heard a sound behind me.

I let off a snow-cicle on instinct.

A flame came out of nowhere and melted my arrow in midair.

Jagger whistled as if he were impressed with me. He was

standing behind me in the snow in front of the Claret. He was the source of the flame. But how?

"What the hell, Jagger? I could have frozen you! How did you . . ."

He raised his wrists, and inexplicably a stream of flame came from each of them. I put out the fire with a blast of snow that cut a little too close to Jagger. He jumped to the side.

I'd grazed his hand with my flash of snow. His face didn't betray the pain.

But he showed me the frostbitten evidence. He pulled a vial out of his pocket and poured it over his wounds. The skin healed up in an instant.

"What is that? How did you do that?"

"It's a healing vial. Small magic," he said matter-of-factly.

"Not that. The fire."

"Fathom and Margot have been working on it. Kind of a magic-science combination."

I took Jagger's hands and looked at the two metal cuffs that were around his wrists. There were symbols carved into the metal that made me think of the Tree.

The metal itself looked familiar, too. It was the same burnished metal that I'd seen on the Enforcer.

"The Enforcer's suit must be made out of this stuff."

When I touched the metal, the symbols glowed and a green light danced out of it. My claws retracted. Hastily, I took my hands away.

"Oh," he said, as if this were new information.

But I wondered if it was what he had wanted all along. For a split second I wondered if I was just there as a guinea pig. Practice for the main event. The Robbers could try out their snow defense powers on me before moving on to King Lazar.

"Relax, Princess. I have no intention of using this on you. You are one of us."

I wasn't comforted. I liked the idea of the Robbers' building an arsenal against the Snow King, but at the same time, I realized their weapons could also be used against me.

"We should get back to training," I said flatly.

Our heist took on a new color. The Robbers had claimed that we could get into the Duchess's palace and get the mirror without incident. But after the Enforcer's visit to the Claret, we were all aware of a potential clash of fire and ice. Even if that fire was manufactured. It was five days until the Duchess's Ball, when our mission would take place.

"We should get back inside. We need to prepare for tonight," Jagger said.

"What's tonight?" Were we stepping up the plan because of the Enforcer?

"Tonight is your first real test as a Robber."

27

EVERY HOUR WE DREW closer to the Eclipse of the Lights. The clock was ticking down, and I could feel the shift in all of us under the pressure. The Claret girls were plotting a new mission that was tied to the bigger one: to infiltrate a VIP party. We each had to lift as many coins as we could from the partygoers. But they weren't just any coins. They were coins that granted us entrance to the Duchess's Ball. The one where we would steal the mirror.

"You can be of help, but there's one thing that's nonnegotiable," Fathom told me in no uncertain terms. Jagger had deposited me in a room that I had never been in before when we got back inside. Fathom had been waiting for me.

The room was circular like mine. But white like Fathom's lab. And empty except for a single chair and a mirror.

I noticed right away that there was something different about Fathom's face. She was smiling. For the briefest of seconds I

thought that our encounter with the Enforcer had changed something between us. Bonded us.

She caught my stare. "What?"

"You're smiling."

"Oh, that." She produced a vial. It was cherry red. "Smile
vial. I call it permafrost. Strikes the right balance, so your mark
always thinks you're happy to see them. Even when you're not."

So, no bond then, I noted to myself.

"What am I doing here, Fathom?" I asked.

She motioned to the chair and produced another vial. This
one filled with platinum liquid.

"You have to wear a different face."

A silver case filled with more vials appeared beside her at the
ready. This was a Robber makeover.

"And seeing how you are with Jagger, you should definitely
take the inhibition bottle when we go. It is possible with enough
time and imagination to break your own heart," she assessed,
holding out the vial to me.

"What are you saying about me and Jagger?"

She shrugged. "Just an old Robber expression. I don't know
what made me think of it."

"I am not in love with Jagger, if that's what you're thinking.
We're just . . ." I didn't know how to sum up whatever we were
to myself, let alone tell Fathom.

"I've seen you two together . . . Once upon a time I loved a
girl like that. Her name was Anthicate. She's Margot's daughter.
We were partners. We were friends. We were as thick as thieves,
literally. We pulled all our scores in tandem. And then she just

left in the middle of the night. No note. No good-bye. And the next thing we heard was that she crossed the Tree."

Magpie. She loved Magpie. The idea of anyone loving Magpie was maybe the most surprising thing that I had learned on this side of the Tree. Almost as surprising as the idea of Fathom loving someone. Maybe they were perfect for each other. But it sounded like, in the end, Magpie had stolen her heart.

I opened my mouth to say something about Magpie. But I hadn't even talked to Margot about her. Did Fathom deserve to know that her so-called love was still stealing at Whittaker? Would it make her feel better or worse? And did I really care how Fathom felt? Things had shifted since the Enforcer's appearance. She had been the kindest of the Robbers so far, but if she really loved Magpie, she probably wouldn't love the fact that I had almost frozen her in my world.

I let the opportunity pass. I let her keep talking without saying a word.

"I can't tell you what to do with Jagger. But I'd be careful. Robbers don't fall in love. Robber Rules."

I wanted to correct her again and tell her that I didn't love Jagger, but she could see the red in my cheeks at the mention of his name and she could probably hear the quickening of my pulse or maybe even my thoughts themselves.

"Out! It's magic time!" Howl entered, singing and pushing Fathom out.

I tried to push Fathom out of my head like Howl had pushed her out of the room.

"Now let's make you one of us," Howl said as she ran a hand

over her punk-rock Mohawk. "Why did you wait so long to do this? I did it the second I got here."

"When you got here? From where?" I demanded.

"Robbers live in the present," she countered, attempting to squash my curiosity with another Robber Rule. She quickly changed between faces to illustrate her point. Howl traded her pretty pink hair for lavender. Her full lips for thinner ones. Her violet eyes for gray ones. The effect was fascinating and a little disturbing, and as her identity shifted and her usual lightning tattoo faded away, I glimpsed a large birthmark on her cheek. "I can fix your scar, too," Howl said, looking at the white spiderweb of marks that still graced my arm.

I shook my head.

"I was touched by your King—thus the permanent reminder. A lot of us were.

"When we were pretty young, a group of us got caught selling our wares a little too close to the palace. The Lights were not on our side that day, and the King happened upon us. He was feeling generous."

"Oh, Howl . . ."

She switched faces again, a pretty heart-shaped one with darker eyes rimmed in purple kohl and studded instead with crystal lashes, but the expression on it said she was done telling the rest of her story about her interaction with the King.

"You should ask Jagger to show you his scar. Rumor has it he had some one-on-one time with the King."

"Have you seen it?" I asked.

"I haven't. But Margot has. Well, if you won't let me fix your scar, at least let me cover it. See?" she said, and pointed to a tattoo of a snowflake where my scar once was.

"I love it. Thank you."

But I felt the familiar scratching of my scar and covered it before Howl could see it light up.

Jagger had been hurt by my father? That was another little fact he conveniently left out. The list was getting longer by the second.

"Now, what to wear?" Howl pondered, whisking me off to a room she called the Closet.

Outfits that seemed to suit every type of person in Algid hung from racks inside the deep, brightly lit room. There were maid and soldier uniforms, as well as some very uncomfortable-looking corsets. There was an outfit for every kind of heist.

Howl reached into the rack and pulled out a corset whose bones were held together with as little lace as possible. Also, the bones looked like they might be actual bones.

Howl's new eyes flashed, a challenge.

"Exactly where are we going?" I asked.

"Where the wild things are, Princess," she said.

As I took the corset, I realized that we weren't just Robbers; we were actors. I wondered about Jagger and the role he was playing. I wondered if I'd ever see his real face . . . and if I'd ever know the real Jagger.

28

THE MISSION WAS IN a speakeasy called Rime in Dessa. The coins we were to obtain came in the form of gold coins bearing a picture of the Duchess herself. Apparently, the invitations were in such demand that once received, they never left your person. Of course, unless they were stolen from you.

There was a disco ball made of snow in the center of the ceiling. It throbbed with fluorescent light that was just a beat out of sync with the music.

The place was Algid's answer to a nightclub. There were giant snow globes with girls in high heels dancing in them. The gaunt girls' white-lined eyes seemed vacant.

Howl whispered, "They dance until they die."

At first I thought it was hyperbole—another attempt to scare the newest Robber. But seeing the ribs of one of the dancers poking through her sheer dress, I thought maybe Howl was telling the truth. I couldn't help but make a comparison between my life and theirs. Whittaker had its horrors, but whatever happened to those girls inside and outside those globes made me shudder.

"Why?"

"You saw what happened in Stygian. They police the wrong things here."

Howl puffed up her rainbow-colored hair and puckered up her lips, getting ready for her set. She'd been hired as a singer for the night. And she was ready. Her barely there dress had a web of blue strips that covered her strategically, and she wore a pair of boots that laced up to her thighs.

I knew this was a mission. I knew it was a scary box to check off in order to get me closer to what I wanted. But it was also my first night out, ever. The part of me that was excited about my first real night out was quickly squashed by the sight of the girl's ribs.

The other Robbers were dispersed around the room, but I could not recognize them. I looked for errant details, such as the wrong shoes or the wrong stitching on a dress. But the Robbers were aided by magic. Their game was flawless. I was the only one fidgeting in my corset and tugging at the hem of my tiny skirt.

Jagger led me out to the dance floor. He took my right hand in his left and then slid his other hand to the small of my back. I felt myself inhale deeply again. I tried to cover, but he noticed everything.

The plan was for us to garner the attention of one of the VIPs, who sat up in the balcony. They were the high rollers.

The other girls made quick work of it, pairing off with the

men one by one. Maybe it was their superior, magically enhanced dancing skills, or maybe it was the length of their skirts. In Fathom's case, it was just sheer manipulation.

"Watch and learn," Fathom said before slipping into the throng of people. She found her mark, the friend of the man she was talking to.

The face she wore was pretty, but it was more than that that drew her mark to her. She was having a dialogue with one man, but having a completely nonverbal conversation with her mark at the same time. She caught his eye with a single glance and didn't break her gaze. When she touched his hand, her mark tapped his friend on the shoulder, sending him away.

Could I do that? I wondered, watching Fathom from the dance floor. Jagger followed my gaze and then spun me into him.

"You don't have to be Fathom to do this," he whispered.

I didn't have to be myself, either. I remembered *The End of Almost.* I remembered how Rebecca reinvented herself on almost a yearly basis. I just needed to do the same. Quickly.

I had never been shy. But I was more a blunt force like my snow than a seductive one. Still, I tried. And the new face helped the pretense. I caught a glimpse of myself in one of the mirrored columns that punctuated the dance floor.

The eyes that stared back at me were smaller and an electric blue. My hair and lashes were triple the length of my own, and tiny crystals decorated every tip. The lips had a more pronounced bow and a smile that was stretched wide with magic.

Even Jagger was hiding behind a different face for this mission. His eyes were a different color and his skin was darker, but his eyes had a spark and his smile had a place that stopped between happy and knowing. I think I would recognize him anywhere. I still couldn't pick out all the Robber girls from the crowd, even though I'd gotten a glimpse of them back at the Claret.

I spun away from him and exaggerated my dancing and my sense of abandon for the benefit of the audience on the balcony. Or at least I thought I did. It felt good to be here. I was outside Whittaker. I was dancing in a club with kids my own age. Music was blasting in my eardrums. This was me doing something kids do. This was me doing something normal. Except for one thing: the part where I was distracting creepy guys so the Robber girls could get their part of the job done.

One of the men on the balcony finally nodded at me. I let go of Jagger's hand and climbed the stairs to the VIP area.

This was a test. I knew that. I had failed many of Dr. Harris's tests before—sometimes on purpose. But this test mattered. It would affect my ability to stay with the Robbers. As long as I was with them, they were my very best chance of getting Bale and getting home.

"Do you know who I am?" the man from the balcony asked, not bothering to stand up from his couch.

"Someone important," I replied coyly.

The guy was some sort of dignitary and a definite creep. I could see it in the way he treated his people. I could see it in the way he took up space, as if he owned the air around him. Objectively, he was handsome. Chiseled jaw. Shiny black hair. Piercing eyes. But he was less attractive with every word and every move he made. He berated the bare-chested guy who delivered a bottle filled with blue bubbly on ice. He leaned back on a sofa made of a pelt of pale-gray fur and stretched out his arms as if he were waiting for company. Namely me.

My mission was to distract him. But the idea of being any closer to him did not appeal to me.

"Aren't you a pretty thing?" he said to me as I reached his couch.

Compliments didn't come my way often. Even though I abhorred this man, I felt my cheeks flush at his words. I reminded myself that Rebecca Gershon would take the praise as a given. I raised my head haughtily and tossed the weight of my new, magically extended hair.

"Shall we take a walk?"

I pointed down to my ridiculously high heels, which weren't the best for walking.

"I have something for that," the creep said, fishing for a bottle of magic.

I shook my head.

"You're not one of those Eluddites, I hope. You know, the kind who don't use magic?"

I laughed as if he had said the funniest thing in Algid.

"Hardly . . . I just like to have all my senses. I don't want to miss anything."

"I think I'd like you for my collection," the creep said, pointing to the girls in the snow globes.

Anger brewed in me. I thought about freezing the glass to free the girls suspended from the ceiling, but I knew I couldn't or they'd fall to the ground.

Luckily, I didn't have to do anything. The globes began to descend on their own, which annoyed the creep. He yelled something in the direction of his followers until I distracted him with a spill of my drink.

"Stupid girl. You'll regret that," he warned, making a grab for my wrist.

At that exact moment, Howl hit a piercing note that echoed through the place. Glasses began to shatter all at once. The thick glass of the globes cracked, too, and the girls pushed their way out like chicks from eggs. Everyone in the club began to scatter for the exits.

The creep opened his mouth to call for the bouncer, and I saw my opportunity.

"Stop right there," I demanded.

The creep laughed, but then he stopped abruptly as the edges of his coat frosted over and the cloth hardened, stiff as a board.

It wasn't exactly as I had planned. Everything could have gone terribly, terribly wrong. But like Margot had suggested, I focused my energy on the objects around the person instead of the person itself . . . and it worked! I had frozen the jacket instead of the jerk of a man inside it. And the terrified man didn't dare move.

My confidence brimmed as I stepped away from him. I had used my frost to keep him in his place. For the first time, I had truly controlled my magic.

I grabbed the coin and showed it to him. It was against Robber Rules to show the mark what you stole from them. The point was to get away clean. But that ship had sailed when Howl screamed.

The man laughed when he saw the coin. "Cinderella wants to go to the ball."

"Nice doing business with you," I said quietly. "If you scream, if you so much as move, then I will come back and freeze the rest of you."

When I hit the door, Jagger was already beside me.

"Isn't this the part where you tell me how great I did?" I said to Jagger as we raced out of the club.

But he was not smiling.

"You didn't listen to my instructions."

"I improvised."

"Robber Rules . . ."

"Versus results? I got results."

I could see the intense bit of a smile forming underneath the approbation as he retorted, "The idea is to get in and out without anyone knowing we're here. Now, the King's guard will be looking for us. For the girl with the power to freeze. He's already on your trail. Now you've brought him a step closer to all of us."

The hair on the back of my neck perked up. Jagger shivered as if he could feel the cold, too.

"I didn't think of that."

"Next time, think."

"So there will be a next time?" I said to him.

He didn't smile fully, but I could tell by the light in his eyes that he wanted to.

Two of the Robber girls met us outside the club. They were

carrying a snow-globe dancer. Her eyes were hollow. She was proof of my father's wrongs.

"This is Cadence," Jagger explained as her face morphed into someone new. She had short blue hair and a pretty, soft face that was stained with tears.

"She's one of us."

"I didn't know it was a rescue," I said.

The Robbers worked so hard to pretend they didn't care. But it seemed every time a Robber Rule was broken it was so they could help one another.

"This was a robbery, like any other. Lucky break that Howl hit that high note," Jagger downplayed, but his voice was laced with a hint of a smile.

The take for the night was the girl they were carrying out in their arms.

The bouncer let us pass, not recognizing the girl and her new face.

29

"ARE YOU GOING TO tell me how I screwed up this time?" Jagger said after we were safely back at the Claret.

"Not this time," I said cheerfully. I had passed the test. I had actually completed my mission. I was one step closer to going home. So why wasn't I more ecstatic?

The Robber girls had poured out their wares on the floor of the common room like the one Halloween before I went to Whittaker.

Queen Margot had smiled and nodded, but then turned away and looked at the forest, which was lavender today. Her expression was a somber one. Cadence wasn't enough. The Duchess's mirror was what she wanted now. And the other two pieces of the King's mirror. But to what end? I had told myself I didn't need to know the story of the Robber girls, of Margot, but the more I knew them, the more I wanted to know.

The girls abandoned their magic treasure and tended to

Cadence. Some took their vials and used them to restore her beauty. Others brought her food and clothing and whispered soothing words. Fathom inspected her like the scientist that she was. I looked away, feeling like I was spying on something private. Something that I was outside of.

"Is she going to be okay? What happened to her?" I asked Jagger.

"'Okay' is relative. Algid is not always kind," he said vaguely.

Cadence's color had returned. She didn't have the same glow that the other girls had, but the sickly gray I'd seen under Dessa's snow-globe strobe light was already gone.

"You killed it in there," Jagger said brightly to me, raising his arms in a victory cheer.

Jagger's shirt rose up, revealing something I hadn't seen before. A long, jagged scar ran the length of his muscled torso. Was this the scar from my father?

"What happened to you? Why didn't you tell me that King Lazar hurt you?" I demanded, changing the subject. But it was essentially the same one. They knew my story. I didn't know theirs. I was a Robber in name only.

He opened his mouth to say something and hesitated.

"So help me, if you say Robber Rules, I will freeze you where you stand."

Jagger's voice was quiet but steady. "It's mine, Snow. It may have been given to me by the King, but it's mine to carry. And to talk about or not talk about."

I took it in. He was right. He didn't owe me his story because he knew mine. But it didn't stop me from wanting to hear it.

"I liked freezing that guy. I saw what he was and I thought he deserved it. He scared those girls. I liked making him scared," I blurted.

Jagger knew who I was, and I could actually tell him things that I could not say to Kai—or anyone else, really.

"I see what King Lazar did to you, and I want to scare him, too," I said, meaning it.

Jagger hastily tucked his shirt in. I stopped him, wanting him to know that his scar wasn't anything to be ashamed of or anything to cover up. Lazar was the one who should bear the shame. My hand was on the center of his chest. I had closed the gap between us.

"I want to scare him, too. For you," he said.

He took a step closer and touched my scar with one hand, and he brushed my hair back with the other. He looked intently at me. So intently that I completely forgot about the scar and my father. I heard myself sharply inhale. All I wanted was to be with him.

"You still think that you kiss people and they go insane?"

"Something like that," I countered. Bale wasn't crazy because of me. But he was forever tied to me. He was kidnapped because of me. And on and on . . . I was danger. I was someone who could break things and people with a single touch.

"Maybe we should test it again . . ." Jagger leaned in toward me.

We were so close that I could feel the heat radiating from his body. All it would take was another inch for our lips to meet. When he closed his eyes, he looked so vulnerable. So beautiful.

I remembered who I was and what my kiss could do. What I could do. I pulled away in time.

We had been inching toward the kiss since we'd met and I'd stopped our momentum. I felt an ache in my chest for what we had missed. For a second, Jagger's face fell, too. But he recovered with a smile.

"So you like me enough not to turn my heart to ice? I'm touched," Jagger joked.

"It's not funny," I said, feeling anger at my edges. I had not frozen Kai, but I could have. His joke had come a little too close to the truth.

"You are not crazy, Snow. You were just lied to. You are not evil. You have magic. It's not a curse. It's a gift. I may be a liar, but I know this much is true." Jagger said the words like he was absolving me of my guilt and my fear—just by telling me the truth I think I'd been waiting to hear my entire life.

When he leaned in again, I was not sure I could resist him.

He kissed me on the cheek. It was as close as I could let him get to me. But he made it no secret that he wanted to be closer.

30

OUR NEXT MISSION WAS the important one: stealing the King's mirror piece from the Duchess. I'd never met this cousin and had agreed to rob her anyway. Aside from the King, she was my only other family in this world. And unlike the King, she had never done anything to me.

What will Queen Margot do when I bring back the Duchess's piece of the mirror? I wondered. It wasn't worth anything without the other two pieces, according to the River Witch. I suspected she had a plan to get the other two pieces, but as long as it didn't involve me, I didn't really care. This was the last thing I needed to do before the Claret would help me free Bale and bring him home.

It was time. I found Margot in the Bottle Room.

♛

She offered me a green vial. "It's a new etiquette spell. It gives you instant manners. You're going to need it where you're going. The

Duchess is royalty, and even though you are in name, well . . .
Let's just say you could use some help in that department."

I shook my head. She wasn't wrong about my manners. But
there was no way I was taking that vial.

"This heist won't work unless you do exactly what I ask when
I ask it," she said.

"This heist won't work unless you tell me everything."

I had spent so much time in the dark that I didn't want to go
into this mission blind. I needed to know everything that would
happen . . . that could possibly happen.

"You are a Robber now. We will go over the plan at length
with the others tonight, but please ask away."

"What exactly do you want me to do?"

"I want you to help us get the mirror from the Duchess's
palace. It's that simple. And that hard."

"But who is she? Aside from my cousin."

"She is very graceful. Her people love her."

"And is she very evil?"

"From what I have heard, there is not an ounce of evil in the
girl. Apparently, that trait skips a generation." She laughed; I
didn't.

I wanted her to know I was serious. "If she's not evil, then
why would she keep the mirror for the King?"

"The Duchess is keeping it from the King. Not *for* him,
we believe, but nobody really knows what her true motives are.
This is a very dangerous thing since she lives by his mercy.
The Duchess is your age, but in our land that is the marrying
age. We are crashing the Penultimate Ball."

"The Penultimate Ball?"

"It is the ball before the Last Ball. After this ball, the Duchess will have met every unmarried man in Algid. She must choose a husband, or her parents will be less than pleased."

For the millionth time since I'd crossed the Tree, I realized that Algid was not like the fairy tales. My cousin, whoever she was, was being forced into her happily ever after.

"You will attend the ball. We will be with you every step of the way—except the last step, of course. You must find where she has hidden the mirror on your own. With a bit of luck, your magic will help you find it. Whatever happens, don't get caught. We've already tried this once and failed."

"You don't know where she keeps it? What kind of heist is this?" I sighed. This sounded about as imprecise as the prophecy.

"Any more questions?"

"What will you do with the mirror, exactly?"

"The King's mirror piece will give us enough power to move the Claret forever. We will be protected until the end of time."

Margot raised her red eyebrows as if to ask if that were all.

"So let me get this straight," I said. "You want me to break into my cousin's house and rob her of her mirror piece. This mirror piece belonged to the King, my father, who's trying to kill me. And the last time you tried to break in, your Robbers got caught . . . ," I recounted, realizing how completely insane this was. Knowing more had not exactly calmed my fears.

"Precisely," she said with a smile.

All the mirrors in the Bottle Room frosted over at once as I felt the enormity of what we were attempting.

"Soon, you will be done with your part of the deal and then it is our turn. May I offer you some free advice?"

I shrugged.

"I can't pretend to know what happened to you on the other side. And I can't pretend to know how to wield snow. But I know from experience. From mine and my girls. And even Jagger's. You don't have to forgive, but you have to move on. Everyone here—we are moving on from something. Everyone here has chosen this place," Margot said simply.

"Or they didn't have anywhere else to go," I countered.

"Sometimes, my dear, that is still a choice. You don't have to embrace the Robber life. But embrace something. This entire land has been ravaged by what happened a long time ago, but we do not dwell; we live. Sometimes we have to steal our future. In my experience, it is never given freely. No one is handing it out. You and your Bale? You could have a place here at the Claret."

"We are going back to New York," I said firmly.

"Very well. You will be missed. By one Robber in particular more than most."

"Thank you," I said, surprised by her sentimentality. Perhaps all the daughter talk was getting to her.

"I wasn't talking about myself," she countered with a laugh.

And in a flash, I knew exactly who she was talking about. And the thought made me blush.

31

THINKING ABOUT DOING SOMETHING and actually doing it are two different things.

Kayla Blue had said that on *The End of Almost* when she was on trial for murdering her husband. But we weren't just *thinking* about robbing the palace. We were actually doing it. As I stood in the Throne Room alongside my Robber sisters and Jagger, it finally felt real. And a lot more involved than our Dessa raid.

I looked down at the gilded table covered in architectural drawings of the Duchess's castle. We all crowded around the table with Margot at the head.

Markings appeared all over the plans. There were circles where we were supposed to go. Margot moved the ink around by raising her hands. On closer inspection, I could see that there were beautifully drawn representations of each of us on the paper. As she spoke and instructed the group where to be and when, the drawings shifted as well. Mesmerized, I watched as the ink drawing of me moved from the ballroom up the stairs to the Duchess's bedroom.

I couldn't help but notice that there were more blue markings than ones of any other color. The Duchess's guards would be everywhere.

"What's that?" I asked, pointing to a tower on the map.

"We have people in there," Jagger explained.

I squinted and saw drawings of tiny Robber girls behind the barred window of the tower. I reached out and touched the window, feeling for the Robber girls stuck there. A tiny room with no way out.

Jagger caught my eye with a small smile, bucking me up and reminding me of the no-sentimentality Robber Rule.

"We may as well get them out while we're there," Margot said leisurely. And a murmur of assent went around the table.

"I thought you weren't in the business of saving people? First Cadence and now them? Robber Rules . . . ," I challenged.

How much is Robber bravado, and how much is true? I wondered, looking around this place where everyone claimed to be out for themselves. At the end of the day, it seemed like they wanted to help one another. They just didn't want to admit it.

"Princess, you will go with Jagger in disguise into the palace and mingle with the guests. The rest of the Robbers will be there in disguise, as well. Jagger will keep the Duchess entertained, and you will sneak upstairs, find and open the vault, and get the mirror."

Snow formed between my fingers at the thought of putting my hand in the lock again.

"How will I find it?"

"The prophecy says it will reveal itself to you. But I am guessing it will be in the Duchess's quarters. People keep their treasures close.

"Then we will double back with the Robbers after you return to the ballroom and find Jagger."

I must not have nodded vigorously enough because Howl was taunting me again.

"Maybe the Princess has a problem robbing her family?" Howl asked.

"Why would it be a problem? She's a stranger. I don't know her from the Fire Witch."

A laugh went up, and we went back to planning. The other Robbers seemed to accept this.

I followed up with a question. "I still don't understand how the Duchess got a piece of the King's mirror in the first place. Why would one of the coven give it to a regular human?"

"The way of the witch is the exception to every rule, I'm afraid. Unpredictable as snow itself. We don't know how or why. We only know the mirror is at the Duchess's because we stumbled upon it when we were robbing the place a few months ago."

Margot said, "Hence the prisoners . . . who you may as well save. The mirror has an effect on all magic. And ours went a little haywire that night."

"If I didn't know better, I'd say that Robbers have a lot in common with heroes."

"Then you don't know us, either!" screamed Howl.

32

EVEN THOUGH MARGOT AND the Robber girls had a plan, they were leaving nothing to chance. Howl took charge of the coins we'd taken from Dessa. What was more interesting was the fact that she was adding magic to the coins—though she wouldn't say what for.

Meanwhile, the other Robber girls were busy trying out new potions of their own. There was a magic bottle to make you smarter and one that made you remind the mark of their favorite thing—anything from a tea biscuit to a field of flowers to a pile of gold bars.

When I wasn't working on my robbing skills, I'd sneak away from the Claret and work on my snow. This time, I had managed to channel my power into making ice arrows.

"Snow," Fathom called. "Look at this."

"Please don't tell Margot. She wants me to suppress it. But I need to figure it out."

"I won't tell. It's amazing. Almost as amazing as what I have to show you."

She showed me a little bottle of snow and a vial containing blood.

I guessed it was mine.

The snow was moving around.

"Tell me that isn't part of a Snow Beast," I said.

"No, it's a mini Snow Puppy."

A second later the Snow Puppy formed. It was kind of adorable except for the giant claws and teeth.

"Now watch this."

Fathom took a drop of blood and dripped it into the bottle. At first, the Snow Puppy repelled, moving upward. But a second later, it attacked the drop of blood. The Snow Puppy slammed itself against the glass sides of the bottle and then exploded into a flurry of flakes.

"Um, how does this help us? I already know that Snow Beasts are never going to be my BFFs."

Fathom looked at me blankly.

"Best friends forever?" I said.

"I think you can freeze Snow Beasts—their hearts and limbs and brains. Your power, once you unlock it, is limitless."

"Well, that would be something, wouldn't it?"

"It would. It could help us defeat the King."

"How?"

"I'm not sure yet, but I think I'm on to something."

We began to walk back to the Claret. The world went black again.

I could suddenly see myself in the common room at Whittaker. It was Bale's point of view again.

"Maybe in the spring," I said.

I knew immediately what memory this was. Bale had asked me if we could run away. And I had said, "Maybe in the spring."

He had stood by me every time I had done something awful at the institute, without blinking an eye. But the one time he had asked me for something, I had said those words.

It wasn't that I didn't want to go. It was that I didn't know what our monsters would do outside their cages. I thought Bale would burn something down. I thought I would do something equally awful. But we were out now. Just like Bale wanted. Only we couldn't be farther apart. And Algid wasn't burning. And my monster, my snow, had taken a whole other form than either of us could imagine.

There was another flash, and I saw Bale's little white house again. This time from the outside. I glimpsed a reflection of teenage Bale in the glass windows staring back at me. Not afraid, smiling with a kind of mad glee.

Another flash. And it was the triangular room. Through the window, I saw the North Lights, which looked almost gray. This time he was quiet. He didn't say my name. He didn't say anything at all.

"Snow," Fathom called, and I opened my eyes.

I was lying flat on my back in the snow.

"Hey, you just fainted or something?"

"I'm okay," I said. But I wondered if Bale was.

👑

When we got back to the Claret, Margot was waiting for us.

"What is it?" I demanded. Having seen Bale again, my patience with her had become threadbare. I was mad at myself for not getting to Bale yet. I was mad at myself for how close I had gotten to Jagger.

She ushered us inside. She wanted us to look at the plans for the heist again.

"You look pale, Your Highness," she assessed.

I pushed past her into the Claret without answering.

👑

That night, I fell into a deep sleep. If I didn't know any better, I would have thought I had drunk one of Margot's sleeping potions.

Somehow I was in Jagger's room. It looked like mine, only his bedding was a dark navy ash. And along one wall was his personal stash of magic bottles.

"You know, when I imagined you in my bedroom, it wasn't exactly like this," Jagger quipped, suddenly beside me.

I whipped around to face him. "How could you?" I asked.

"Look, whatever I did, I am sorry," he said lightly. "Robber Rules, by the way. You should not be here unless I invited you. But let's consider you invited."

He moved toward me flirtatiously.

My breath went shallow. And my heart was in my ears.

"This doesn't feel like a dream. You seem so real," I said with wonder.

"That's partly true," Jagger said smugly. "You are dreaming, and I am in your dream. I took this."

Jagger held up a shiny silver bottle and continued, "This magic lets me walk inside your dreams."

I had wanted to kiss him. And I had cared enough not to. And now this. A betrayal. I had not drunk a potion. He had.

"You were worried about kissing me. We can do anything you want here. No consequences."

He put his hand around my waist and pulled me to him. I felt myself melt the tiniest bit, but I could not let go of the questions as they took hold.

"You did this back in New York, didn't you? You inserted yourself in my dreams. You manipulated them. You manipulated me to make me come here, didn't you?"

"Do you really want to waste the time we have doing this, when we could be not talking?" he asked, leaning in.

"You were right when you said that you didn't understand me. You are such a liar."

"'We breathe out the lies; we stutter the truth . . .' An old Robber proverb," he said, smiling wider. "It means that it's easier to lie than not to."

"For you."

"For most people. They lie to make others feel better. Whatever it is, we lie."

"I don't." I paused and then added, "At least I didn't before I came here."

"It's easy to be good in a bubble, Princess. You were in the Whittaker bubble, but our bubble burst the day you were born."

I felt a flutter somewhere inside me, like I'd swallowed a gazillion butterflies. I wanted to be immune to Jagger. But wanting did not make it so.

I felt a drop of cold water on one of my arms. I looked up with dread. The ceiling of Jagger's room was covered in ice. The ice was racing across the surface, dripping down in long, deadly icicles. And it was heading toward Jagger.

I walked out of the room onto his balcony. Was there anyone I could trust? Was there anyplace I could actually be safe? I had no idea how Jagger truly felt. If he was on my side or if he would ultimately betray me. He had said as much when I first arrived here. So why was this such a surprise? Why did I care? And why did I want to kiss him, knowing all that?

He followed me out to the balcony.

"I'm sorry for invading your dreams."

I touched the banister. It was vibrating along with my pulse.

"You should go," I suggested. "We should talk when you're not in my dreams."

And when I don't want to freeze you to death, I thought.

"You know what this means? It's exactly like Margot said. It's your emotions that fuel your magic. When you first got here, you were so far past caring. You were so hurt by everything that had happened and everything that you'd learned. But now you've started to care again. You care about me, Princess. Otherwise you wouldn't be angry enough to hurt me."

"Get out," I said quietly. I knew he was right, and I also knew that if he didn't leave, I would tear the whole room, maybe the whole castle, apart.

"I will do as you ask. But not for the reason you think," Jagger replied.

"You gave me the nightmares—and then you put yourself in my dreams so you could save me."

He shook his head. "No, the nightmares were already there. I just made it so you could see them and so that you could save yourself."

"So all this is for me . . . right?"

"You were in no way, shape, or form prepared for what is to come—for being in this land. I was trying to help."

"I don't believe you anymore. You lured me here from my world so you and Margot could get the mirror."

"It's what we do," Jagger said unapologetically. "You were the biggest get of all."

"How did you know I would go along with it? How did you know I wouldn't just go more crazy?"

"You were never crazy. Most people listen to the man of their dreams," he said.

"Don't do that," I warned. He pushed and teased every minute.

I had tried singing and yoga and counting and breathing, but the thing that made me most calm was Bale. He was brave enough to walk through the tornado that was my anger and take my hand. His touch was enough to return all my nerve endings to their normal positions. And now he was gone.

Bale and I were both storms. Maybe that was why he could always reach me. Maybe that was why we were each other's calm in the center of what we were. But that changed with a kiss, and

I could not figure out what to do about our reverse fairy tale. What if Jagger held the key? What if Jagger had started all this and not me?

"Please tell me it wasn't me that did that to Bale. Please say it was you."

I felt a little hope push in beside my anger. I was searching for the one thing that might make what Jagger did a little bit less horrible.

He shook his head. "I didn't take him, and neither did the Robbers."

"What about Bale being sick, being crazy? Tell me that you did that to make me not want him anymore."

"I had nothing to do with his going crazy. But I still don't think you did, either. Kisses don't do that on either side of the Tree. I've never heard of anything or anyone having that effect."

I thought about my kiss with Kai and my relief when nothing happened to him afterward. And a tiny part of me wondered what would happen if I did kiss Jagger, even though every brain cell told me not to.

"But I'm not like anyone else."

"No, you're not."

There was too much affection, too much *like* in the way he said it. I didn't know if it was true or another lie.

"Go. Now," I ordered, stepping back into his room.

Jagger's face fell.

"If you ever cared for me at all . . . Leave. Now!" I repeated.

By the time he cleared the door, the icy balcony cracked free and began to fall.

When I woke in my own bed, the sheets were as cold as ice. I sat up and a single icy teardrop fell from one of my eyes. A memory of the dream came flooding back.

"Regardless of what you think of me, I will keep my word," Jagger had said. "I will help you get what you want. You will have your Bale, and you can return to your land. And you will never have to see me again. I promise."

"Robber Rules?"

"No, I promise on you and me."

"There is no you and me," I had countered.

Jagger had smiled a sad smile. "Look at you. We made you a Robber yet."

His words echoed in my head. *We breathe out the lies; we stutter the truth.*

33

I COULDN'T SLEEP. MY head was full of Jagger. And I couldn't
bear the idea of his being in another dream of mine. It was hard
enough to resist him in real life. I walked the halls of the Claret,
impatient for the Duchess's Ball, to rescue Bale, and to go home.

Through the windows, I saw the ever-changing colors of the
trees. Tonight the bark was a creepy yellow against the dim night
sky. The North Lights were even more faded than usual and
emanated a hazy soft focus of washed-out watercolor, rather
than the electric luminescence of my first evening in Algid. Time
was almost up.

Apparently I wasn't alone in not being able to sleep. There
was a light on in Fathom's lab. I knocked and went inside.

Howl and Fathom were on opposite sides of one of the slabs.
They were bent over something. When they looked up, their
faces burnished with more color than their magical blush alone.
What had I interrupted?

"Hey, can I hang out here for a bit?" I plowed on, wondering if this was a romantic moment I'd marched in on or something else.

"We shouldn't let her stay," Howl said, glancing nervously down at the table. There was only a stack of empty slides in front of them. I didn't see what all the fuss was about.

"Queen Margot won't like it?" I asked.

"No, I just can't have anyone fainting while I work."

"I'm not a fainter," I declared.

"Let's see if you can say that after," Howl said, disappearing in a blink.

"Don't mind her," Fathom said, turning around to reveal a supersharp scalpel that caught the light.

"What's the knife for?" I asked, trying to keep trepidation out of my voice. Despite all my bravado, I worried I might actually faint.

"You have already graduated from petty thievery. Tonight you get upgraded to kidnapping."

"What?"

"We have to kidnap the people that we will replace at the ball."

"And what do we plan on doing with them?"

"I'm going to cut their faces off."

After a beat, she laughed.

Fathom motioned behind her, and a light turned on. Lying on the slabs at the back of the room were bodies covered by thin white sheets. I noticeably twitched when the sheets moved. The people she had already captured were still alive!

"Don't worry. They're just sleeping. Usually we use the dead and take their faces. But this is an invitation-only ball. So we need specific faces."

"Oh," I said lamely, wishing that I had stayed in bed and dealt with dreams of Jagger rather than come here. It would have been a lot less scary.

Howl returned with a dramatic poof of smoke and an entire carriage. Inside were two people dressed in all their finery. The woman was leaning against the windows. The man was desperately trying to lock the doors.

"You couldn't have left the carriage outside the lab, Howl?" Fathom complained.

Howl shrugged, whispered something I didn't understand, and threw open the door to the carriage.

"May I present Lord Rafe Mach and his wife, the Countess Darby Mach."

The man stomped out of the carriage, his eyes scanning the room for a way out and sizing us up. The Countess arched her neck upward and held her skirt as she daintily stepped into the lab, feigning grace in the middle of everything.

Howl pointed to two chairs, and they obediently sat down. With a wave of her arm, she and the carriage were gone.

"Don't worry," Fathom reassured me. "They won't remember a thing."

"Will it hurt?" I asked.

The woman looked up at me, suddenly frightened.

"Like a Snow Beast," Fathom deadpanned before breaking into a smile. "But I'm not a monster," she said defensively, and offered the couple two vials filled with a light-green liquid. "Drink this."

They didn't take them.

"Your choice, but if I were you I'd rather not feel what I'm going to do next."

The couple exchanged a look before the man grabbed one of the vials and gulped down the liquid without even a hint of hesitation.

Fathom looked at the Countess almost sympathetically. "Once I had a guy steal the sleeping potion from his girlfriend. It wasn't pretty."

The Countess spat at Fathom before downing the potion.

Fathom shrugged, wiping away the saliva. "And they say Robbers have no manners . . ."

Within seconds the couple fell into a deep dead-to-the-world sleep, slouching against each other.

"What happens next?" I asked.

"Help me get them up on the tables. I have got to remember to do that first next time," Fathom said, irritated.

Together, we lifted the Lord, who was remarkably heavy.

"I hope you like the Countess. Because her face will be yours. Once you put on the face, the spell lasts until midnight. You and Jagger will take their places at the ball. You'll sneak upstairs, and your magic should lead you to the mirror."

"Why me? Why not one of you? You have so much more experience with heists. What if I freeze the ballroom or something?" I worried aloud.

"All the better for us." She laughed.

"I'm serious."

"Always so serious, Princess. You have a special relationship with the mirror. When you get to the mirror, it will only reveal itself to you. In pieces, the mirror can only reflect back a certain amount of power. Legend has it that if the pieces are united, then the power is a million fold. The prophecy says that whoever reunites the mirror controls Algid's destiny. We just want to control our own."

"Don't you already do that? Jagger suggested that you want to get back at the King."

"There's that. But I like to think beyond that. A different life. A better life. One in which we never would have to steal again."

"But will there be enough magic for me to get past the Snow King and find Bale?" I said out loud, reminding her and myself of Queen Margot's promise.

"I don't know how much power the single piece will give you, but we will make sure you are reunited with Bale."

Fathom got to work. I helped her lift the Countess onto one of the tables, and I looked at the face that I would be wearing.

Fathom approached the woman, scalpel in hand. She made a tiny incision on the lady's cheek, removing a bit of skin that she placed on a piece of glass. Effortlessly she slid the glass under an odd contraption that looked like a giant microscope. A beam of light focused down onto the glass.

The piece of skin began to grow.

"This light is powered by a mirror," Fathom explained.

The bit of skin soon became the size of a washcloth and then facial features began to stretch over invisible cartilage. When the process was complete, a perfect mask of the Countess's face stared up at us, unblinking.

"That's incredible!" It was creepy and miraculous at once. All the years, all the needles and the blood at Whittaker had left me not squeamish. I had worn a face of another before, but I had not seen it being made.

"How does it go on?" I wondered out loud.

"Magic," Fathom said simply. "This lucky couple will sleep it off, and you have until midnight tomorrow until the face returns to its proper owner."

"And what happens if I don't get back in time?"

"The mask disappears at midnight and turns to dust. But don't you worry. You'll make it," Fathom said.

I couldn't help but think about Cinderella, and if Fathom was my Fairy Godmother, I had no idea what to expect next.

34

THERE WAS A FORMAL dining room in the Claret, complete with mismatched chairs, a ginormous stone tablet that served as a tabletop, and candelabras that lit themselves the second somebody sat down.

The Robber girls didn't bother with formalities, maybe because of the upcoming heist or because they never stood on ceremony for anything other than magical rituals. There was no dinner bell or announcement. The girls just popped in to eat whenever they wanted.

Howl and I found ourselves at the table at the same time the next day. She informed me that tonight's meal had come from one of the local restaurants in town. Even the Robbers' food was borrowed.

I took a bite of purple pasta. It melted in my mouth with a delicate, sweet, almost chocolaty taste. The minty ale concoction I chased it down with came from the speakeasy we'd robbed.

I shoveled it all down, eager to get back to work and away from Howl.

As if on cue, Howl leaned back in her chair and asked, "How is she? Fathom won't ask you. But I will."

"Who?"

"Anthicate."

"Magpie?"

I had not talked about her, and no one, not even Fathom, had asked me about her. I had spent the better part of two years at Whittaker with Magpie. Aside from whatever information Jagger had gathered about her during his visits, I was the sole possessor of the few details about what had happened to their runaway Robber.

"Magpie and I weren't exactly friends," I admitted.

Howl nodded as if that were no surprise to her. "She broke Fathom's heart. She breaks everyone's hearts."

"So you're not sad that I'm here and she's not," I said, knowing I had taken Magpie's place in the Claret.

Howl smiled.

"I wouldn't trade her for a million snow princesses. But she has her path and we have ours."

I sensed Howl wanted their paths to cross again. But what she did next took me by surprise.

Howl produced a vial on a chain around her neck from her ample bosom and downed it. When she caught my gaze, she rooted around in her pocket for another vial and offered it to me.

"What does it do?" I asked, wondering if the liquid somehow took the edge off missing Magpie.

"Whatever you want it to do," she answered.

I shook my head, and Howl studied my face as if trying to figure me out.

"If I told you a rainbow had ten more colors, would you want to see them?" she asked, genuinely curious.

"I only want to see what's real," I said. "I have had a lifetime of vials. Mine just came in pill form."

"You don't know what you're missing," Howl said blissfully. The effects of the vial had kicked in, and she got up abruptly and left me alone with my purple pasta.

As I stood up to blow out the candles, a memory flooded back. I couldn't stop it. I was looking at the candle on the stone table, but what I saw was a completely different one.

It was my birthday—a couple of months before I kissed Bale at Whittaker. I had had a birthday cupcake with Vern, and my mother had brought me an elaborate piece of cake with a perfect pink flower, which I crushed immediately with a plastic spoon. That night, I had woken up to find Bale sitting beside me in my bed.

How did he get out of his room? But before I could ask, Bale put a finger to his lips, motioning me to keep quiet. I took the hint.

Bale handed me a donut. It was the middle of the night and—hands down—the best dessert of the day. He'd probably saved it from breakfast or talked his orderly into getting it for him. The donut had nearly brought me to tears. And I was not a crier, not even when I took the Grumpy pill.

"Wait!" Bale said.

I sat up in bed and inched closer to him.

"There's more?" I asked, clapping my hands together, which was an uncharacteristically cheerful gesture for me. I was relieved only Bale saw it.

I expected Bale's present to be a book. Bale liked books the way that I liked drawings. It was a travesty the day he would not be even allowed to hold a book because Dr. Harris thought it would end up as kindling.

"Close your eyes," Bale commanded.

"Are you serious?"

"Just close them."

I could hear movement, and when I opened my eyes I saw he had placed a candle in the donut. The flame flickered in the dark room.

No one was supposed to have candles at Whittaker. No one was supposed to have matches. And especially not Bale.

"Bale . . . put it out," I pleaded. Fire was the reason he was here. Birthday or no birthday, he was tempting fate.

"I think it's your move. You can't have a birthday without making a wish."

Bale wanted to give me a little bit of normal. A little bit of what every other kid had and we didn't. A simple birthday wish.

"I already have my wish, Bale."

He looked at the one window in my room, as if to say the obvious wish was for both of us to be on the other side of it. Free from Whittaker.

"Make a wish with me, Bale." I gestured to him, giving him permission. I knew I would have to get the matches from him after I blew out the candle.

Bale leaned over on the bed . . . and then it happened.

My bedspread caught fire. Flames quickly edged along the bedspread's hem, grazing the floor. I jumped to my feet.

But Bale did not move from his spot. It was as if Bale were paralyzed by the flame.

"Grab the water pitcher, Bale!" I yelled as I pulled the comforter onto the floor.

But Bale was frozen. The flames danced in his eyes for a second or two before he finally poured water over the fire, dousing it.

Bale began to apologize, but I cut him off and demanded he give me the matches. He passed them to me with a shaky hand.

"Snow, I didn't mean to."

"I know," I said, palming the matches.

"You have to go back to your room, Bale," I ordered. "The White Coats."

"I won't let you take the blame for this," he said, sinking down onto the floor beside me and taking my hand.

We sat there together just like that until the White Coats came. It wasn't a happy memory, exactly. But it was ours.

The memory done, I blew out the candles on the Claret's dining room table. The heist was tomorrow. I still knew my wish.

35

AND THEN THE NIGHT of the heist was upon us. It was the night the Robber girls were going to rescue some of our own. I was supposed to infiltrate the Duchess's Ball, find the mirror, and steal it. The whole thing sounded ridiculous and impossible.

Howl had outfitted me in another flying dress with feathers. The dress was the palest shade of pink, a color I normally would have run from because it made me think of my mother. But it was the most exquisite thing I'd ever seen. Its bodice had a deep V that managed to be sexy and demure at once.

Fathom had interrupted and given me a locator moth and a blade with a handle made of a burnished metal that looked a lot like the Enforcer's armor. "I know you plan on fighting snow with snow."

"I didn't plan on fighting at all."

"None of us do—except maybe Howl. But it doesn't mean you don't need to be prepared."

She handed me the knife. The handle felt like the wrong end of a fire poker. I released it, dropping it to the ground.

"Ouch! Are you trying to hurt me?"

"I'm trying to protect you. I should have warned you. It's going to hurt, but if you get in a bind . . ."

"I have my snow."

"But there is another way to fight, Snow . . . Fire."

She held the dagger out, and it glowed like Jagger's cuff.

She reached into her saddlebag, which seemed to have an endless supply of whatever was needed and when.

She produced a garter with a holster and slipped the knife inside. She handed everything to me.

I took it grudgingly.

"Aren't you Robbers supposed to be so good that it won't come to this?"

"We're good enough to know that someday it always comes to this. May that day not be today."

She took the knife back and kissed the blade.

A Robber blessing. I was not comforted. But as I hitched up my skirt and slid the garter up my leg, the knife did not burn my skin through its holster. And I hoped that her blessing held through the night.

When she was gone, I looked at myself in the pond glass. Sometimes I was more in awe with the small magic than the big. Robber clothes were different from everyone else's. They were not for the practical purpose of warmth or propriety. They were for beauty and they were for magic. With enough magic, even their skirts could take flight.

I waited until the very last second to change my face in the mirror. Countess Darby's face looked different on me. And it wasn't just the contents of the smile vial that I was pretty sure Fathom had slipped into my water earlier.

I joined the others downstairs. But when my eyes met Jagger's, neither one of us spoke of the dream he had invaded, and I still wasn't sure what, if any of it, had been real. Jagger's hair was short and cropped, and I wanted to run my fingers over the buzz.

"This time we're taking the River," he said as if trying to respect the distance I had put between us.

I thought about the River Witch. I wondered how things would have been different if I'd stayed with her—if I'd believed her from the start. What would she think if she could see me now?

Howl approached. She looked positively radiant in a model-esque face that had razor-sharp cheekbones. "Did you get it?"

"What?"

"The knife. Fathom put a double whammy on that blade. You don't have to know how to fight. The blade knows what to do. This doesn't mean we like you. But you have to be alive if you are going to bring home the mirror."

I realized that the weapon had been her idea. I was half-unsure about taking a weapon from her that had a mind of its own. What if she and Fathom had spelled it to stab me in the heart?

Margot called us together for one last spell.

"It's a oneness spell," Jagger whispered. "When we are on a mission, we all take it so that we can act as one. We are all in one another's heads."

"What if there's something that we don't want other people to know?" I asked.

"We have no secrets in the Robber palace," Howl said and leaned in beside me as we all took hands.

"Relax. There's a trick to it." Jagger took my hand in his.

There was a trick to everything at the Robber palace. And somehow Jagger always held the key or the lock pick.

"Another bottle?" I wondered out loud. I needed to learn quickly, or everyone would know my secret, which was no secret at all, really. That I wasn't done with Jagger.

"No, just your will. The trick to the spell is that it only lets you tell the things that you really want to tell."

"It binds us together so that the operation moves smoother," Howl added.

I felt my stomach flutter as Jagger's hand moved in mine.

Still, I could not back out now.

Margot chanted something, and we all followed suit.

My pronunciation was not as good as the others', and I hoped the magic didn't demand it. I hoped I didn't ruin the spell.

"Sometimes the magic needs the words," Queen Margot said, "because magic is something that has to be fed."

To Margot, magic was something as alive as me or her or the roomful of Robbers.

Sometimes words could be a sacrifice, too, I guessed.

An hour later, we were in a boat on the River to the Duchess Temperly's palace.

The boat glided along another passageway underneath the palace. The walls were muraled with drawings of the Snow King bringing eternal snow to Algid. His face couldn't be seen, and the pictures made it look like the people were grateful for the snow.

I knew Margot believed that I would locate the mirror with my Snow Princess powers, but I wasn't so sure.

"How will I find the mirror in the Duchess's room?" I asked Jagger.

"You'll know. You'll feel it when you get there."

"Won't there be guards?"

"Yes, but they'll be a little busy. With us," Jagger said confidently. "The door to the dungeon may just happen to find its way open."

There was a noise behind us. It felt as though someone were watching us. I reached for the knife that Fathom had given me.

"Take it easy, Princess. It's just an invisibility spell."

"Cadence," I whispered in recognition. It was Cadence, the girl we had rescued from the club. She now was at full Robber girl glow. She wanted to help rescue the others.

"Invisibility spell?" I asked redundantly as Cadence disappeared back into the night.

Jagger nodded and shushed us as we pulled closer to the palace.

Focus. I heard his voice in my head.

Focus. There was an echo from all the rest.

Jagger had said that the palace being on the water had something to do with fortification. Spikes jutted out of its underbelly where the water met the palace, and our boat halted as if it knew it was a breath away from being impaled.

Jagger had used magic for navigation. He used magic for everything.

A thought, errant and wild, crept into my head. *What would he be like without magic? Would I like him?*

"This had better work," Jagger said. He flipped one of the gold coin invitations in his hand, and the spikes split apart. Each spike transformed into a petal, and the petals fell open, revealing a door.

Our boat pressed on—without a moment more of hesitation.

It seemed as if I didn't breathe the whole time.

When it seemed we were finally safe, I inhaled deeply. The scent that filled my nostrils was from flowers growing on the walls of the underground passage.

I thought of Gerde. Had she been here? I reminded myself that she probably wasn't the only person in the world who could grow things, anymore than Kai was the only one who could build them.

We docked alongside a little-used entrance to the castle and made our way to the ballroom.

Jagger pulled me into one of the hollows of the palace. He pushed me gently against the wall and took my hand in his.

"If it all goes south," he began, "drink this and say home . . ."

His hand closed around mine, pressing a tiny green bottle into my hand. For a moment, I thought he was going to kiss me.

"Home is the other side of the Tree," I countered, trying to hide my disappointment.

He looked at me, reading my mind without the aid of the spell.

"It won't take you that far. It will take you back to the Claret. It will take you back to me. I promise you that it will take you only where you need to go. Only if there's no other way."

I bit my lip, considering.

I grabbed the vial.

36

EMERGING FROM THE UNDERBELLY of the Duchess's palace into the luxe main hall was like night and day. Mildewy concrete buttresses turned into marble staircases, tapestries woven with spun gold, and crystal candelabras.

All the guests were announced by an extremely tall man who took our second gold coin invitation. He flipped it over and up into the air. The coin disappeared. A piece of paper floated down in its stead. Fathom's magic worked perfectly.

The coins were apparently part of an intricate magical security system. They knew their invitees and would alert the palace guards of imposters. Fathom had modified the coins so we could enter without incident.

"May I present Lord Rafe Mach and Countess Darby Mach of Glovenshire," he said regally.

"I almost feel guilty for the poor sap," Jagger said as we took the red-velvet-lined stairs down into the grand ballroom.

"Since when are you capable of guilt?" I mused. From what I'd seen, Jagger and the other Robbers did not allow themselves much room for guilt. But I could see what he meant. The real Rafe Mach was missing something quite beautiful.

The ballroom was abuzz with music and dancing. A twenty-piece orchestra played from one corner of the room. There were ice sculptures shaped like the Duchess hand in hand with a faceless suitor, her husband-to-be. Bright-yellow banners hung from the eaves. The chandeliers seemed to be floating on air. I looked for wires, but there were none. Magic.

And in the middle of all the din was my cousin, the Duchess herself.

She sat on a gilded throne looking perfectly poised. Braids woven into other braids formed a hair origami crown upon which her diamond-encrusted tiara sat. Her dress was an intricate brocade in a shimmering pale pink. But what made it special were the dress's straps: garlands of flowers that wound their way down to the bodice. The skirt was also covered with live flower petals.

Across her porcelain face was a delicate gold mask edged with glittery lace filigree. The mask covered her eyes, extended right up to her hairline, and skimmed across the bottom of her flushed pink cheeks. I couldn't see how it was fastened on. It seemed to be floating just above the surface of her skin. She was exquisite.

The Duchess glanced around the room, looking a little lost. She appeared to be my age, and she didn't seem to be having a good time at her own ball. I knew that Algid was different from back home. But the Duchess seemed a little too young to be deciding her forever tonight. My fate, however, would change course before the evening was over if I succeeded in finding the mirror.

The plan had made sense to me in the Claret. But now that I was here, I felt everything in me clench and not just because of the corset under my dress.

"First we dance and then we split up," Jagger reminded me.

He had not stopped staring at me since we left the Claret. And I couldn't help smiling as we took to the polished dance floor. I had a different face and so did he. But he was right. If you looked closely enough, you could see the real person behind the borrowed face. And we were both looking very closely. I liked the feel of his hand on the small of my back, so much so that I missed it when the dance required us to part.

"Um, don't you think it's weird that you brought a date to a suitor ball?" I realized suddenly.

Jagger could see my nervousness, but he talked right through it. Keeping his hand on mine, he smoothly led me into the fray.

"In Algid, everyone is eligible to marry the Duchess. If she takes a liking to me, she'll execute you."

I narrowed my eyes at him. He was joking, but I needed to hear his laughter as confirmation.

"I think the Duchess will assume that I believed I had no chance. It will read as humble," he said.

I laughed out loud. If the Duchess was even remotely as intelligent as she was rumored to be, there was no way she would think Jagger was humble.

Fathom's voice interrupted our thoughts. *We have a problem.*

What's that? Jagger replied.

An uncloaking spell.

I couldn't see Fathom, but I could sense her on the dance floor among the swirling skirts and colorful tuxedos and white gloves.

How is that a problem? I asked before I realized what it meant to my fellow Robbers.

"She's going to strip us of all our magic so she can see who's at her ball," Jagger explained. "It's pretty clever. She's doing it for her suitors. Which I have to say is a tad hypocritical considering she never takes off the mask." There was trepidation in his voice. "After it happens, can you do me a favor? Don't look at me, Snow. Can you do that?" Jagger said earnestly, his eyes brimming with concern instead of their usual mischief.

I almost stopped dancing. I forgot the steps and nearly tripped over my own heels, crashing into Jagger's muscled chest. He caught me and righted me on my feet as if I were light as a feather.

He never took off his mask, either. Was he afraid I would see the real him? Was it vanity or Robber Rules? I recalled the scar on his chest. Had Lazar carved up even more of him? Was that what he was keeping from me?

"But don't I need to see you so that we can escape together?" I asked, instead.

"By the time we get back to the boat, I'll be back to myself."

"Okay," I said. I wanted to tell him that I didn't care how he looked. Because I didn't. I wanted to tell him that I didn't care what was under his mask any more than I cared about what was under the Duchess's. I only cared that he wouldn't show me his face after he had seen all my dark places. All my secrets. But I couldn't open that up in front of the roomful of people. Especially with the entire Robber crew listening in.

Something caught my eye at the entrance of the room beneath the floating chandelier. I knew that every eligible man in the Kingdom was required to be here—even the servants—but still, I was surprised to see one man in particular. My heart began to race uncomfortably.

I knew Kai's rail-straight posture anywhere, but the clothes he wore were new. Kai looked like a proper gentleman. He was no longer dressed in the rough burlap fabric that he wore back at the cube.

But just then Kai bowed in front of the Duchess. He asked her to dance.

"Old friend of yours?" Jagger said between dances when he realized my distraction. "Looks like your architect's situation has changed."

"Whoever do you mean?" I asked, knowing better but pretending not to. Where was Gerde? Where was the River Witch? Had they come here for me?

Spinning away from Jagger for a moment, I asked one of my fellow dancers, a woman in a pink monstrosity, who Kai was.

"Oh, that's the King's new architect."

"The last one blew away in a snow-nado. Very tragic," someone else murmured.

Was Kai working for the King now? Or had he been working for the King all along? My mind spun along with the music.

I pushed away the last thought. I didn't believe it. Unless . . .

I felt a sudden tightness hit me in the chest. Unless our kiss had changed him, after all.

"He never stays long at these things. He's either terribly shy or his heart belongs to another," the other dancer assessed. "I mean, why else would you not put yourself in the running for the Duchess? She clearly likes dancing with him. Look at the color in her cheeks!"

The Duchess's cheeks are barely visible beneath her mask, I scarcely bit back.

"Snow, are you still with me?" Jagger asked, bringing me back to him.

"Of course," I said, but part of me was still following Kai.

The architect doesn't matter. He can't matter. Howl's voice was in my head.

I'd forgotten about the oneness spell. Howl was watching me. So were all the other Robbers, probably. I felt my cheeks burn, knowing that they had all heard my thoughts. Especially Jagger.

Next time, you'll know how to shield yourself, someone said.

Next time we'd be going after Bale.

The idea of Kai dancing was almost as absurd as me dancing. But seeing Kai's arms around the Duchess brought back our time together. Brought back the kiss.

"You kissed him?" Jagger asked lightly, but his eyes betrayed an intensity that I couldn't help but read as jealousy.

"He kissed me," I countered, but I felt myself flush.

"Well, I don't think your kiss drove him crazy."

I could see the jealousy in Jagger's eyes. I looked at his lips reflexively, considering a kiss, despite where we were. Despite Kai in the Duchess's arms. Despite Bale.

"I almost froze him."

If Jagger was surprised, he didn't show it.

"You didn't have control of your snow yet. You do now."

I almost laughed. That was a lie. I was getting better, but kisses were supposed to be about abandon. About letting go. I'd seen it on TV, and I'd felt it with Bale and even a little with Kai. And if my lips ever touched Jagger's, I just knew that control would be the last thing I was capable of.

"I thought we were supposed to put him out of our heads," I countered, pretending that we were still talking about Kai.

But we both knew we weren't talking about my kiss with Kai. We were talking about the one Jagger hoped to have with me.

"He's not distracting me," Jagger said, sounding light.

But I was sure that Jagger was lying.

"Could have fooled me?" I laughed.

Jagger pushed me backward on the dance floor, at the same time pulling me closer to him.

When we passed Kai, I did not strain to look for him again.

"For the record, a life without kissing is no life at all," Jagger said, slipping one of his hands away from me and into one of his pockets. He pulled out his watch.

He nodded at me. We couldn't talk anymore. Or dance. We had to move. There was a mirror to steal. Everything else had to wait. I let go of Jagger's hand and slipped up the staircase, which spiraled to the second floor. As I climbed each step, I glanced out the window and saw that the lawn was covered with tents beyond the River. Everyone wanted to see firsthand who the Duchess would choose.

Now, Snow! Margot said.

I hope she doesn't blow it.

I looked back from the window and down at Jagger in the ballroom. I wouldn't be around to see Jagger uncloaked. But despite my promise, I wished I could see his real face.

At that moment, all eyes were on the Duchess, who was addressing the crowd.

"I want to thank you all for coming. It is an honor to have you in my home. We all know that magic has an unspoken place in this Kingdom. But when it comes to love and the future of Algid, it is important that there are no rose-colored glasses. I must see clearly whose hand I am taking before I step toward the future. To that end, when the clock strikes midnight any spells that have been cast will be unraveled."

It was ten minutes until the clock would chime.

Ticktock, Snow, Jagger's voice said in my head.

I wondered if they would just abandon the mission. Robber Rules: No one sees anyone else's real face. But Jagger stood his ground and so did all the Robber girls. The mirror was that important.

Ticktock, Princess, Jagger's voice said as he made his way toward the Duchess.

I'll get the others, Fathom said.

The dungeon, someone answered.

I felt my heart speed up. I was just as worried about the girls as I was for myself. It wasn't just the oneness spell. At some point in the last few days, I'd learned what it was to care about not just one or two people, but a whole bunch of them at once. Even Howl.

I put Jagger out of my head. But as I reached the top of the landing, someone put his hand on mine and bowed low in front of me.

It was Kai. He hadn't stayed to dance with the Duchess, after all. Kai gently pulled me to his rail-straight frame and took my hand in his. The music and party continued below us, the lilting notes drifting up to where we stood. Before I knew it, Kai and I were dancing. To my surprise, somehow we still fit together well. And he moved with an ease that I did not expect. Meanwhile, I fumbled, stepping on his feet and cursing beneath my breath. When I looked up at him, I reminded myself that I was wearing another face. Kai thought I was someone else. And that someone else should apologize.

Kai wrapped his arms around me. He was stiff, but he knew all the steps. I wondered if Gerde had given him some sort of dancing root or if it was one of the things that he was just annoyingly good at. But I was happy to see him. His blue eyes locked with mine. The timing was wrong, but the sight of his overly tall figure lifted something up in me. It broke through the intrigue and the danger.

"No offense, but you don't seem the type," I proffered.

"What type?"

"The waiting-for-the-Duchess-to-pick-you type."

"It seems that the Duchess is running out of eligible men. I was invited like everyone else, and an invitation in this Kingdom cannot be ignored."

He was lying. I was doubtful that the King would send an invitation to the River Witch's caretaker.

Some part of me felt insulted. I hadn't thought of Kai with anyone but me. And he was treating my alias, the Countess, just like he treated me. Or maybe, just maybe, he could sense me under the pretty perfect shell.

"And where did the King's men find you?" I asked.

"You found me. You have forgotten me so soon?"

I nearly stopped in my tracks, but I kept dancing. Was he talking about the Countess or me?

Kai continued, "You asked the very same question the last time I saw you. At last week's ball, remember?"

"How could I forget?" I asked as demurely as I could manage.

"And yet you don't remember our last dance. We did it here in this very spot. You promised to tell me more when we met again—and yet it seems I have one of those faces that doesn't stick."

I was the one with the less-than-sticky face.

"I could never forget you . . . I just have traveled very far. And I am dizzy from all the dancing. You try wearing a corset."

"Of course. I do not envy the price you pay for your beauty. But I do enjoy the results."

Was Kai flirting?

I suddenly wanted to tell Kai everything. But what would I say?

I was now a holder of a whole new set of people's secrets. The Robber girls' story belonged to them, just as Gerde's belonged to her and Kai.

"I don't mean to be presumptuous, but you have that look. Like you want to say something," Kai said.

"And why would I share it with you?"

"Because sometimes it's easier to talk to a stranger."

"But then we wouldn't be strangers anymore."

"Precisely. Or maybe you're not a stranger, after all. Maybe I already know who you are and what you can do. What you must do."

"Excuse me, I think I need some air," I said and made myself break away from Kai.

"We will meet again. I am sure of it," Kai said mysteriously.

Ticktock, Princess, Jagger's voice sounded again.

But something drowned out Jagger's monologue. The crowd collectively gasped. For the briefest of seconds I believed that we had somehow been caught.

Steady, Jagger's voice said.

I followed the craning of necks and the tiptoeing of high heels of the crowd as the music and dancing came to a halt. The reaction of the crowd had nothing to do with the Robbers among them.

Six soldiers in the King's royal red were shouldering something golden down the staircase.

It took my brain a second to catch up with what it was seeing—who I was seeing. The soldiers were not carrying a box. It was a cage with ornate brass bars that curlicued around its captive.

"*Shhhhh . . .*" Jagger again hushed me.

Kai froze beside me.

And I could see why. What they were carrying was the real reason he was here.

It was Gerde. Gerde was in the golden cage. She was naked and trying to cover herself with her hands. There was a wild look of panic in her big gray eyes.

My heart broke. I wanted to ask Kai how it had happened. How had she been taken? But I remembered that I wasn't wearing my own face.

I wanted to freeze the whole room to get her out.

I know she's your friend, but you can't help her now. We're here for the mirror. We're here for your Bale, Jagger's voice again interrupted.

If he had been standing beside me, I think I could have frozen him, too. He was demanding that I choose between my friend and my Bale.

Kai could save Gerde. Wouldn't he? But how? He didn't have magic, and Gerde's cage was surrounded by soldiers.

If you make our presence known, we are all dead, Snow.

I couldn't find Margot's face in the crowd, but I knew it was her.

You said yourself that distraction is the better part of a heist, I countered.

Controlled distraction. Not chaos, Margot defended.

I looked at Gerde in the cage. My friend was trapped in a room filled with the most refined people of Algid. Margot had instructed me to take an etiquette vial just to fit in with them. But they were more barbaric than the River Witch or the Snow Beasts out in the woods. Gerde was the entertainment for the evening.

"The King is delayed, but he sends you this gift," a soldier announced.

The Duchess's mask rode up slightly. "What kind of gift is this? She's just a girl."

One of the soldiers prodded Gerde with a spear. Its sharp tip glistened under the glow of the floating chandelier.

Don't, I said in my head, willing Gerde not to show them her beastly self.

The Duchess inspected Gerde through the bars.

"Not just any girl," the soldier said with a flourish of pride and poked through the bars at Gerde again.

I could see Gerde's tiny face set in a hard line. She was resisting—but she was also mad. She flinched as the prod pierced her flesh, drawing blood.

The guests didn't react.

The King's soldier prodded again. And again. And on the third time I could see the change begin. I almost looked away. I could see Gerde searching the crowd for Kai. She found him and held on to his gaze while the change occurred. Just like I'd watched her find him when they were together at the cube. Kai always calmed her down and brought her back from the brink, back to herself. This time there was nothing he could do.

When Gerde's transformation was complete, she reached through the bars with her fur-and-feather-covered arms, trying to get at the soldier.

The Duchess smiled beneath her mask as if this were the very thing she had always wanted.

And the crowd remained mute and still. Was this

commonplace in Algid? Girls being given as presents and then tortured in front of them? Were these people hiding their feelings, or did they just not have any?

"What a marvelous find. Thank His Majesty for me," the Duchess said finally, clapping her hands.

She looked to the crowd, and they began to clap, too. I could not bring my hands together. Snowy webs were forming between my fingers already. I could see that Kai wasn't clapping, either. He gulped hard; his Adam's apple moved. I assumed he was swallowing his objections, reminding himself of whatever plan he'd cooked up to free her.

"The King will be pleased that you are pleased," the soldier said with a slow smile, prodding Gerde again to get her to move to the back of the cage. Apparently, seeing the beast was a treat, but seeing it maul the Duchess would be too much.

King Lazar had reached a new level of creepy. He gave people as presents. The ball, which moments ago had seemed so beautiful, had taken a grotesque turn.

I'm sorry, Margot, I said in my head.

I focused on the lock. With a little luck maybe I could make a key of ice and slip it to Gerde.

But before I could do anything, Kai dropped into a low bow and ran down the stairs to his sister.

And then the lights went out.

First things first, said Margot.

I had a mission to finish.

Ignore the chaos, I told myself.

Use the chaos, Margot's voice said in my head.

I pushed myself away from the recent past and rocketed toward my future. I rushed up the next set of stairs as quickly as I could, trying to look like a flustered girl in search of a powder room after the big commotion, not a thief ready to rob the Duchess blind.

"It looks like we have somehow run out of magic," the Duchess said as her servants brought in a sea of candles. She smiled wide, but I assumed she knew that magic didn't just disappear. It was taken.

"Luckily we still have the liquid kind. Champagne for everyone . . . ," the Duchess continued, assuring the crowd that the party would go on.

I could hear Fathom's voice in my head, confirming that our plan would do the same.

Our people are finally coming home, Fathom said, sounding more sentimental than I'd ever heard her.

As servers brought in another round of bubbly on what looked like floating trays and the band started up again, I cast a look back down to where Kai had been and then to Jagger. *He is so good at playing his part*, I thought as he presented himself to the Duchess, dripping with charm. The connecting spell let us move concurrently and share a consciousness, but not everyone was as good at cloaking their thoughts as Jagger.

I hoped I was able to conceal my feelings for him. And from him. And from everyone else in my life.

37

THE THIRD FLOOR OF the Duchess's palace was even more glamorous than the lower levels. I stopped myself from touching the gilded petals that stemmed all over the walls. They reminded me of the flowers on the Duchess's exquisite dress. I looked around before releasing the locator moth that Fathom had given me. The magical insect took off on its silvery wings and flitted around. I followed it to the door of my cousin's room.

I quickly closed the door behind me and surveyed the scene. A plush canopy bed sat in the center of the room. A portrait of the Duchess hung on one wall, her face hidden behind her mask, as usual. An overflowing jewelry box sat on her dressing table. The contents of which were probably worth millions. I scanned the room for the Duchess's safe.

Margot had said to use magic, so I called on my snow.

Frost left my fingertips and searched the room for the mirror. I watched as it wound its way under and over every surface of the room. A misty fog poured under the bed, into the ornate armoire and out again, and behind the curtains.

It finally settled in the middle of the pale-gray rug that covered the center of the floor. I pulled back the rug and found nothing but wooden floorboards. The frost gathered on one section of the wood.

Magic likes poetry, Margot had said.

"Open for me. I want to see."

I touched the floor and several wooden planks fell silently into the dark below. I rolled backward, barely avoiding the drop.

I grabbed a candle from the Duchess's nightstand and peered into the hole. There were no stairs. There was just blackness.

I waved a hand down into the dark, and a staircase of ice formed a spiral down to a bottom I could not see.

I descended carefully into the dark. When I finally reached the last step, I found a long hallway at the end of which was an arched doorway edged in icicles. Though the entryway appeared open, I knew safe passage would take more than merely walking through. Margot had said the architect of the safe had warned her of this very spot.

I placed my candle on the floor and reached out my hand. The icicles dropped down like a guillotine. They stopped in midair right before touching me. I was not harmed, but I could not pass through. Not yet.

Margot had said that the safe required blood. Royal blood.

I took out the dagger Fathom gave me. It burned in my hand, and I quickly cut my palm. The pain was doubled by the hot blade. I gritted my teeth to keep from screaming. I opened my hand in the doorway again. This time when the icicles fell, one shard gently dipped into the blood on my palm. The icicles all retracted at once, and I stepped through the doorway.

I expected another magical booby trap, but instead I saw an enormous room filled with mirrors.

There were pieces of every size and shape. Some were mounted in frames. Some were leaning against the room's walls. Still others were piled high to the ceiling.

It was genius, really. If anyone other than the King or the Duchess got this far, how on earth would they know which mirror was the right one? How was I to know?

I examined my reflection in mirror after mirror—to no avail. There was the woman's face I'd stolen in every one.

I sank down to the floor of the room. I had not come this far to give up now. I called on my snow, but my frost encircled me and went nowhere.

"Mirror, mirror on the wall, watch the mighty Snow Queen fall . . . ," I quipped. "Sometimes you have to break things to find what's unbreakable."

The words weren't mine. They belonged to Dr. Harris. He'd said that after Bale had broken my wrist. He had meant to illustrate how strong I could be. But I remember taking offense, thinking he was calling Bale weak. So I'd broken a glass paperweight on his desk.

I called on my snow again and held my breath and closed my eyes.

"Break," I ordered and tucked into a fetal position.

There was a long pause. Spell work was still new to me.

Every mirror exploded at once. My ears filled with the cacophony of broken glass. The seconds ticked by, and I could feel the draft caused by the movement of the glass around me. But not one shard scratched me.

I opened my eyes. When I stood, all I saw was a blanket of broken mirror. I walked the wreckage looking for the one left unbroken.

In the corner of the room, I spied a tiny little compact. It was gold with a symbol on the outside that looked like one of the markings on the Tree. At first I thought it was a flower. But it was actually an odd-shaped snowflake. I held my breath before opening it and exhaled when I saw my reflection. The mirror was intact. But the face in the mirror wasn't the Countess's borrowed one. It was my own.

The King's mirror piece could see through the face that Fathom gave me. It could see the real me.

I clamped the compact shut and carefully climbed up the ice stairs. I didn't know how long I'd been down there, but I didn't have a moment to lose.

Just as I rolled the rug back across the wooden floor, the bedroom door banged open. The Duchess strode angrily into her room, followed by a pack of dangerous-looking and heavily armed guards dressed in the same blue that decorated the palace. I hastily hid the mirror in the folds of my gown.

"What are you doing in my bedroom?" the Duchess questioned.

I hesitated, formulating a lie and tried not to stare at the glittery mask that now seemed to be embedded in her skin.

"Look, I'm sorry, okay. I made a wrong turn and ended up in here. I don't mean any harm. I was just heading back to the ball," I lied and moved to walk past her.

She nodded, and one of the guards stepped in my way.

The memory of her laughing at Gerde flooded back to me. If the Duchess didn't believe my story, some part of me wanted to freeze every last one of them.

The clock struck midnight.

I blurted a curse as my face changed back to normal, but at the time normal was the last thing I felt.

The Duchess breathed in sharply, and the color drained from her rosy cheeks.

She turned to the guards and ordered them out. "Leave us!"

The lead guard hesitated, not wanting to leave his mistress unprotected.

Did he recognize me? Did she?

The Duchess gave him another stern look, and he and the others marched out the door.

We stared silently at each other for a long moment. And then the Duchess spoke.

"Well, Snow. Long time, no see."

I could hear the voices of my crew abandoning me, not on purpose, but because they had no choice.

She's caught!

They know we're here.

Where's Snow? Jagger pleaded.

Where is she? Fathom echoed.

I won't leave without her.

We're surrounded.

Get on the boat, Jagger.

No! Jagger protested.

You'll thank me later, Fathom's voice said.

Fathom, you hit him too hard, Howl said.

Princess . . . Jagger drifted off.

And then there was silence.

They were gone.

I looked at my cousin, the Duchess. I could be her guest, or I could be her prisoner, or I could start a storm and make a path back to the Robbers.

"I know that you came with Robbers, and I know what you came for."

"Then why did you send the guards away?" I asked. There was no point lying now.

"Because we're family. We're blood. And that means something to me. We have so much catching up to do. But first, you must return the mirror," she finished, holding out her hand.

My heart stopped. The entire time we were talking, the Duchess knew I had stolen her mirror. My instinct was to freeze her, to freeze the guards that were probably still waiting outside the room. I raised my hand, feeling the frosty ice fill my veins. But something was holding me back. This was wrong. I couldn't—wouldn't—use my snow. The Duchess hadn't done anything to me. I struggled indecisively while she tapped her foot against the rug expectantly.

"Why don't we do this, Snow?" the Duchess suggested. "Give

me my mirror, and I will tell you what it means, why I have it, and why you cannot. Everything in Algid depends on it."

The opportunity to learn more about this cursed prophecy was too much for me to turn my back on. Reluctantly I drew the mirror from the folds of my dress and began to hand it to her. Something stopped me, though: the image of her in the ballroom with her gift. I didn't know what kind of person I was handing the mirror over to—no matter what answers she promised.

"Back in the ballroom, you seemed very appreciative of Lazar's gift. How do I know that you aren't saying all this for him? That you won't let him kill me?"

"You don't. Sometimes trust is a choice."

"Funny, I thought it was earned."

"Besides, you're the Snow Princess, right? If you don't like what you hear, you can just freeze me and take off with the mirror."

Her blunt logic made a certain amount of sense.

I opened my palm. She grabbed the mirror and turned it over in her hands with a kind of reverence.

She opened the lid of the compact and said, "Watch and learn."

The Duchess leaned in and blew on the glass. It liquefied, slinking up and away from her, forming a giant mirror as tall as me. The edges were shaped like a puzzle piece. This was still only one third of the whole. I'd already heard about the mirror from the River Witch and from Jagger.

The Duchess and I were both reflected in the glass.

Then it was my turn to inhale sharply.

Her mask was gone. In the mirror, the Duchess looked exactly like me.

"I don't understand. It's a trick," I said.

"It's the truth. The mirror tells the truth, among its other qualities," she said simply, as if this were an everyday occurrence.

She pulled off her mask with effort. The edges of the lace were tiny tentacles that seemed to want to hold on. The mask was a living thing, or at least a magical one.

The Duchess had my face. The same eyes. The same nose. The same lips. It couldn't be, but it was.

"What the hell!" I said out loud as she dropped her mask to the floor.

And then she said the one part of the story that was the only explanation.

"We're sisters."

The Duchess was my twin.

38

"CALL ME TEMPERLY. I never expected you to show up at my ball. And with a band of Robbers, no less. It was so clever of you to find friends who are not allied with the King. That is no easy feat in Algid. And I hear that they are a dangerous lot. Do they really steal faces?" Temperly said.

I suppose she could tell that I was still reeling, or perhaps it was just royal etiquette to fill the silence. The Duchess was my sister. She may have been surprised by the company I kept, but I was no surprise to her. She knew about me.

Her cadence, her manner of speech, was different from mine. More formal. Less likely to start a string of expletives at any moment.

"I never expected you. Period," I countered, finally finding my voice.

Maybe it was a trick. Maybe it was like the faces Fathom stole. It was magic. But something in my gut told me that it was true. The spell had undone my disguise, and the mirror had shown her real face. It just happened to be mine, as well.

"How is this possible?" I demanded.

Her face fell. "I grew up knowing all about you, of course. You were a bedtime story, a cautionary tale. You were everything I ever heard about, and you didn't even know I existed. But then, no one does," she said almost bitterly.

"There were two babies. Only our mother knows about me. And the witches. And now you. When I was born, she secretly gave me to one of the witches. The witch thought she'd chosen well. A good family at the edge of Algid raised me as their own. Our father can never know about me, either, even though I am the one without an ounce of snow," she explained.

My eyes began to water. I realized I hadn't blinked since the second she took off her mask.

My mom had saved both of us. But she had not taken my sister with us. Did she think this was safer? If *I* was having trouble with our mother's choices, I could not even begin to imagine how Temperly had lived with this for all these years. I had been locked up. But she had been left behind.

My heart clenched. Another impossible thing piled upon all the rest and threatened to topple me. But I centered myself and stared into my sister's face, trying to find something about hers to differentiate it from my own.

"Is that why you hide your face and pretend to be someone else?"

"Yes. Because of the prophecy. One glimpse and the King would know who I really was."

"This is mind-blowing," I said. "How did you end up a duchess?"

"I never imagined he would take such an interest in me. I am sure our mother never planned for this. The witch didn't think twice about putting me with a family that was distantly related to the King. So many people are. But as the years waned, the King had gotten rid of so many of his relatives, including the Duke and Duchess who had adopted me. In a twisted bit of fate, it turns out that the Duchess that he thinks I am is the last of his line."

"And the King . . . in all this time, has never seen your face?"

The man I had heard about would get curious at least once in all these years. I was shocked he never saw who she really was.

"The King has no room for me in his thoughts. He has his Snow. He has the memory of our mother. Those are the only two things he cares about in this world or the next."

She blinked at me with wide eyes. This moment was less strange for her because she had always known about me. She had been waiting for this day. For me.

"When I was little, I used to dream that you would come and switch places with me . . ."

"And you would go live a glamorous life beyond the Tree? You didn't miss much. I was in an insane asylum." I finished her thought, my voice dripping in sarcasm.

"I dreamed I would go there and you would come here, and you would kill our father," she continued without missing a beat.

Sarcasm she did not know. But bloodlust was a different story.

"Do you know what it is like to be the only one in our family without power?"

But that wasn't the only thing Temperly was without. She was without love. I didn't know what Mom was to me, really. She'd kept so many horrible secrets, but in her own way she'd done it to protect me all along.

"How can you be sure the prophecy is about me? Why not you?" I asked, studying her.

My tone was wrong. It was almost hopeful. I couldn't help but wonder what it would be like if this whole thing was some kind of mistake. If the burden of this place, of this prophecy, belonged to someone other than me.

She held out her hands and shook them futilely. She had no snow.

"It's not about me. It's always been you."

She believed in the story and the prophecy that had done all of this to us. What if it wasn't true? What if we were all playing parts of a fiction? All these lives ruined. Maybe if we didn't believe in the story and instead just believed in one another, things would be so very different.

Temperly continued, "I have had to spend my whole life like this . . . waiting for you and the Eclipse of the Lights."

I thought of Whittaker and then looked at her beautiful room. My eyes stuck on a mint wrapped in silvery paper on her silk pillow. At least her prison was gilded and opulent and had every comfort imaginable. She had chocolates, and I had the seven dwarfs, a pill for every emotion. I bet she had a dress for every one, instead.

"Yeah, it looks so horrible. Getting dressed up in couture every night, dancing with the Kingdom's most eligible, starring in your own version of *Princess Bachelorette* . . ."

I remembered her dancing in Kai's arms. I blushed with sudden jealousy. Kai wasn't the point, I told myself.

Temperly blinked hard, perhaps unused to anyone contradicting her.

"I used to get drugged up on a daily basis, and I was literally locked in a room every night," I added.

"It's strange, isn't it?" she said, looking at me. "We both had our prisons."

But mine wasn't as bad as hers in a way. I'd had Bale. And in a way, I'd had Mom. Even though I never really appreciated her until I got here.

"But no one is telling you who to love," she said quietly. This was her cross to bear. The thing that defined her life. The thing that made her beautiful life not so beautiful.

"Your options are pretty dreamy. That guy you were dancing with . . . ," I silver-lininged. Even I felt a pang of understanding now. I could not have survived Whittaker without Bale. How did she survive Algid without anyone?

"Which one?" she asked, half-annoyed, half-interested.

It was a good question. She'd been dancing with Jagger, too. But it was Kai that came to mind first.

"No matter. I can't love any of them . . . ," she rolled on. Her eyes cast down to the gray carpeting as if it had suddenly gotten interesting.

"I don't understand."

"I love someone else. Someone the King and people would never approve of." I rocked back on my heels. The Duchess had layers and secrets. I'd let the gown and the manners fool me. She was more than she appeared.

"Who?" I asked.

"When I was very young, I met someone from another land. We fell instantly and madly in love—only he was taken by the King's men."

"The Enforcer?" I asked, shuddering just thinking about him and our first encounter.

Oblivious, the Duchess perked up at the mention of his name. "The King's right hand? I hope my love never meets him. According to legend, he might not even be a man at all. He might just be an invention of the King. Maybe just a suit of armor filled with animated snow. Regardless, the King is said to be able to see through the Enforcer's eyes just like he can see through the Shells."

"Shells?"

"When Lazar gets inside your brain for long enough, legend has it that he can wipe it clean. The result are Shells. I've never seen them, but they're supposed to roam the forest."

"Do you really believe that?"

"I have seen him do incredible things with his snow. Impossible things . . . and I think I've felt him trying to glimpse my thoughts. But perhaps it's just my imagination. The more you see of evil, the more evil seems limitless. I guess the same goes for good, but I haven't seen as much of that."

I nodded.

"Do you know . . . are you . . . sure that your love . . . that he's still . . ."

Alive, I thought but couldn't say out loud. I'd seen what the Enforcer could do.

Her eyes went wide at the thought of the Enforcer hurting her love, or worse.

"I have sources in the King's palace. My beloved hasn't had an easy time of it. But he's surviving."

"I am so sorry, Temperly," I said, meaning it.

Suddenly we had so much more in common than I had ever thought possible.

"So you're going to keep doing this to buy time while you find a way for him to escape?"

She looked away from me again. I wasn't sure if it was too painful for her to talk about or if there was something else she wasn't telling me.

"I don't know how to get him out. There are no efforts except hope. The people of this land depend on me to keep the royal bloodline going. The King and I have a peace. But the people are growing restless. They want a wedding and perhaps a baby to pin their affections to."

"So how long do you plan on holding them off?"

"Forever if I must," she said with a sigh. The weight of what she'd been carrying finally seemed to press on her more as she spoke about it. As if the act of telling me had brought all her pain to the surface.

"The people have been waiting for the Snow Princess to come back and save us. Now that you are here, perhaps my prayers have been answered. Perhaps all of them have been."

"I am not a savior."

"We shall see about that. You must think me terrible for not doing anything to get my beloved out."

"I do not judge," I said quickly, but some part of me was questioning what she was and was not doing. I had after all crossed the Tree for my love. I could not wait on hope. In her scenario, I was the hope. At the same time, I was ignoring the prophecy that said I was supposed to save this land and all its people.

"There is more to this than you think. Much more . . ."

"Like what?" I asked.

She paused and bit her pretty lip. She wrung her hands that were shaped just like mine but seemed somehow more delicate. "Don't you think I want to take my guards and fight against the King? I want to save my love from that prison on high and never look back. But if I were to fail, then it would not be just me who suffers. It would be the whole land. There are people who depend on me."

"But aren't they already suffering?" I remembered the little boy in the square. If the Duchess thought that keeping quiet was helping her people, she was wrong.

"You don't know the King the way that I do. It could be so much worse. This, comparatively, is mercy."

I nodded, accepting it. But something in my gut twisted. Maybe a touch of shame of my own. This was supposed to be my fight. And I wouldn't take it on, either.

I tried to push it away. I concentrated on the Duchess, whose bottom lip trembled as if she were fighting back tears. I wanted to halt them.

An old story that I'd read back in Dr. Harris's library popped into my head.

"There's a tale where I come from about a woman whose husband goes away and is presumed dead. She waits for him to come home, but she's pressured to marry again. She promises that once she finishes her father-in-law's funeral shroud, she will comply and pick a new husband. So every day she wove the shroud, and every night she unwove it."

It was the Greek myth of Odysseus and Penelope. But the Duchess looked as if I was reporting something real and important. Something possible. In truth, the Duchess was already weaving and unweaving her own little engagement drama for the people and the King to believe every day.

"And how does the story end?" she asked quietly, her voice laced with expectation. She was rooting for the girl in my story because she was rooting for herself.

"It takes a long time. Years. But she and her love are reunited. I think Odysseus might slay all the suitors. I can't quite remember."

I left out the part where the hero slept with a couple of other women on his journey while Penelope was weaving her shroud. But I didn't want to undercut the romance.

"No matter," she said quietly.

"The point is that I do love someone, but I love my people more. And he understands that. The world is bigger than us."

Despite everything I had done in the last few days, I still believed that my world was just me and Bale. Wasn't it?

But looking into my sister's identical face, my plan was blown to bits. I felt the wrong emotion for the millionth time in my life. I had not wanted to save the land. I had not wanted to save the Robbers. I wanted to get me and Bale free. I wasn't noble or magnanimous.

But I had a sister in the world now. Did that change anything? Did it change everything? It didn't have to. I didn't know her. And yet I felt something like gravity in her presence, pulling me into her story, letting her into mine.

"We may look alike. We may share the same DNA, but we don't know each other and we aren't anything to each other," I blurted defensively.

"And we never will be unless you get out of here at once."

She waved her hand, and the mirror shrunk back into the compact. She extended it to me.

"You're giving this to me?"

"Take it. You need it to find the other witches and broach a peace."

"What will happen to you if the King discovers I have the mirror and that you were involved?"

She paused and then said, "Whatever happens, I will know that I have finally done something."

Temperly thought her long nightmare was finally over. She thought that I was here to fix everything. She could not be more wrong. I couldn't take the mirror without telling her my truth.

"I don't want to kill our . . . King Lazar. Not that he doesn't deserve it. But the King has someone of mine, too. I just want to take my friend and go back to the other side of the Tree. His name is Bale."

She shook her head in disappointment.

"But you can come with us . . . if you want," I offered.

I couldn't imagine this royal girl back in upstate New York. Not that I could really imagine myself there again, either. I couldn't go back to Whittaker. I didn't know how me and her and Bale would survive back in the real world. But it had to be better than Algid. For all Algid's magic, there were equal parts of potential pain.

"So you're going to give the mirror to the Robbers? You know that you can't trust them."

"You just said that I had found friends who were enemies of the King. They have the same goal."

"You're not what I thought you were," Temperly said.

"Temperly . . ."

"I thought you were a hero."

"I never claimed to be. What about you? You had the mirror all along. You didn't need me or the power of snow to broach a peace with the witches."

A look of hurt crossed her face, and then it settled into something like shame.

"You're right. I didn't have your power. And the prophecy says it has to be you."

I felt the frost again—the inside-out squeeze of anger and fury. No one was going to tell me what to do or where to go or who I was.

But she was right. I wasn't a hero. Far from it. And right now, she was standing in the way of what I wanted. I needed that mirror. It was my and Bale's passport out of Algid. I wasn't going to save the world, and neither were the Robbers.

A ring of frost began to form at my feet and make circles around us. Temperly looked down, startled, then back up at me.

I could see that she knew I could just take the mirror if I wanted to.

"I need you to give it to me, Temperly. I am sorry. You can come with me—or you can stay here. But I will have that mirror."

Temperly's face crumpled. But it wasn't disappointment this time. It was fear.

"Guards!" she yelled, clutching the mirror to her chest. And then her eyes darted to someone behind me.

When I turned, I saw King Lazar standing in the doorway. My father. Or rather, our father.

"No!" she uttered, her hand flying to cover her face. My face. She reached for her mask on the floor and quickly put it back on. The pretty lace tentacled itself back onto her skin.

I watched as her body language shifted back to regal poise. She bowed deeply again. The curtsy held something more: an opportunity to slide the mirror into the pocket of one of her skirts.

I looked at Lazar's face. But his expression was stone-cold. It didn't betray anything. I didn't know what evil was supposed to look like. But I hadn't pictured this.

I had never seen my father—at least I didn't remember him. I was only a baby when my mother had taken me away. But I didn't need to remember what he looked like to know my biological father. His face was handsome and younger than I expected. I had always thought that my features were the spitting image of my mother, but something around the eyes and about the shape of the face I had in common with him. And the smile, the one I rarely used, was on his face right now, smiling at me.

Stephen Yardley, the man who claimed to be my father and made visits every other month to the Whittaker common room, and I had not one feature in common. He was round where I was angled. He was large where I was small. Maybe he hadn't just been disappointed in his madwoman of a child. Maybe he didn't want me to figure out the truth: that we were not connected at all.

Looking at Lazar, I wished that I was wrong about Stephen Yardley. I wished for a blood tie where there was none. And I wished to rid myself of the tie with the one who was standing in front of me.

My father's armor had the same symbols carved into it as the Tree and as the Enforcer's armor, but his was a burnished red instead of the Enforcer's black.

His skin was weathered like he had been exposed to the sun, and there were markings on his face and arms that reminded me of the marks I'd seen on the arms that took Bale.

Looking into the cold blue eyes of my father, I knew that it was always supposed to come to this. Did I really think I could get in and out of Algid without facing him? Just because I didn't believe in fate didn't stop fate from showing up in a suit of full armor five minutes after I'd met my secret twin sister.

"So there are two of you. That Ora was always a clever one. And right under my nose. What a quaint family reunion . . . ," he said finally, his voice deep and sure.

"You are not my family," I said evenly. I didn't want to show any emotion. He didn't deserve to see it, but I couldn't hold it in.

The frosty pattern on the ground cropped up into spikes. Snow flurries floated through the air. All my doing.

"Your snow begs to differ. Come now, is that any way to greet your father?"

Temperly looked from me to her father, our father.

The veins in his face rose beneath his skin and filled, making his blue blood visible. With a wave of his hand, streams of ice created a globe around Temperly. She was trapped.

She pressed her hands against the ice and mouthed something at me.

Kill him.

39

I WAS STUCK FOR a moment staring at my sister in the ice bubble.

His snow is different from yours, Fathom had said.

And she had examined both of us up close. Did I not have the same gift? Or was it just that he'd had longer to practice?

"I think this will give us some time to talk," he quipped behind me.

He reminded me of someone. My first thought was Storm on *The End of Almost*, because Storm was the biggest, baddest villain Haven had ever seen, but the thing was he didn't know he was a villain. He thought every evil thing he was doing was right. He had his reasons, just like King Lazar apparently did.

I was pretty sure that Temperly hadn't figured out if she liked me or not. I wasn't sure if I liked her, either, but looking at her now I could see she hated Lazar as much as I did. Maybe more.

I sent a sharp icicle at the globe to crack it open. But it deflected off the rock-hard surface and landed on Temperly's rug.

"Let her go," I demanded.

"I'm afraid I can't do that." The King ignored me and Temperly, whose poise was completely broken. She was banging against the ice.

I threw a snow-cicle at him, which he deflected with a wave of his hand.

"I have plans for you, Snow," he said as I sent another icicle in his direction. He deftly stepped out of its arc.

Meanwhile, Temperly's soldiers entered the room in response to the commotion.

"Your Highness," the lead guard said, seeing his mistress trapped in a snow globe.

The King froze him first. The others raised their swords, and the King froze them in formation, their mouths still open, their swords drawn.

It had happened so fast, I hadn't even managed to raise my hands to counteract him.

I realized it was my turn to run. Lazar raised his hand toward me. Perhaps to stop me. Perhaps to hurt me. I considered the door. But the sight of Temperly in the globe stopped me. I dropped an icy wall between him and the door. I didn't know how long it would hold. But I could see his smiling face through the ice wall. He was amused by my efforts.

I made another attempt to crack the globe with a blast of ice, but the surface remained unblemished. Behind the ice wall I could already hear the King powering away at my handiwork.

Inside the globe, Temperly was shaking her head, telling me to save myself and go.

Then I remembered my dagger.

I hitched up my dress and slipped it out of the garter sheath that Fathom had given me. I took a deep breath before holding the hot handle in my hand. The blade glowed as I pierced the ice. In an instant, it cracked like a giant ice egg and I pulled Temperly out.

Still holding her hand, I fled the room, walling it up with more ice after we crossed the doorway.

She looked at me. Her face was a question: What now?

"You stayed for me?" she said, surprised.

I didn't answer. I just yanked her along the hallway. We heard loud crashing sounds coming from the ballroom as we made it down the hall. We raced out to the balcony.

For a split second I thought that the partygoers were oblivious to King Lazar's arrival, but it was just the opposite. Some of the dancers were running hysterically. A few were standing completely still. Instead of the waiters who had circled through the floor carrying hors d'oeuvres, now there were Snow Beasts serving up their own specialty: fear.

The cage that had held Gerde was empty. And there was no sign of Kai. I hoped they were safe.

My eye caught on someone who wasn't running or standing still. She was fighting. It was Fathom. She was sandwiched between two Snow Beasts that were deciding between fighting for her or sharing her for supper. Of course her weapon of choice was a disappearing vial. One second she was standing in between the Beasts. The next, she was sitting on top of one of them with her dagger in hand. She stabbed the beast. It fell, and she disappeared again. Then reappeared atop the other one.

I blinked. The other Robber girls were there, too.

They had come back for me, and they were fighting the Beasts. Interspersed among the Beasts were the King's guard. A few of the remaining members of Temperly's guard fought with them.

Each Robber had apparently taken a different potion depending on their fighting style of choice or some combination.

I saw Howl blur by, dagger in hand, slitting a soldier's throat. She had clearly taken a speed potion.

Margot was dancing with another soldier she'd apparently seduced with a waltz spell. Her dagger was raised behind his back.

I turned away before the knife went in. Instead I searched the room for one figure: Jagger. But I found the Enforcer instead. He ruled the Snow Beasts with arms raised, conducting his symphony of pain.

Temperly made a small sound. I wondered if she had ever seen anything like this. The battle raged below. It was Robber girl versus Snow Beasts and soldiers. And the girls were grossly outnumbered.

"Hide! I'll get the Robbers, and we can get out of here . . . together," I ordered. As long as she was with me, the King couldn't use her against me.

She hesitated, unsure . . . A wild thought crept in, and I wondered what it would have been like if we had been on the same side of the Tree growing up. If Mom had taken her to New York, or if we had somehow managed to hide out from Lazar somewhere in Algid together.

Temperly's face registered what I assumed was impatience. Her eyebrows shot upward. But maybe she was anxious. I didn't know her expressions. Another thing that Lazar had stolen from us. But I didn't have time to make up for the time we'd lost. At least not now.

"Wait . . . Give me the mirror," I demanded.

"I have to ask. Were you saving me or the mirror back there?"

I hadn't actually thought of the mirror since Lazar had shown up until this very moment.

I said, "Can it be both?"

I didn't know why I wasn't kinder. We were walking into a battle. This could have been the very last conversation I ever had with my sister, and still I was cruel.

She began to hand the compact over and then she stopped to say, "Find the Witch of the Woods. And I'll find you."

"Temperly, I can't promise that."

"All of Algid is counting on you—not just your friend," she said, pressing the compact into my palm.

I nodded.

"And they're counting on me, too," she added. She began to head toward the ball instead of away from it. "I'm going to help people get out."

"You'll get yourself killed. I can't protect you," I warned, not sure I could keep an eye on her and fend off everyone else.

"I don't need you to protect me. *They* will."

"I thought I was the crazy one. Who is 'they'?" I asked.

Temperly leaned out on the balcony and let out a low whistle. Some of the suitors turned in unison and looked up at their

Duchess. They immediately drew their swords. One of them went for one of the Red Coats, stabbing the King's soldier in the jugular. Another turned on a Snow Wolf and made quick work of it with a sword. Another Snow Beast rose onto his haunches, and one of the Robber girls threw a glowing dagger into his exposed underbelly.

So this was what the mysterious look had meant when Temperly talked about her suitors. She wasn't just idly waiting for me, after all; she was building an army.

"You've had a plan this whole time," I said.

"The King proposed that marriage would create an alliance between families. But I thought, why not create more than one alliance?"

"You know that a lot of those men are in love with you, Temperly," I said lightly.

"I know. But such is war. May their hearts be the only casualties today," she said.

But despite her bravado, despite the suitors who apparently made up her resistance, when she turned back to me, her face wasn't filled with determination. There was fear written all over it. It was still disconcerting to see a face that looked like mine look so scared.

She was not me, I reminded myself as Temperly released me and made her way down the stairs. Whatever we did or didn't have in common, we were both stubborn and I didn't have to argue with her. And maybe, just maybe, it didn't matter how you looked going into battle. It just mattered that you went.

I followed her down into the fray.

40

DESPITE WHAT I HAD said about not helping her, I cleared a
path for Temperly as she edged her way around the ballroom. I
used my snow to knock a beast that was sniffing in her direction
out of her way. Her guards did the same, taking out a Snow Lion
that lunged at her and pushing another Red Coat to the ground.
She opened a door in the corner of the room, and with her
suitors' help began ushering costumed ladies through the door to
a safe exit.

Temperly had no dagger, no training. But she did not run
away from the fight.

Her eyes met mine and she nodded.

Across the room, I saw a Snow Jackal jump on Howl. It was
on top of her, its open mouth dripping ice-laden saliva. The
monster leaned down to take a bite of Howl.

I pushed through the mess of beasts and soldiers to Howl.

I grabbed my knife again just as Howl twisted away from the

Snow Jackal's jaws. The beast sank its claws into a clump of her hair.

I raised my dagger over it. When the hot dagger pierced its skull, the Snow Jackal tore apart and split into pieces.

Snow Beast guts fell all over Howl. But she grinned, happy to see me.

"We came back to save you," she said with a smile, still flat on her back, exhaling heavily, the enormity of the close call hitting her.

"Obviously," I said, giving her a hand up.

"How's that dagger treating you?"

"Burns like hellfire."

"Good! Then it's working. Fathom will be thrilled."

I could see Fathom across the room, disappearing and reappearing around a soldier. He slumped to the ground in her wake. He dropped without even registering a look of surprise. Fathom had moved so fast that her opponent didn't even know he was dying.

My reunion with Howl was short-lived, as an oversize Snow Bee came at both of us. She daggered it with one hand. Then fished something out of her pants pocket and tossed a glowing blue vial at me.

"What is it?"

"You're going to need to be a better fighter. Fast."

"I have my snow," I said defensively.

"Suit yourself, but everyone—even Your Highness—can use a little help sometimes."

In truth, I wasn't sure how the vial would make me feel. It

might make me faster, but I needed all my senses sharp when the King broke through the ice trap I'd made for him back in Temperly's bedroom. Just like all villains, he would be back.

I took the vial and slipped it into my skirt pocket. I felt it make contact with the compact.

I heard a cracking sound upstairs and knew that the King was breaking through at least the first of the ice walls. We didn't have a lot of time.

"Thought you could use an assist, Princess," a voice came up behind me. He bashed the nose of a Snow Beast that had just set its sights on me. It stumbled backward and roared forward again, but in a different direction.

I knew the voice belonged to Jagger before I turned around.

"You came back! You said that Robbers never do."

"Hopefully I will *live* to regret it." It was meant to be a joke, but he wasn't smiling. "The place is surrounded," Jagger said.

"I noticed that right after I learned that the Duchess is my secret twin sister," I whispered, waiting for the words to have their effect.

For the first time since I met him, Jagger looked genuinely surprised.

"I have the mirror. We need to get all the Robbers and go."

Jagger's eyes lit up, but then he looked around the room. "We can't leave all these people to die."

I could hear the other Robbers around me, fighting and grunting. I did not want to hear Temperly's guests dying.

"Careful. That sounded almost noble," I said.

Jagger caught himself, as if "noble" were the dirtiest word in all of Algid.

"We don't have enough travel potion to take everyone back. Let's get our people to the tree line. Margot knows a way through the woods on foot back to the Claret," he corrected.

Before I could say anything more, the air above the ballroom began to swirl. And in an instant a spinning white funnel was heading toward me.

When I looked up, the King was on the balcony.

"Snow," the King called my name, and it echoed through the ballroom.

Jagger squeezed my shoulder and then began throwing glowing daggers in the direction of the balcony.

I sent a tornado of my own in the Snow King's direction. My tornado met his in the middle, and they clashed together, forming a larger funnel that neither of us controlled.

It dipped down into the center of the ballroom where I had danced with Jagger. Now the evening's theme had changed from heist to carnage.

Amazingly, the funnel touched down in an area clear of guests. A few remaining suitors threw themselves to the ground to avoid getting picked up by the icy vortex.

Kai, I thought. I searched for him even as I tried to wrest control of the giant tornado. I could feel Lazar's pull on the cyclone, too, but I forced it from him and pushed it toward the stage. It tore through the wall, opening the ballroom up to the world.

Some of the partygoers saw the opportunity as a chance for freedom. They rushed for the gaping hole in the wall.

It was a fatal mistake. As the debris cleared, I could see how much so.

The field behind the castle was full of hundreds of the King's men and even more Snow Beasts. They were waiting for us.

I watched in horror as the beasts attacked a woman in a pink dress. I tried to send snow to rescue her, but the beasts were already clamping down on her. One had picked her up and was tossing her around in his mouth like a chew toy. I recognized the woman. She was the one who had gossiped with me about Kai on the dance floor.

The sick, dull ache inside me deepened.

Behind the palace there was a field of Snow Beasts—too many for me to count. And behind them was another wave of the King's soldiers outfitted in the same color as his armor. It was a sea of red.

I turned to Jagger and shot him a look that said maybe it was time to retreat.

He and the Robber girls had wanted to face Lazar on their own terms with the help of the whole mirror, not just the piece I had in my pocket.

"The only way out is through. By now the King's men have sealed off the moat. The plan is to get to the tree line. Don't be a hero, Snow."

The other girls assembled beside me. Margot, dusting off her gown, took her place next to me.

"It's not going to be nearly as pretty as we are," she quipped. Not exactly a pep talk, but I assumed that was just another thing that Robbers did not do.

Jagger sprinted ahead for the gap. He was fast, not as fast as Howl, but it was as if every step had more power than the last. He got to the gap in seconds and threw something. It landed in front of one of the beasts.

The package exploded and ripped through the animal, blowing the snow to bits. Fragments of ice and bone flew everywhere.

Jagger smiled back at me, ever cocky, but the pieces began to drag themselves together again in his wake. And his smile faded. He jumped through the gap and raised his cuff to blast some fire over the pieces.

I joined Margot and the others in a race to the gap, but they were all enhanced by vials and they were there in seconds. Only Margot stayed beside me, perhaps protecting her investment until the mirror was in her possession.

"Thank you for coming back for me," I blurted.

"Who says I came back for . . ." Margot stopped midsentence. There was a garrote around her slender neck and a soldier standing behind her pulling the wire tight.

I produced a tiny snow tornado in the palm of my hand.

"Is that supposed to scare me, Princess?" he asked.

"Just imagine what it will do when it's inside you. Let her go, or I will tear you apart from the inside out."

He dropped the wire and backed away.

Margot laughed.

I stared at her for a long beat. I had saved her and she was laughing.

"It's been too long since we had a good fight," she said thoughtfully.

I took a last look back at the ballroom, which was destroyed. The door that Temperly had disappeared into was shut, and her guard and suitors were nowhere to be found. The balcony where the King had stood was empty, too.

As Margot and I made it to the gap, a figure larger than the beasts stood imposingly in front of Jagger. It was the Enforcer. With one swift move, he knocked Jagger to the ground.

In the distance, Cadence was in trouble between two Snow Wolves.

Margot nodded at me before racing off to Cadence's side with speed that I did not possess.

"Jagger!" I yelled. I couldn't tornado my way to him without hurting people. I had to run and jump through the gaping hole in the Palace, just as Jagger and the other girls had.

But once I crossed into the field, a soldier was on me—his sword inches from my heart as he debated whether or not to kill me or take me back to his King.

I looked back to find the Enforcer still on top of Jagger. The Enforcer's fists were raining down on him. Jagger had magic, I reminded myself. The Enforcer used brute force, but Jagger was quick.

Jagger dodged the Enforcer's fists as he tried to pummel him. And without warning, he pushed the Enforcer off him. The Enforcer was thrown into the trunk of a nearby tree, which shook from the impact.

Jagger apparently had taken a strength potion. It explained how his daggers earlier had sailed such a far distance.

Undaunted, the Enforcer returned to his feet and began to make another run at Jagger as fast as the armor would allow.

The Enforcer opened his mouth, and I stopped cold. Fire blasted out of it in Jagger's direction. Thinking quickly, Jagger grabbed a chunk of the palace wall and used it as a shield.

What was the Enforcer—part dragon? Why hadn't he used his fire on me in the square?

I sent some snow to extinguish the Enforcer's flames. But a sound overhead distracted me. I looked up. The King had left his spot on the balcony and was flying above me.

On his back were wings made of ice.

I shot snow arrows at the King as he came for me, but they pelted off his wings. He took a sudden dive, but it wasn't from one of my arrows. I looked beneath him. On the ground stood Margot. Her hands were outstretched toward the King, and waves of light like the sun were radiating toward him.

She was casting a spell. She was melting his wings.

He fell to the ground in front of her.

I knew in a heartbeat that she'd made a grave miscalculation. The King was sprawled on his back, but he would be back on his feet again in seconds. She might have brought him down from the sky, but she put herself directly in his path.

Margot continued punishing the King with her heat rays, which worked on his wings but did nothing to his armor. He kept advancing.

I summoned my tornado to bring me closer to them, but by the time I touched down, the King had sent paper-thin ice discs spinning into the air. They sliced into Margot with incredible accuracy and speed. I was too late.

"Until we meet again, Your Majesty," she said with a deep bow before crumpling to the ground. As I had always suspected, it sounded as though she and the King had a history.

It had not been like in the movies. The King had taken her without so much as a word of preamble.

There were tons of tiny cuts all over Margot's body. And ice shards stuck out of every single one of them.

I looked up at my father, who was savoring the moment, watching my pain with as much interest as Vern watched *The End of Almost.*

I pushed him back with a walloping torrent of snow that shoved him hard against a tall snowbank. I concentrated on the snow above him, causing it to avalanche down. He tried to push back, but he disappeared under the weight of snow and ice.

I knew that this wasn't the end. He would not go gently under that avalanche. But I'd bought a few minutes before he could dig himself out of the temporary grave I'd built for him.

Cadence had managed to put down the soldier she was battling and had draped herself over Margot. The girl's eyes were wide and wild.

"Can we save her?" I asked as Fathom joined me at her side. Tears poured down her face.

Blood was already Rorschaching around Margot, staining the snow redder than red. There was so much blood. Too much.

Margot opened her mouth to laugh with difficulty. My chest stung, and I swallowed hard.

"My magic . . . ," Margot whispered.

Queen Margot's face began to contort. Within seconds she looked like a normal person. She wasn't old or young or beautiful. Her hair was short, and she wore glasses. A pattern of freckles covered her pretty olive skin. The freckles killed me the most. I liked them. I hated that she covered them up.

This Margot, the real Margot, looked ordinary, but her eyes were still the same: hungry and calculating. She looked down at herself, aware of the transformation. Her power was gone.

I reached for her. She needed help. I called out to the others to help her. Fathom must have a potion to heal her.

"I'm fine," Margot vowed. But her eyes didn't seem to be able to focus on me. Robbers were always confident, even when they weren't. Robber Rules.

Her body was weeping blood the way the River Witch wept water.

The battle raged on around us, and suddenly Howl appeared beside me, yellow bottle in hand. There was blood on one of her cheeks and on her pretty feathered coat.

"Go. I'll help her."

Howl, always ready with a million little bottles, tipped a potion to Queen Margot's lips.

Margot began to sing.

She brings the snow with her touch,
They think she's gone, but we know
She will come again,
She will reign in his stead,

She will bring down the world on his head.

Oh come, Snow, come . . .

I saw Margot differently then. Not just because she was stripped of her magical enhancements, but because she was stripped down to who she was.

Some part of me had hated Margot for bargaining for Bale's life when I first met her. But now I understood what she was trying to do. She was fighting for her people, for her castle. She was a queen—even more than the Duchess was a duchess or the King was a king. She had laid down her life for her people.

"Your Majesty, you have done your Robbers proud," I said to her with a bow, kissing her cold hand.

When she looked up at me, she was smiling, but her dull green eyes were drained of their light and mischief. Queen Margot was gone.

41

THE DARK SKY WAS silent. It was suddenly very cold. I was never affected by temperature drops anymore, but this one I knew was not merely external.

"You need to go," Howl said, shivering.

I had never seen her cry before. But frozen tears decorated her magically enhanced lashes.

"*We* need to go," I insisted.

"I won't leave Margot. Help the others. And by all means, finish him!" She slipped off her feathered cloak and continued, "Take this. There are more potion bottles in the lining. Bring them to the girls."

"We'll be okay," I said. I didn't want to take the coat. I didn't want to see Howl cold.

She shrugged the coat back on and began chanting under her breath. She tenderly placed her hand on Margot's chest.

Around us, the other Robbers had heard about Margot's death

and fought with enhanced vigor. Jagger threw the Enforcer halfway across the field using his magically enhanced fire-cuff hands.

Howl was right. It was time to finish this. I headed directly for the spot where I had buried my father in the snow.

I was ready and waiting for him when he burst out of the snow. He was breathing heavily, limbs wobbly.

The King blinked hard. He looked at me and at the snow on the ground between us. It rose and fell like the hollow of someone's chest.

I concentrated on the snow as the pain flowed through me. I had never lost anyone close to me before. The pain was tinged with something else: guilt. If I was honest with myself, I had never particularly liked Margot—but she had died fighting for me. There should be a special word for this kind of sorrow.

Turning my attention to the mountain of snow behind me, I felt an immediate flash of pain when I thought about what King Lazar had done to me and Mom. But anger alone was not enough to fuel my magic. I thought of the peace I'd found with the Robbers. Finally, I thought about Kai and his buildings. Each one began with a simple snow brick. I thought about snowflakes. I thought about them multiplying. And as I thought about all of this, the snow began to stir. Finally, I thought of the light going out of Margot's eyes.

My Champion rose from the ice in a jerky Frankensteinian fashion. She looked like me. This Champion had my face.

She was bigger and taller than me—possibly taller than even Vern. She was the fiercest, scariest version of me carved roughly out of ice and snow. She moved with my anger. With my pain.

With every ounce of grief and regret that I felt over Margot. Over Bale.

My Champion tested her limbs in the air and then crushed the nearest Snow Beast with a clap of hands around its icy skull. I could hear the ice break and see the beast's head begin to fall apart.

I saw surprise register on the King's face.

I felt a surge of something in my chest. Was it hope? Pride? Maybe the tide was turning. Maybe I had done something he could not.

But the King looked back at the field with new determination.

The remaining Snow Beasts gathered together. Their icy hides began to merge. The group was becoming one larger beast, bigger than my Champion. It was a Snow Wolf that stood a couple of stories high.

I cursed under my breath as the giant Snow Wolf knocked down my Champion with one easy swipe of its claw.

My father laughed and advanced on me, believing that he had the battle in hand.

But I focused on the field again. Everywhere I looked, a new Champion rose up from the snow.

There was a tiny bit of red just above the King's eyebrow. It was a caked smear of red like the paint in the Whittaker common room that I sometimes got to use when I had been good. The color was Cadmium Red Deep, I recalled. But this wasn't paint. It was Margot's blood. The sight of it made me angrier.

The King flew at me. A gust of snowy wind pushed my back to the ground. I struggled to get up. I felt tired. My limbs felt heavy, as if the ice in my veins were no longer propelling me but was weighing me down. I tornadoed away from him to regroup, to catch my breath, and to regain the strength I had somehow lost.

I landed on a bridge that crossed over where the moat merged with the River. My hands gripped the iron railing. I felt completely and utterly drained.

But the King followed me to the bridge, snow carrying him through the air without wings, like a current. He landed softly beside me.

The King sensed my weakness, too. I closed my eyes for the slowest of blinks, gathering strength I did not have as I rolled away from him. But he was too fast. He was over me again.

I needed to get to my feet. But I was spent.

I did what Rebecca Gershon would do when she faced Storm in this exact situation. (Well, not exactly. She had been kidnapped, but not by her demented patricidal father.) I tried talking to him, stalling as I waited for my power to return.

"Why did you bring me to Algid? I never would have known about this place if you hadn't taken Bale," I said.

My father cocked his head, considering. "You were always coming back here, Snow. It's our fate."

Below us, I willed my Champions to defeat the beasts and the King's soldiers. My snow was gone for the moment, but my Champions still followed my will.

The giant Snow Wolf ate one of the Duchess's soldiers as proof of its new combined power. I heard the Robber girls chanting something. At first I thought they needed me.

But no. It was Margot's name they were calling. What sounded like fireworks suddenly followed.

A dozen grenades exploded on the King's mega Snow Wolf. The Robber girls were now focusing all their efforts on one target instead of several. The Snow Wolf blew up into a billion bits of ice and frost. The blast spread so many pieces of it so far that even if it could find its way back together again, reconstruction would take time.

I looked coldly at the King. "You were never meant to find me. And I'm not sure I'm buying into your insane prophecy, anyway," I replied.

"It is fated, my dear Snow. It is what will be. And you are just as magnificent as the prophecy said you would be," the King said without a hint of irony.

I realized something was wrong. My feet slipped on the icy surface of the bridge. My body felt even weaker. My hands shook when I called for more snow. Trembling, I reached for the vial that Howl had given me.

The King knocked it out of my hand.

A thin liquid spilled onto the light coating of snow that covered the ice. I reached down and scooped a handful of blue snow to my lips. I didn't feel anything.

"No cheating, Snow. It was hard for me at first, too. Until I met your mother, I killed countless people by accident," the Snow King teased.

And now he kills on purpose, I thought.

I concentrated on what little snow was on top of the ice, whipping up the smallest of tornadoes. It took him by surprise and pushed him back toward the railing of the bridge. He tried to hold himself steady, but his feet slid backward and he was soon straining against the side of the bridge. I hoped the railing would break, for my father to fall into the water below. It would be perfect. It would be poetic.

But it was not to be.

My snow stopped swirling. I reached out my hands again and nothing happened. The air and the snow stilled and remained motionless. My father stood upright.

"You possess such raw force. I can see that you have had some training, but whoever taught you really should have told you the most important thing."

"What's that?"

"That you can't make life without sacrifice."

And then I understood what he was saying. I had sacrificed my snow to bring my Champions to life.

The King took another step toward me and restrained my arms. He shouldn't have been able to reach me. I should have been able to stop him before he got so close.

But I couldn't. I looked up at the sky and concentrated on the cloud formation that was just beneath the North Lights. I willed it to come close to bring me more snow. But the clouds remained in the same spot. The North Lights themselves were a moody dark blue. They looked melancholy.

"Don't you worry, daughter. Your power's not gone. It just takes a little recovery time. Unfortunately for you, you have run out of time. The throne is and always will be mine."

And for the second time in Algid, I felt a wave of cold wash over and through me. The King was trying to freeze me.

I kicked him as hard as I could, but even when he released

me, I could still feel the cold burrowing into the corners of my heart.

My fingers felt paralyzed. My face felt twitchy, but every muscle was stuck in place. This was different from the battle with the Enforcer. The King was not going to hesitate for any reason. Certainly not out of love for his daughter.

His eyes weren't just cold; they were distant. They burned with an intense wanting that I didn't quite understand.

He came back again for more. And this time I was the one pushed toward the edge of the bridge. My body was half-suspended, and I could see the water below.

This is not how I end, I told myself.

I reached for his face with my claws and for my knife from my dress pocket. I managed to shove the dagger deep into his side, where the chain metal gaped open just enough for my blade to slide through to his flesh.

The King roared in pain. I knew how he felt. The burning of the blade, the unforgiving heat that no amount of cold could temper. He responded with a head butt.

The pain radiated through me, and my ears rang. The King put his hands around my throat, but he didn't squeeze. He froze, overtaken by the dagger that I withdrew as forcefully as I had stabbed him. I felt myself slipping into whiteness.

I thought of Bale and of me and him at the institute in happier times. Of the kiss near the window at Whittaker. Of the first time he had held my hand when we were so small. I would never get that back if I let myself go into the whiteness.

A new rush of strength surged through me. It wasn't much,

but enough to create razor-sharp snowflakes. I concentrated, and the King's face came back into focus. He was not faring well, either. His face strained with the effort of freezing me. My snowflakes fell from the sky onto his face. They were as hard as diamonds and as sharp as glass. They cut into the skin on his face and hands, just like in one of my dreams. Tiny red dots surfaced on his skin. My pulse quickened. I had drawn blood. Cadmium Red Deep. Same as Margot's.

Clutching his face, the King released me—and I turned my snow on him.

I tried to freeze him, but nothing happened. I had run out of steam. I had run out of snow.

My spiky flakes stopped falling from the sky.

"You don't know me," I said, baiting him.

I remembered *The End of Almost*. He had told me I was out of time. But I could make my own time. I could stall him.

"But I do, Snow. More than you know. Sometimes you have to break things to find what's unbreakable," he added.

The last words were not his. They were Dr. Harris's. Had Temperly been right? Could Lazar really get inside anyone's head? Had he gotten into mine?

Before I could process my questions, I got a new answer. With a crush of skin and bone, Lazar's face re-formed as one I knew very well: Dr Harris.

"No . . . How? I don't understand . . ."

"No, you wouldn't," he said in Dr. Harris's voice.

"You . . . were there all along . . ."

"Oh no," he said, transforming back into the King. "I only

borrowed the good doctor's eyes when I needed to. I could not cross the Tree. Nor could I kill you there. It had to be here in Algid. But I could not go long without seeing my love. When love shuts a door, it opens a window."

The look on his face softened when he spoke of my mother. It was not a manipulation this time. He was still in love with her. Or at least his twisted version of it.

"So Dr. Harris was a Shell?" I demanded.

That part of the legend was true. The King could see through people. Maybe even control them.

My mind raced. Dr. Harris had been a little too interested in my mother. But I never thought this was possible. I never imagined this.

"What an ugly word. I did not harm Dr. Harris." He shook his head. "He is very much alive and well on the other side of the Tree. I found that with enough concentration, I could visit the minds of the very weak. Like your good doctor."

"Mom didn't know . . . ," I muttered, more to myself than to him.

I thought of Mom and Dr. Harris's last few interactions and how much she had been relying on him lately. He had spent years wearing her down, gaining her confidence. Her trust. She'd crossed into another land to protect us, only to have him stalk her through Dr. Harris.

"You're a monster. You're the sick one," I said.

My eyes stung. I tried to make sense of my father's evil.

"Don't cry, dear. I hate it when you cry. You never cried at Whittaker, even when Bale . . . Well, you know what happened to him. Don't think that I didn't care about that boy . . . and for you. Why else would I have brought him to me? I have plans for him. But I blame Ora. I did not want to know you. I did not want to feel anything for you. It's harder to dispose of you now."

"What do you want from me?"

"What I've always wanted. I want you to die."

He gave me another shove—one that pushed me over the edge of the bridge. My claws came out and grabbed hold of the side of the bridge just in time. I hung there for a second, trying to pull myself up as he stepped back and reached out with a sword made of sharp, heavy translucent ice.

He wielded it at me and in a flash cut off the snow claws on my right hand. I continued to hang on with my left. Beneath us the River raged.

Maybe I could let go and the River Witch would fish me out again. But would she know where I was? Would she get to me in time?

The River suddenly froze over. Spikes sprung up like a bed of nails. Clearly there would be no River Witch rescue or death by drowning if I fell now.

"The truth is, I did not expect to like you so much. Or to see so much of myself in you," he said, giving me an admiring look even though he intended to kill me.

"So now what? You love me, so you're going to spare me?" The words came out bitter and sarcastic. My arm felt weak, but I held on.

"I'm afraid I can't do that," he said, raising his sword again.

I made one last effort to summon my snow with my free hand.

"Go to hell," I spat at my father as the hilt came down.

Without warning, my father was thrown up and away from me. I couldn't see where or how or why.

Jagger appeared over the top of the railing, "Miss me?" he said, kneeling down and pulling me to safety.

I threw my arms around his neck. I had never been so happy to see him in my life.

"You have no idea," I said, sinking into his strong, lean chest.

"I'd never leave you, Princess. Never," he said with a solemnity that made me want to trust him. And more.

"A shame, really, how love creates an opportunity for weakness," the King interrupted from beyond the bridge.

I looked at Jagger, who was studying me intently. He had come for me. But a small part of me still wondered if he was here for the mirror and nothing more.

A scepter made of ice formed in the King's hand. He pounded it against the base of the bridge. I heard a clash of thunder in the distance.

"Run," Jagger said, grabbing my hand and making for the opposite side of the bridge. I followed, not understanding, but trusting Jagger's steps on the bridge as I had on the dance floor.

"What is it?"

"Thundersnow. Where there's thunder, there's lightning . . ."

I heard the crack behind us as the bolt hit the bridge. It began to split down the center. We were forced to run in the other direction toward my father. Just as he intended.

We could hear part of the bridge fall onto the frozen River below as we ran, our every step just an inch ahead of the tumbling snow. When we almost reached the other side, Jagger and I jumped and landed on the snowbank. Our bodies tangled together in a painful but welcome fall.

I felt a sliver of snow come back to me just as Jagger willed me on.

"Get up, Snow."

And as he pulled me to my feet, I saw a new danger. The King had gotten ahead of us and let loose a barrage of icy discs like the ones that had killed Margot.

I returned fire, but a couple of my icicles only dropped a few of the flakes.

The King sent another round of spiky discs in my direction. They would cut us to bits unless I could counter them with my snow.

Jagger produced a sword and with vial-aided dexterity, cut each approaching disc down.

The King laughed and threw a squadron of icicles next.

I wasn't fast enough. I managed to shoot off a single snowcicle. But I had nothing left to shield me from the King's next wave.

"Robbers don't usually show such loyalty, boy," the King said.

"You have no right to speak for my people," Jagger spit back.

"Leave him out of it! Hell, leave me out of it. I already told you, I don't want any of this. You can keep your stupid crown. Just give me Bale and let me go."

"I'm afraid that isn't up to you. I have to be sure the prophecy is over. I can't leave this up to chance or the Eclipse of the Lights. You have so much power already. In a few days, it might be too much . . ." He raised his hand again.

Jagger pulled back and threw a fire dagger at the King. It hit his armor but did not even leave a mark.

I shot off some more snow and concentrated on the ground behind him. A half-formed Champion rose behind the King in the snow, ready to impale him with an icicle. But the King was stronger and faster than me. He sent an ice spear straight to my heart.

The spear flew through the air. Closer. Closer. My Champion fell to the ground.

No! I thought. *Not now. Not like this.*

At the last second, a blur of mat-black armor jumped in front of me. The spear went straight through as his body fell to the ground. Jagger let off a round of fire, stunning the King momentarily.

It was the Enforcer. He had saved me, and in the process he'd sacrificed his life for mine. I leaned down and removed his helmet.

I heard a far-off scream that I realized was my own.

The Enforcer was Bale. My Bale.

42

BALE LAY IN THE center of the ground, not moving.

My hands shook over the gaping hole that went right through his armor.

I looked up at Jagger. "Please help him . . . This is our deal. The mirror for Bale. Robber Rules."

Jagger's handsome face was twisted in confusion. "Even after all this? You still love him?"

I didn't answer. I couldn't say what Jagger wanted me to say.

"Even if I could, I don't have a vial for this, Snow. The wound's too deep."

I needed Bale to wake up so I could start hating him or he could give me a reason to keep loving him. Nothing made sense. How could he work for the Snow King? How could he hurt that kid in the square? How could he be the one that Gerde and Kai had told me such awful things about? The one who'd come and hunted me at the ball?

Was he still the Bale I knew? The one who'd grown up with me on the other side of the Tree? Or was this the part of him that I'd always seen but could never quite reach—the part of him that loved fire and loved to watch it burn everything in its wake? Was that what appealed to Bale in Algid?

There was no sound. No movement. Bale was still.

My snow was still, too.

My breath caught. I held Bale in my arms, life pouring out of him, leaving me.

I should have known the Enforcer was Bale. The heat that poured off him in the battle and now. He had saved me twice. It made sense, finally. He chose not to kill me in the square.

Had he chosen this life? Or was he under the King's control?

I had not come this far to let him go now.

With a sigh of resignation, Jagger tore a piece of his own shirt and placed it over Bale's wound, applying pressure.

"Well, isn't that a surprise," the King said menacingly, having recovered from Jagger's attack. "His love for you is stronger than I anticipated."

The King came at me again. He cast a sorrowful look at Bale. But it wasn't enough to stop him from finishing what he started.

I rose to my feet to face my father again, maybe for once and for all. I closed my eyes and summoned a snow sword, which appeared in my hand. It was covered with symbols like those on the Tree.

The King conjured up a sword of his own. His weapon clashed against mine. I had never done this kind of fighting before, but like Fathom's dagger, my snow sword seemed to know which way to move and when. Or maybe it was sheer will. I found my footing and pushed my father back. I matched him strike for strike, but he pushed back in return, forcing me up a hill. From my vantage point, I could see the Robber girls were all winning. The tide was turning in our favor. I considered sending a wave of snow to wipe out the giant Snow Wolf in case it had re-formed, but it seemed too much of a risk.

I pressed forward against the King, the weight and speed of my sword outpacing his, finally. My father's eyes widened as he lost his footing and fell backward into the snow.

I raised my sword over him unsteadily. All it would take was one slice down and he'd be dead. I wondered and hoped that the beasts and Shells would fall the second that the King did. But I had never killed anyone, and I wasn't sure I could kill him now, no matter how much he deserved it. I had hurt people in my life, but never permanently.

I steeled my grip on the sword's hilt and channeled every ounce of strength I had. I had no choice. There was no alternative. There was no cage that could contain a power like his. And he would never stop coming after me and Temperly and the Robber people. This was my destiny.

"Don't, Snow."

It was the one voice that always stopped me in my tracks. It was my mother. Here. In Algid.

"You can't," she said.

"Mom, he's evil. He tried to kill *me*. I have to end this," I said, readying myself for the final stab.

"You can't kill him . . . ," she repeated. "I love him. He's your father."

I blinked up at my mother, repeating the words in my head to make sure that I had not misheard them.

"You love him?" I demanded. She couldn't know what she was saying. She couldn't mean it.

Mom nodded and raised her hand, and a wave of fire swept down the hill and scorched everything in its path. Mom had fire and she was using it against us.

My snow Champions were cut off at their knees, and the Robber girls were running in every direction. Jagger was still by my side, unsure what to do or say.

"This isn't happening," I said, pushing my lips together as pain registered in my heart. Snow began to come down heavy and angry around us.

"Hello, Ora. Welcome home," the Snow King said, the tip of my sword still hovering above his heart.

Looking at him, an idea formed.

"You're doing this. You're inside her head. And when you are gone . . ." I drifted off, hope rising. My mom could not do this, say this, of her own volition.

"Your father could never get inside my head. Could you, love?" she said, addressing him affectionately.

He smiled a smile filled with years of love and longing.

I regrouped my blade and put my weight behind it, wanting to erase the smile and what it meant. Forever.

"I'm sorry, Snow, but I can't let you do this," my mother simply announced. Then she melted my sword with a wave of fire.

I should have stabbed him through when I had a chance. Now I was defenseless. My snow was used up. And my mind reeled at the knowledge that my mom was starring in her own twisted fairy tale: *Happily Ever After with the Enemy*.

Ora helped the Snow King up and continued, "Neither of you will kill the other. At least not yet. Let's not forget the second part of the prophecy: *Should the sacrifice come exactly when the Lights are extinguished, whoever wears the crown will rule Algid forever.* Timing, my dears.

"Snow, you don't have to die. The prophecy says that you may choose us, our side, and make us stronger than ever before. But if you choose the other path, on the Eclipse of the Lights you *will* die."

"Let me get this straight, Mom," I said. "You locked me away and waited more than ten years to get the timing of your sacrifice right?"

Bile rose to my mouth. My mother wanted to kill me, too. She just had a timetable for it. The story that the River Witch and Jagger had told me unraveled. My mother had been cast as a hero when she and my father were both actually villains plotting my demise.

"Patience may be a witch's most vital spell," said my mother.

The River Witch had been right about my parents being bad for each other, but it was not my father leading my mother into the darkness. They were equals in the dance. They, like that couple in one of Vern's old movies, were the Bonnie and Clyde of evil.

The pain in my chest had not gone away. Every word felt like another knife, and yet I found myself asking for more.

"Mom, I don't understand," I said. "Tell me the truth. You owe me the truth."

"You're right, Snow. But I'd rather show you."

A flash of a dream accompanied her words. And all of a sudden I could see her memory.

My young, handsome father was standing by the River, holding a screaming baby in his hands. Just as he was about to toss me in, my mother grabbed me and jumped off the cliff toward the rushing water below.

But this time instead of the silence of the dream I knew, there was sound. I could hear the rush of the River. I could hear my mother's desperate, ragged breath.

I could hear her as she whispered to my father before she jumped. The words chilled me to the bone and made sense of my entire existence.

"Not yet, my love . . ."

My whole life turned on a sentence.

I opened my eyes and she repeated the words, to me.

"Not yet, my love."

The Snow King broke the spell, bringing us all back to the palace grounds. "I know what the prophecy says, but there is no way Snow will pick our side."

Mom raised an eyebrow. "Because there is so much good in her?"

"Because she has so much power. Too much. There is no way she'll give her power to us when the Eclipse comes. She's strong, and she's only going to get stronger. It's too much of a risk. We have to cut our losses. You must see that now."

Ora turned to my father. "We must wait. Now that Snow knows this truth, there's yet another truth, another past, to attend to. Our other daughter has the mirror, and she is running—something you would have sensed if you had been doing what I asked instead of this . . ."

"You knew about my sister this whole time?" I spat at the King.

"Oh yes." He laughed. "But she was of no consequence. Until now."

"Enough of this! Go, Lazar. Find Temperly and our mirror," Ora demanded.

No matter how powerful he was, it was clear that Mom was the driving force in this dysfunctional relationship. In this plot, she was the mastermind.

The King sighed, and the air around his feet began to swirl. A snow tornado formed around him. It rose into the air, and my father was gone.

Beside me Jagger raised his sword. I pushed it down.

"You don't understand," I said, confused for the umpteenth time. "I have the mirror. Mom lied to save me, didn't you, Mom?" I slipped the compact out of my pocket to show Jagger the proof.

"Open it," he demanded.

I clicked open the gold lid. The mirror was gone.

I thought of Temperly's face when she had passed it to me. She had somehow slipped the mirror out—another betrayal. Temperly had gone on her own to try to make an alliance with the witches.

My sister had run, and our mother had just sent the King after her. Now Temperly was in danger. My mom had been the biggest lie of all.

No! my brain screamed. My head hurt. I looked down at my arms where the blue veins were more prominent than ever. I wondered, if I got angry enough, if I got hurt enough, would I transform into something else, like Gerde? Like the River Witch? I thought I had reached my pain limit when I saw Margot die in the snow. But apparently there was no limit. There was only an abyss. It was too much. I wanted to go back to Whittaker. I wanted to go back and unknow all that I now knew.

"Snow," Jagger said in a whisper, urging me back to him.

I looked at the man who had saved me so many times in Algid. He was calling to me. But I only had eyes for Bale.

I ran to Bale's side and pulled the wretched armor off his body. I noticed water pooling around his head, the red hair I had missed now a matted mess. I still reached for it. "Bale, I don't care what you did. Just come back to me. Come back to me so I can hate you. Come back to me and convince me that this is wrong. Just come back, Bale," I ordered him.

What mattered was that he breathed in and out again. It didn't matter what he had done.

An interminable pause followed. I felt a pain in my chest.

Bale's eyes fluttered open. He shook his head, a bit of recognition mingled with confusion.

"Snow."

He said my name, and for a split second the world mended.

"Bale. My Bale." I held on to the moment, knowing that the flood of bad things was coming back. I ran my palm over his cheek. It was hot to the touch.

"Sorry . . . ," he spoke again.

But the word complicated things even more.

I was sure that fire was the only thing Bale might love more than me. Would he have given anything, done anything, in exchange for that power?

"I'm so s-sorry, Snow," Bale stuttered.

He withdrew a vial made of ice from his pocket. The star with razor-sharp points on his left forearm glowed with an intensity I had never seen before. I realized then that it wasn't a star—it was a snowflake. And before I could stop him, he tipped the potion to his lips.

Bale disappeared. He was gone again.

I felt something break in me. I didn't know that there was anything left to break.

I closed my eyes, and my mind flashed to a vision of the past. Bale's past. I saw Bale's house again. I heard his jagged breath. Only this time, I saw streams of fire shooting out of Bale's—little Bale's—raised arms. No matches.

Bale's house was set against a forest of purple trees. The house was in Algid.

Then just as suddenly, the vision shifted to Bale now, sixteen-year-old Bale, who stumbled into the house.

And then the vision faded to white.

"Snow . . ."

It was my mother's voice, calling me back. Calling me away from him.

I pushed the voice out of my head. I needed another minute with the vision to figure out where Bale was in Algid.

"I can help your Bale," my mother coerced.

"Did you and Lazar send him to me? To spy on me? To make me love him? Was that you, too?"

"Does it really matter how? You love him."

I looked at the outline in the snow where Bale had been. I did love him. I'd crossed the Tree for him. And even now, I loved him still. But did the how matter, like Kai had once said?

"I can take you to him. I can heal him. Come with us, child. Wait for the Lights. When you come into your own and you come to our side, we can be the family you always wanted. Algid is your home."

She reached out her hand to me.

"Don't believe her. She will kill you, Snow," Jagger piped in.

My mother looked at him sharply. "Like she can believe you?"

I looked from Jagger to my mother and back. I knew what to do. I took my mother's hand.

She beamed at me beatifically. I squeezed her hand tighter. I felt something cold and imposing transfer from me to her. The look on her face said that she felt it, too. I took a step back as her expression changed from satisfied to confused to pained. She tried to pull away, but to no avail. The color drained from her hand in an instant, and her fingers began to harden. Her skin turned blue as the cold moved up her body.

When the cold had taken hold completely, my mother was frozen solid. It couldn't be undone. I expected the regret to flood in. But instead there was just sadness and hurt. Freezing her didn't take the pain away. It made it more permanent. Just like the one scar on her face from the day I walked through the mirror that was visible even through the ice.

I let go of her hand. It was done.

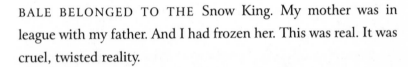

43

BALE BELONGED TO THE Snow King. My mother was in league with my father. And I had frozen her. This was real. It was cruel, twisted reality.

My knees buckled. Jagger caught me in his arms. It was too much. It was all too much.

"Just breathe," he ordered, holding me tighter. But what he was really doing was ordering me to live. To survive.

"I can't . . . ," I said with a sob.

"It's over," Jagger said, looking around the palace grounds. "The battle's done."

Howl approached us with the full report. "The King's soldiers surprised me. They took Margot and Cadence and Fathom. I couldn't stop them. I used up everything I had trying to save Margot. I had nothing left."

Jagger squared his shoulders. "We should gather the girls together."

"Is the Snow King dead?" Howl asked.

"No," I said. "I couldn't do it."

Howl paused, processing. A look of rage replaced the sadness. She looked at Jagger and pounded her fists into his chest.

"You were supposed to keep your eye on her. This whole thing could have been over. The King should be dead, not Margot," Howl said, releasing her hurt and anger on Jagger.

"Snow knows about Ora," Jagger warned, looking at my frozen mother.

"What?" I demanded.

A new layer of dread formed in my soul like the thin layer of snow over the bridge.

Jagger reached out to me. "It's not what you think."

My chest ached. I could hear my heart in my ears.

"Did you know about my mom and the Snow King?"

"I suspected they were working together."

"Then why didn't you tell me? How could you not tell me?"

"I didn't think it would help for you to know," he said matter-of-factly.

"Liar," I threw back.

"Okay, truth: I didn't want to stall the mission," he said. "I didn't think you would go on, if you knew. I thought you would go back to the other side of the Tree. I didn't want you to leave."

Jagger had told me who he was from almost the first second we'd met, and yet still it surprised me when he betrayed me.

"Don't blame him, Snow. Once a thief . . ." Howl trailed off.

I felt the anger drain out of me. I looked at Bale's blood on my hands, and I felt so tired.

Jagger took a step toward me.

"Stay away from me!" I shouted.

"I know you don't mean that, Snow," he said, a little too carefully.

"Don't touch me. Don't ever touch me again," I demanded.

He stepped back. Did he think I was going to freeze him, too?

I almost did.

I took one last look at my mother. And then I turned around and headed for the River.

44

I WAS STILL WEARING the Robber girls' feathered dress that had been touched with magic. I let it pick me up and carry me to the spot where I had first met the River Witch.

I pulled the empty compact out of my pocket. What had I done? What would I do next?

The water rippled, and I saw the reflection of the only one I could turn to.

"You were right, about everything," I said simply.

"Fear not, child," the River Witch said. "This will be your home. And we will make you Queen."

ACKNOWLEDGMENTS

To my editor and publisher, Cindy Loh, for your faith and brilliance. Snow would not exist without you. Also, for divine taste in food.

For my team at Bloomsbury, especially Cristina Gilbert, Lizzy Mason, and Erica Barmash, thank you for embracing and supporting Snow!

To Joanna Volpe, my powerhouse agent, there are not enough thank-yous! You know what you did and what you do!

To Pouya Shahbazian and the rest of my team at New Leaf, thank you for taking such good care of me and blazing a trail.

To Ray Shappell and Erin Fitzsimmons—for making covers so beautiful that people have to pick them up.

To my family and friends, thank you for being there and for understanding when I haven't been there. Mommy, Daddy, Andrea, Josh, Sienna. Your love and support is everything to me.

Bonnie Datt, for being a lifeline, for making me laugh, and for being a true friend. Nanette Lepore forever! Annie, Chris, Fiona, and Jackson Rolland, I love you to 5,000 and more.

Lauren, Logan, Joe Dell. Laur, I am so glad that our friendship really is forever. Carin Greenberg, for sharing your smarts and lunches with me. Paloma Ramirez, you moved away but we will always be close! Daryn Strauss, for being a star and always making me feel like one. Leslie Rider, for showing up and showing by example how to be brave.

Kami Garcia, for being a goddess on and off the page. Kass Morgan, thank you for the last-minute read and the kindest of words.

Jennifer Armentrout, Kiera Cass, Melissa de la Cruz, Margie Stohl, Melissa Grey, Valerie Tejada, Sasha Alsberg, and Josh Sabarra and the countless other writer friends who teach and share and cheerlead.

My *Guiding Light* family, Jill Lorie Hurst, Tina Sloan, Crystal Chappell, Beth Chamberlin, and all the fans who still keep the light alive.

Lexi Dwyer, Lisa Tollin, Jeanne Marie Hudson, Megan Steintrager, Kristen Nelthorpe, Tom Nelthorpe, Ernesto Munoz, Mark Kennedy, Maggie Shi, Leslie Kendall Dye, Sandy and Don Goodman, Mike Wynne, Matt Wang, Seth Nagel, Kerstin Conrad, Chris Lowe, Steve McPherson, Lanie Davis, Harry and Sue Kojima, and all the other friends I will think of the second the book is published.

For the bloggers and the Tubers, thank you for bringing new life to the book world and for helping get my books seen.

For my readers, thank you for crossing the Tree with me. I would write if no one was reading me, but you have made every step of this journey that much sweeter. There is nothing like knowing that something you poured your heart into is in the hands of a reader and that person feels something. It's the closest thing to magic I've gotten to experience.